The Vexations of a Shut-In VAMPIRE princess

D1490741

©riichu

Komari

The Shut-In Vampire Princess

Hobbies: Reading and writing
Aspiration: To become a novelist
Persona: Genius Commander
A total knockout beauty.

©riichu

Crimson Lord and Supreme Commander, Terakomari Gandesblood

"How did I end up in this situation?!" –Komari

"YEAHHH!!!"

"Let's go!!!"

©riichu

A
torrent
of magic, staining
the skies a
deep crimson...

©riichu

0
Prologue
[001]

1
The Shut-In Vampire Princess Goes Out
[009]

2
Komari's Charming Comrades
[053]

2.5
A Fox Face in the Dead of Night
[075]

3
A Mutinous Uprising
[083]

3.5
Inverse Moon
[119]

4
Party Crasher
[123]

5
The Darkness of the Shut-In Vampire Princess
[145]

6
Millicent Bluenight
[171]

7
Blood Curse
[197]

0
Epilogue
[235]

[The Vexations of a Shut-In Vampire Princess]

©riichu

The Vexations of a Shut-In Vampire Princess

1

Kotei Kobayashi

Illustration by **riichu**

YEN ON

New York

1

Kotei Kobayashi

Translation by **Evie Lund**
Cover art by **riichu**

HIKIKOMARI KYUUKETSUKI NO MONMON Vol. 1
Copyright © 2020 Kotei Kobayashi
Illustrations copyright © 2020 riichu
All rights reserved.
Original Japanese edition published in 2020 by SB Creative Corp.
This English edition is published by arrangement with SB Creative Corp., Tokyo
in care of Tuttle-Mori Agency, Inc., Tokyo.

English translation © 2022 by Yen Press, LLC

Yen On
150 West 30th Street, 19th Floor
New York, NY 10001

Visit us at yenpress.com
facebook.com/yenpress
twitter.com/yenpress
yenpress.tumblr.com
instagram.com/yenpress

First Yen On Edition: April 2022

Yen On is an imprint of Yen Press, LLC.
The Yen On name and logo are trademarks of Yen Press, LLC.

The publisher is not responsible for websites (or their content) that are not owned by the publisher.

Library of Congress Cataloging-in-Publication Data
Names: Kobayashi, Kotei, author. | riichu, illustrator. | Lund, Evie, translator.
Title: The vexations of a shut-in vampire princess / Kotei Kobayashi ;
    illustration by riichu ; translation by Evie Lund.
Other titles: Hikikomari kyuuketsuki no monmon. English Description: First Yen On edition. |
    New York, NY : Yen On, 2022- |
Identifiers: LCCN 2021058967 | ISBN 9781975339494 (v. 1 ; trade paperback) |
    ISBN 9781975339517 (v. 2 ; trade paperback) | ISBN 9781975339531 (v. 3 ; trade paperback) |
    ISBN 9781975339555 (v. 4 ; trade paperback)
Subjects: CYAC: Fantasy. | Vampires—Fiction. | Princesses—Fiction. | Humorous stories. |
    LCGFT: Vampire fiction. | Fantasy fiction. | Humrous fiction. | Light novels. Classification:
    LCC PZ7.7 .K676 2022 | DDC 741.5/952—dc23/eng/20220107
LC record available at https://lccn.loc.gov/2021058967

ISBNs: 978-1-9753-3949-4 (paperback)
        978-1-9753-3950-0 (ebook)

10 9 8 7 6 5 4 3 2 1

WOR

Printed in the United States of America

1

Vexations

[The Vexations
of a Shut-In
Vampire Princess]

Blood, spurting. The air, thick with the roars. Magical spells, flying every which way.

And heads, rolling.

Across the heart of the sprawling grasslands, a fierce battle was unfolding.

The Eastern Army, composed of brawny beast-folk. The army of the Lapelico Kingdom.

The Western Army, composed of a select vampire elite. The Imperial Army of Mulnite.

"Gah! The heck kinda creatures are they?!"

But the outcome of the battle was already a foregone conclusion.

The beast-folk's morale had already weakened to a breaking point. And it took only a glance at the scene to understand why. The heaps of dead bodies strewn about the battlefield consisted almost entirely of Lapelico Kingdom soldiers.

"Fire, Fire! Burn the Trembling Forest to the ground!"

"Shit, more magic?! Let's kill 'em all before they can cast it! Let's… GAHHH!"

"Tony? Hey, Tony! Stay with me, Tony!"

As the bear-man rushed forward, waving his sword, he suddenly burst into flames. The remaining beast-folk could do nothing but stare slack-jawed in shock, overwhelmed by the colossal discrepancy in combat skill on display. Still, no one made any attempt to lay down their weapon. Perhaps they still had some soldier's pride left in them. But as the air began to tingle with the ethereal singing of the vampires, many of the beast-folk gulped audibly, before all stiffened and trembled in mortal terror.

"Screw this! I'm getting outta here!"

"Ice, Ice! Freeze the hearts of our enemies!"

As a tiger-man attempted to desert under enemy fire, an arrow of ice struck him in the back of the head. His body fell to the ground with a heavy *thud*. The sight of this fresh corpse made the bulky beast-folk unleash animalistic howls of terror. The chain of command had collapsed. A deer-man threw aside his weapon. A cat-man howled at the skies. A lion-man began to tear out chunks of his own mane.

Yet still the vampires showed no mercy.

Instead, they doubled down on bombarding the beast-folk even as they fled in a blind panic, taking sadistic delight in shooting them, crushing them underfoot, setting them on fire, and even blowing them up. It was as if there was no greater thrill in life for the vampires than this.

"Gyaaaah!"

"Don't! I don't wanna die yet!"

"Aargh! My tail! My freakin' TAIL is on FIRE!!!"

"Fire, Fire...!"

It was an all-out massacre.

Even the Supreme Commander of the Eastern Army (a chimpanzee-man) must have been wishing he could throw in the towel and go home. They could always reanimate with the power of the Dark Core, of course, but that didn't change the fact that getting your head lopped off was painful indeed.

And who enjoys getting hurt?

Nobody.

"Battle report! Battle report! The enemy forces have been decimated! At this exact moment, Lieutenant Bellius and Captain Mellaconcey are rushing the enemy's stronghold! The victory of the Komari Unit, of which we are all proud members, could not be more certain!"

As the victory message rang out clear and true across their stronghold, the vampires unknitted their brows and began to smile. "Not bad," exclaimed one. "Excellent," stated another.

It was located on the very western edge of the grasslands atop a small hill.

The Mulnite Imperial Army's battle fortress, that is.

"It looks like we've done it, then!"

"Yep. Beast-folk really are far too easy."

"Did you see that? Now *that* is the stuff the Komari Unit is made of!"

The strategy the vampires unleashed played out as follows:

First, the mighty warrior Lieutenant Bellius attacked the enemy stronghold with a daring front-on assault. This drew out the majority of the beast-folk forces, leaving Captain Mellaconcey free to sneak around the rear and infiltrate the fort. Then, taking advantage of the weak defenses, he easily captured their supreme commander, thus winning the engagement.

It was incredibly simple, but still more than enough to flummox the simpleminded beast-folk.

"Time for a victory party once we get home?"

"Heh-heh-heh, let's mix some liquor with beast-blood and have a toast!"

Confident in their triumph, the vampires slung their arms around one another and laughed with crass abandon.

But among the revelers was a single male vampire whose face was a stiff mask of absolute seriousness.

"It's too soon to celebrate. Our victory hasn't even been officially called yet."

Silence fell.

He wore an imposing military uniform and was so tall and thin that he resembled a stark winter tree devoid of leaves and branches.

His name was Caostel Conto, a self-proclaimed "monster" and member of the Imperial Army's Seventh Unit, aka the Komari Unit.

"War is a clash of minds. We can never truly know what kind of ace in the hole our opponents could be hiding. Have you no shame, crowing over an undetermined victory? Cretinous fools!"

Caostel's undeniable logic had the same sobering effect as a bucket of ice water poured on their heads. Cowed, the rest of the troop hushed.

"It's true that Bellius and Mellaconcey are formidable fighters, with a long history of greatness in combat. But anything can happen. No game of chess was ever won in only a single move. And this is still our first skirmish. Failure at this stage is simply not an option. Is that not right, Supreme Commander Terakomari?"

All eyes shifted to a single individual.

She was sitting to Caostel's left.

Draped across the ornate, sparkling throne, she stirred.

"Eh? Whassat?"

The young woman lifted her head, as if roused from a deep daydream.

Eventually, she seemed to realize that everyone was staring at her.

An attending maid leaned in and quickly whispered something in her ear.

"Lady Komari. *Psst. Psst. Psst...*"

"Huh? ...Ah. Yes, of course."

The young girl cleared her throat loudly before speaking.

"All right, listen up, everyone! Caostel's right. This is our first battle! Nobody wants to go home a loser, right? So let's give it our all!"

《《《《《《《   》》》》》》》》
....

Her high, clear voice rang out across the bloody grasslands.

All at once, her entire audience was overcome with overwhelming emotion.

She was beautiful—simply beautiful.

Golden hair, sparkling like trapped moonlight. Translucent white skin, pale as a corpse. A nose that looked as though it had been chiseled out of marble. And more striking than any other feature, the trademark crimson eyes of the Mulnite Empire's ancient vampire bloodline. Truly, there was no finer specimen of the vampire race than she.

Her full title: Supreme Commander Terakomari Gandesblood.

"…Uh, why's everyone so quiet all of a sudden? You *are* gonna do your best, aren't you?"

The hint of concern in her voice made all present suddenly gasp.

To fail to promptly respond when their beloved and respected supreme commander was trying to rally them—such a slight could never be properly compensated for, not even if they all got stark naked and committed ritual seppuku while dancing the hokey pokey.

They all roared in response as one, loud enough to shake the very earth beneath everyone's feet.

""""""*Yes, Supreme Commander! We'll go all out!*""""""

Supreme Commander Terakomari flinched for a second, but then she merely readjusted her limbs in her cozy chair, letting their overzealous, impassioned response wash over her.

Caostel dropped to his knee at her feet.

"Supreme Commander. I have but one request."

"Oh, wh-what is it? Spit it out."

"In the event that Bellius and Mellaconcey have failed…would you, Supreme Commander Terakomari, apprehend the enemy commander yourself?"

Time stood still.

"…Huh? Why?"

"As I have already explained, there are no certainties in war. Even such a sparkling gem as Terakomari Gandesblood, with all her might, her abundant wisdom, and her status as the supernova who is surely the obvious candidate to succeed the throne…even such an exalted one as she, could, were the fates unkind, find herself defeated by that uncouth chimp of an enemy commander. And yet! If you were only to take this opportunity to demonstrate your proficiency, in this, our first major clash, then it would make the name of Terakomari Gandesblood ring out the world over!"

The crowd all gasped appreciatively at this.

"Yeah, but…I don't think I should…"

"Moreover, to speak from my heart of hearts, I myself am dying to see it! The true power of Terakomari Gandesblood! I want to burn the image onto my retinas forevermore! The glory of the Crimson Lord, who, at the tender age of fifteen, has achieved the highest rank of supreme commander!"

"*I want to see it, too!*" "*Me too, me too!*" clamored the other soldiers, all gazing at their leader with the utmost admiration.

But for some reason, Supreme Commander Takamori seemed hesitant. "Er, yeah, but…," she hedged awkwardly. Nevertheless, Caostel was dead set on encouraging her.

"There is no need for bashfulness! Let us crush that poxy country of insignificant hybrid-folk! With but one mighty deed from our commander, we can elevate the reputation of the great Mulnite Empire across the land! After which historians will proclaim it thus: That your battle was the catalyst that marked a new dawn, a new era, for the world!"

"""""""*YEAAAAAAH!!!*"""""""

Inspired by Caostel's rousing speech, the vampires cheered raucously. Applause broke out, and before long, the din was deafening. Then a chant broke out— "*Ko-ma-rin! Ko-ma-rin! Ko-ma-rin!*"

In the midst of all the clamor, Supreme Commander Terakomari Gandesblood simply sat there. Then finally…

"O-okay, then…"

The cheering and applause came to an abrupt halt.

Everyone strained their ears to hear what she would say next.

Looking around at her subordinates, the supreme commander heaved a deep breath. Finally, she gave her shoulders a little shake and spoke.

"Since you all have such high expectations for me, I guess I'll have to give it my all. But I'm only going to act if both Bellius and Mellaconcey have failed. If, and only if, the two of them fall by some freak chance, then I will put all my energy into giving the enemy the pummeling of a lifetime. That's right, you all have nothing to fear! I'm the

©riichu

greatest, after all! I could fell even the mightiest enemy in about, oh, three seconds!"

"Three seconds…?"

"Ah, I misspoke! I meant one second! One! I could kill 'em all in, uh, one second each!"

It happened instantly.

The previous racket of cheering and clapping resumed anew as if it had never even paused.

—*YEAAAAAAAAAH!!!*

—*Ko-ma-rin! Ko-ma-rin! Ko-ma-rin!!!*

"Oh, ah-ha-ha… Oh my… How did things end up like this…?"

And so the curtain opens on the nerve-racking trials and tribulations of Terakomari Gandesblood…

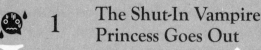

1 The Shut-In Vampire Princess Goes Out

The Vexations of a Shut-In Vampire Princess

The world has always seemed completely irrational to me.

Roughly fifteen years ago, I was born to a renowned aristocratic family of the Mulnite Empire.

The Gandesblood family.

First thing that probably jumped out at you is that our name has the word "blood" in it. A little on the nose for vampires, don't you think? With a name like that, our family has to suck. Well, they do literally suck, so I guess the name's pretty consistent.

The Gandesblood family has served as commanders in the Imperial Army for a thousand years. If you dig up our family tree a little, you'll find that all kinds of famous Gandesbloods have been written about in the history books. In fact, my own mother served as a Crimson Lord and commander of her own unit until five years ago.

Anyway, all the irrationality begins from there.

I feel like I shouldn't even have to explain this, but I'm actually a peace-loving, justice-seeking sort of vampire. I couldn't possibly be more different from those warmongers in my ancestral lineage. But my family members keep piling pressure on me. *"Komari's going to be a great commander one day,"* they all say, *"And she's going to slaughter those foreign fools in a massacre like you've never seen! She'll pen her name in the vampiric!"* I mean, give me a break.

At first, I really did try my best to live up to everyone's expectations of me, but I quickly had to give up.

I just don't have what it takes, you know?

First of all, I can't use magic.

Second, I'm a completely uncoordinated clumsy klutz.

Third, I'm super short.

And it's pretty obvious how I developed those handicaps.

I can't stomach drinking blood, you see.

The Gandesblood dining table has always been plentifully supplied with decanters of blood (origins unknown), but I could never understand the mentality of people who drink the stuff. My problem with it is basically the smell, and the way it looks, and just…ugh, everything about it.

Why do I have to force myself to drink such a foul liquid? Why am I expected to pretend to actually *enjoy* it?

And how can the others glug it down without gagging?

My *darling* younger sister, Lolocco, is fond of saying: *"Those who can't stomach blood are missing out on one of the finest things in life, hee-hee-hee."*

Just…shut up. Get off my back. I'm fine with tomato juice.

In society's eyes, though, I know it looks like I'm the heretic.

And this nonconformity of mine has bent my future path out of alignment.

No blood for a vampire means no growth, either.

Blood contains essential nutrients for vampires, so missing out on them leads to stunted growth and arrested development. My lack of any kind of magical ability, my clumsiness, and the fact that even my little sister towers over me in height…it's all because of malnutrition stemming from a lack of blood in my diet.

My life has been nothing but a series of bitter experiences.

At school I was picked on day in and day out, and sometimes I even got beaten up without provocation. So yeah, my classmates bullied me pretty badly. But I had to just endure it by myself somehow, since my dumbass relatives were all expecting such great things of me. I wasn't strong enough to hold up in that kind of environment, though.

So I decided to become a shut-in. Major introvert.

That was about three years ago.

In vampire society, power is everything. But I couldn't drink blood, couldn't use magic, I was clumsy and a shut-in. I just didn't belong. I was much more suited to entombing myself in my safe, comforting room and writing novels.

Yes, that would have been better for everyone…

It was morning. I awoke with my biological clock.

But I couldn't get up. Just couldn't do it. Wrapped snug in my blanket, I closed my eyes tight, squeezed the dolphin-shaped body pillow Daddy had bought me, and decided to settle in for a relaxing morning spent lolling about in bed. I was way too comfy to move.

I was a member of the idle rich, after all; someone totally disconnected from the harsh realities of the world.

Just as I was starting to drift back to sleep, I noticed something strange.

My belly itched. I scratched and scratched, but still the sensation persisted.

I was so itchy, I woke right up.

A bug had probably bitten me while I was sleeping, or something. Peeling back my pajamas, I peered down at myself reflexively through half-closed eyes.

"…Huh?"

Then I froze.

A strange pattern had bloomed on my skin just above my belly button.

The mark was very odd. It resembled the wings of a bat, dripping with blood. I had the feeling I'd seen it somewhere before, and the realization hit me a moment later. It was the national emblem of the

Mulnite Empire. The one that emblazoned the banners at the Imperial Palace.

I rubbed at it, but it wouldn't come off. Maybe I was dreaming.

"Good morning, Lady Terakomari."

My heart almost leaped out of my chest as a voice rang out.

I turned to see an unfamiliar girl standing in the corner of the room. Dressed in a maid's uniform, she had a cool gaze and a frosty aura about her.

But wait, did we have a maid like her working for us?

I glared at the girl, on high alert.

"Wh-who the heck are you? And what are you doing in my room?"

The maid arched an eyebrow.

"I apologize for not introducing myself sooner. My name is Villhaze. I'm with the Mulnite Imperial Army, and my rank is junior lieutenant, Third Division. I have been sent here to serve as your maid from today onward, Lady Terakomari."

What she was saying made no sense to me. Villhaze looked around my room with curiosity.

"Forgive me for my remark, but this room is quite a mess, is it not?"

Wow, how rude.

"What are you after? Is it money?"

"Please don't be startled. I'm here to help you, Lady Terakomari."

There was no way I could trust her. She could have been a burglar, or some kind of sadist sent to kidnap me. I needed to contact Daddy, ASAP. Plus, I needed to pee. But there was no way I could take a leak and leave this girl unattended in my room. Great, now what? Wet my pants?

"…Listen, Villhaze or whatever your name is. Wait here a sec, okay?"

"We don't have time to delay. You're to come with me to the Imperial Palace at once."

The Imperial Palace. Nothing about that sounded good.

Blessed with a nose for danger from birth, I attempted to slink away

©riichu

quietly like a cat. But just then, the maid got her arm around my neck and forced me into a headlock.

"Release me! I hafta go pee!"

"No time for urinating. Listen to what I'm saying, please."

"I'm gonna pee my pants! You want to just let that happen?!"

"You can listen to me while you're wetting yourself. I have no issue with that."

"You…you sick pervert!"

"No one is watching. Feel free to let it flow."

"*You're* watching!"

What the heck was wrong with her? Maybe she really was some kind of sicko trying to snatch me away. It would make sense. After all, I'm a total knockout beauty (that's what Daddy says to me every day, so I know it's true).

"There's no time. Just settle down, please."

"No way! You're here to abduct me, aren't you? Since I'm so incomparably gorgeous and all?"

"Sorry, but have you ever heard of modesty?"

As the girl and I continued our tug-of-war, someone else spoke.

"Unhand her now, Vill."

A low voice resounded from the hallway. Relieved that someone had come to save me, I turned to find a tall vampire standing there, dressed in a black coat. He took a step inside my room. Yes! Daddy! Tell her off! She's a sicko pervert maid who's trying to kidnap me! As I tried to communicate all this to him with my eyes, the girl immediately released me.

"Waah!"

I fell flat on my face, sliding across the floor. Ouch. That stung. My eyes were filled with tears, and I couldn't see.

The sicko maid completely ignored me and bowed her head low before Daddy.

"My deepest apologies, Lord Gandesblood. Lady Terakomari was quite reluctant, so I'm afraid I had to use force to bring her along."

So she *was* trying to kidnap me!

"Try to be gentler with my daughter. Everyone knows she's a serious shut-in."

"Ah, indeed. She's a dedicated homebody."

Could everyone stop calling me a shut-in right to my face? It's so rude. Besides, I'm the kind of recluse who could go outside if I really felt like it. I stay in only 'cause I have zero reason to go out. Why, I could go and hitchhike around the whole world by myself if I wanted.

"Now, Komari. Are you hurt?"

As I struggled to my feet in an undignified manner, Daddy approached with arms spread wide in a grandiose gesture. He even dusted me off and patted me down, which did nothing for my self-worth.

If he wasn't my dad, he would have been carted off to prison for manhandling me that way.

"Hmm. You seem all right, but should we take you to the doctor for a checkup? It would be terrible for anything to happen to such a knockout beauty, after all."

"Er, no thanks. I'm fine."

"Are you really okay, Lady Terakomari? Do you feel any strangeness at all around the stomach region?"

I scowled at the girl. Her sympathy was the last thing I wanted. But then I quickly remembered.

Oh yeah. That weird pattern on my belly. It was still super itchy.

Quick as a flash, the sicko maid reached out and peeled back my top.

"Oh dear. You mustn't scratch it like that! You'll ruin that silky skin!"

"Don't just pull my shirt up without asking, you perverted maid!"

I knocked her hand aside and quickly retreated three steps. She simply stared at me with her ice-cold eyes in response. Creepy. She had a super-threatening aura.

"Daddy! What's her deal?!"

"This is Villhaze, and she's going to be your personal maid starting from today. She'll do whatever you say, Komari, so use her well."

Whatever I say? But when I demanded to be released from her head-lock, she just completely ignored me.

"I don't need a maid. Especially not one as creepy as her!"

"It doesn't matter what you say, Komari. These orders come straight from the Empress. You'll just have to put up with it."

"The…Empress? What are you talking about?"

"Allow me to explain."

The weirdo maid took a step forward.

"Lady Terakomari, do you know of the Crimson Lords?"

"Um, yeah, but what's that got to do with anything?"

The Crimson Lords. The seven mightiest vampires in all the land, the mightiest and most exalted figureheads of the Imperial Army. But what did they have to do with this?

"Now you are one of their number, Lady Komari."

"Say what now?"

"Congratulations! It's very impressive indeed to be appointed as a Crimson Lord at just the tender age of fifteen!"

"Just hold on a sec… Why? And how?"

"Well, your father pulled a few strings…"

That's when Daddy started to smirk in this totally gross way.

"Komari, you mentioned something before about wanting to find employment, didn't you?"

My heart pounded in my chest.

"Um, did I?"

"Oh yes, I remember it well. It was during last year's Christmas party. Lolo asked you if it wasn't about time you got a job, and *you* said…"

"Employment, huh…? Of course, I understand the importance of labor. But I have a rare, scholarly intellect. There aren't too many jobs out there that are suited to me. Though if there was one, I guess it would have to be Empress of Mulnite, right? Yeah, I wouldn't mind working if I could be the Empress. That would be a sweet gig."

I felt my cheeks growing hot.

Now that Daddy had brought it up, I *think* I remember saying something like that.

"Ah, I was so moved to hear you say that, daughter dearest! My introverted Komari! My little shut-in! My daughter, who has been holed up in her room for three long years, finally showing some initiative toward work at long last!"

How could I have even responded to that? To be completely honest, I've never had the slightest inclination toward actually working. Sure, I might have been shooting my mouth off at the Christmas party and said something like, *"I wouldn't mind working if I could be the Empress, heh-heh,"* but that was just because I was drunk. Yeah, intoxicated. On, uh, apple juice.

"Y-yeah. You're right. I did say that. But what about it?"

"Well, not too long ago I went to see the Empress and asked if she wouldn't mind abdicating so you could have your turn on the throne."

Have you lost your mind?!

"But I'm afraid to say that put her in a very bad mood indeed."

Obviously.

"But I hung in there, Komari! Anything for my little girl."

Please, Daddy! Don't go taking crazy, unsolicited risks like that just for me!

"Anyway, I explained to the Empress what a genius you are. About that 'rare scholarly intellect' you're always telling everyone you have. About how you lock yourself up in your room all the time meditating and ruminating, totally ignorant of society. And of course, about how you're a bombshell for the ages. And when I laid all that out to her, the Empress was very impressed. In fact, the exact word she used was 'fascinating.'"

Fascinating?! I'd never been so insulted!

"In other words, the Empress is all aboard the Komari train now. But obviously it's not proper procedure to hand over the throne to a young lady who hasn't even been fully evaluated yet. So this is where your tenure as a Crimson Lord comes into play."

The sicko maid nodded along.

"It is exactly as Lord Gandesblood says. Mulnite Empire tradition dictates that only someone with a distinguished military record can be crowned. Furthermore, serving as a Crimson Lord is an essential prerequisite for the position. Thus, you have been assigned a member of the Seven Crimson Lords so that Her Highness can evaluate your abilities. Incidentally, I have also been assigned to assist you as your personal maid. I am pleased to make your acquaintance."

My head was spinning.

The Crimson Lords. I knew about them. They were an elite group of absolute war demons who slew other races in the Dark Core Zones all around the world. But I'm a peace-and-justice-loving vampire. There was no way I'd fit in with that band of barbarians.

I was completely unfit for that sort of work. *Duh.*

This conversation was completely beyond me. Also, I really needed to pee. So I decided to ignore the both of them and head to the little girls' room. On my way out, though…

"Hold on!"

Horrifyingly, the sicko maid dropped to her knees and grabbed me around the thighs.

"I am your personal maid, Lady Terakomari, sent to aid you during your military rule! Please, please say you'll join the Crimson Lords! Otherwise, I'll have no reason to live!"

"G-get off me! Stop *shaking* me! You want me to pee on you?!"

"I am your personal lady-in-waiting, Lady Terakomari! I am honored to accept your urine!"

"What?! Daddy! Help me!"

"But Vill here is an exemplary servant, the perfect fit for someone with your exceptional level of intelligence. She's going to help you get ahead in life, Komari."

"The only place I want to get to right now is the bathroom!"

"Please, Lady Terakomari, I beg you to join the Seven Crimson Lords and become a Crimson Lord!"

"Never! Never, never, never!"

I gave the sicko maid my fiercest "don't mess with me" look.

"In fact, let me take this chance to say this! I'm going to become a novelist! In fact, I'm working on several novels right now! I'm just going to stay right here in my room and write a whole bunch of stories, without going outside and without dealing with other people! Me, seeking employment? I was clearly just paying lip service! You actually took me seriously? How dumb are you?!"

It wasn't until I'd already finished ranting that I realized...

Realized that both the pervert maid and Daddy were staring at me with flabbergasted expressions.

I felt a pang of regret.

Being a shut-in for so long can make a person's mind a little loopy, I guess.

The way I used to be, up until a few years ago...I would have *never* yelled at Daddy. The mere prospect would have seemed absurd.

"S-so anyway...the point is, I'm *not* becoming a Crimson Lord. No way."

"But..."

"Just...get off my back!"

"But, Lady Terakomari, if you don't join the army as a Crimson Lord, you will be fated to die by explosion..."

"...What?"

What did she just say?

Blowing up? Me?

"Vill is right, Komari."

Daddy was gazing at me, brows knitted with concern.

"It's compulsory to make a contract with the Empress in order to join the Crimson Lords... This contract stipulates that, in exchange for partaking in the perks of the Crimson Lord status, you swear your complete fealty to the Empire. And if you break that contract for whatever reason, you'll magically combust..."

"Er, but I don't remember signing anything..."

"She snuck in late last night to do it."

"…Who did?"

"The Empress. She sealed the contract with a kiss while you were sleeping, Lady Komari."

"Whaaat??!!"

A smooch? Are you freaking kidding me? Like on the lips?! Okay, yes, a kiss is a classic magical contract sealer, we all know that, but how messed up it is to sneak in and do that while someone's *sleeping*?!

"…Wait a minute! Sealing magic should only be binding if both parties agree! I don't recall consenting to anything!"

"Your father accepted on your behalf, as your representative."

"Daddy! How could you?!"

I turned and started pummeling him with my fists, but he just laughed. *Oh, ha-ha-ha you colossal idiot!*

Now it was all coming together. The weird symbol that had appeared on my stomach was proof of the contract. Unbelievable. Talk about a violation! I could totally sue for this!

"This is the worst thing ever. My life is completely over!"

"Lady Terakomari, please accept a personal letter from the Empress."

The weirdo maid handed me a gaudy, ostentatiously designed sheet of stationery. I quickly scanned it.

> *Komari, I have decided to appoint you to the Crimson Lords. It has already been settled by blood oath. At this juncture, you have no way of defying my orders. If you do not wish to be blown to bits, you will take up your position in the Crimson Lords and do your utmost to impress me so that you may succeed me as the next Empress. Your potential as supreme commander and Crimson Lord aside, I must admit that I have already evaluated your looks most highly. You are indeed the most beautiful girl in the whole empire. Simply watching you as you slumbered gave me full-body tingles.*
>
> *By the way, I have heard the rumors that you are loath to imbibe blood. This is highly irregular for a vampire. Still, I have made allowances for this odd*

circumstance. Instead of exchanging blood to seal our agreement, as is tradition, I instead shared my saliva with you, by way of a kiss of the extremely juicy variety. This is exceptionally special treatment indeed, so you should savor the lingering taste of my noble spittle upon your lips. See that you comprehend the honor it is.

EWWWWWWWWWWWWWWWWWW!!!

"Isn't that nice, Lady Terakomari?"

"It is *not* nice! It gives me the creeps! I hadn't even had my first kiss yet..."

"Well, it was as good a time as any, and now you can join the Crimson Lords. Oh, you're going to be such an exalted member of society! I'll be able to puff out my chest with pride and brag about my daughter now!"

Daddy was roaring with laughter, but it sounded far away and muffled to my ears.

Supreme commander. Crimson Lord.

Why did I have to take up such a violent vocation, of all things? If I simply had to have a job, why couldn't it have been a more peaceful one? Like working in a cake shop or something...

"Congratulations, Lady Terakomari. Now, let's dive straight into your upcoming schedule. First, you have an audience with the Empress two hours hence. Afterward, you'll be meeting your subordinates for the first time. Tomorrow, you have your first battle with the neighboring Lapelico Kingdom. And then after that..."

The sicko maid was grinning as she reeled off the itinerary they'd prepared for me. None of her words made any sense to me.

Why? Why was this happening to me? I never should have said all that stuff about wanting to become the next Empress. And how did Daddy manage to convince the current Empress to consider me anyhow? Even his connections shouldn't have stretched that far. Could it be blackmail? *Daddy, no!*

But ruminating on it wasn't going to change anything.

This was my current reality now. Stark, harsh reality.

All those years I'd spent desperately trying to avoid real life had caught up with me at last. With a vengeance.

"Noooo!!!"

My last vestiges of self-control abandoned me as I fell to my knees and wailed in despair.

But only for a moment. I still had to pee, after all. I quickly got to my feet and scuttled off to the bathroom.

This time, no one tried to stop me.

One hour later.

"Hey, you. Whatsyername. Villhaze."

"You can just call me Vill."

"Oh, okay… In that case, you can just call me Komari. Everyone in my family calls me that."

"Certainly, Lady Komari."

"Um… Anyway, Vill…how many subordinates am I getting? Like five?"

"Five hundred."

I almost fell on my butt. Not only was that a big number to process, but the bright sunlight was also making me feel dizzy. I hadn't been in the sun in a long while.

"Ugh, it's far too bright outside."

"Oh, Lady Komari! Please, hang in there! I am escorting you right to the bathroom."

"Why the bathroom of all places?!"

"Because you seemed to want to go so very badly."

"I already took care of that!!!"

An hour had passed since the sicko maid came crashing into my life.

Oh, reality was truly unbearable.

I kept pinching my cheeks, hoping this might just be a dream after all. But all that did was make them sore. No, this was real life, my idiotic fate…to join the Crimson Lords under orders from the Empress, on pain of being blown up. Okay, so I probably deserved it on some level, but wasn't this all just a bit too cruel?! I clutched the hair on my temples in despair.

"Ohhh! I don't *want* to be a commander in the army!"

"Well, do you want to die?"

"No…but…"

Of course I didn't wanna die. That's why I was outside in the first place.

Let's go back an hour. Realizing there was no way I could dodge my impending military service, I announced the official end of my shut-in period in front of all the servants, who broke into uproarious applause. Even Daddy was bawling. My elder sister and brother appeared from who knows where and started congratulating me. Despite my despair, I actually started to feel a tiny bit pleased, maybe even moved. Although hearing my younger sister—who had also shown up to wish me well—mutter *"Is Big Sis Koma gonna die?"* was going to stick with me for a while. Don't jinx me like that.

Daddy explained what was expected of me. It was only one thing.

"Every three months, you must do battle with one of our enemy countries and emerge victorious."

That was the minimum duty expected of a Crimson Lord, and if I couldn't manage that, I would automatically explode and become a star in the heavens high above. It was all so cruel that I couldn't help bawling a little. But there was an additional clause as well.

"If you can win a hundred battles, then you will earn the right to stand as the heir apparent to the Empress."

Right now, that part of the deal meant less than nothing to me.

"Please, let us make haste. There are only twenty minutes until your audience with the Empress."

I quickly swung myself up the steps of the horse carriage Vill had called for. I hadn't ridden in a carriage in, like, three years. Actually, I hadn't even been outside the house in that entire time. Unused to physical exertion, I couldn't suppress heaving a huge sigh as I stumbled over and flopped down on the seat.

Then we drove for a while before arriving at our destination.

I gazed up at the Imperial Palace for the first time. Under the circumstances, it looked creepy and foreboding in its splendor. Our house was pretty big, to be sure, but it seemed tiny when compared to this sprawling castle.

After announcing ourselves to the guards, they smoothly escorted us to the audience chamber.

Oh yikes, now I was getting really nervous.

"Aha! Welcome, welcome, Komari! As lovely as ever, I see!"

The Empress leaped lightly off her throne and came bounding toward me, a huge grin plastered on her face.

She resembled a young girl around the same age as me, with distinctive bright blond hair. But I knew better than to let her angelic looks deceive me. The Empress was a true demon who'd slain countless enemy commanders during her time in the prior generation of Crimson Lords. Even worse, she was a notorious lady lover, who, upon seeing a cute girl, would defy all laws of decency and decorum and immediately start groping her. Yes, she was a witch! A sapphic witch! And…whoa! She was all up in my business! Too close! Back off! *Oh gosh, she really is a pervert!*

"Komari, darling! I am *so* happy to meet you at last!"

Her nose was less than an inch away from mine. I could feel her breath on my cheeks. She smelled sweet. Her eyes were the color of moonlight. I felt a strong urge to run screaming, but that might have been misinterpreted as *lèse-majesté*, which could have earned me a spot under the guillotine.

"Uh, excuse me, Your Majesty, but don't you think you're a bit too close?"

"What's wrong with an Empress and her top commander being close?"

"Uh, I don't mean that, I meant in terms of physical proximity…"

©riichu

"By the way, I'd very much like to fondle your breasts. Do you mind?"

As she spoke, she reached out brazenly toward my chest. Oh yeah, I was spot on. She was an undeniable pervert. I was going to have to exercise extreme caution whenever she was around.

"Your Majesty, please be moderate in your japery. Lady Komari is about to weep."

Just as I was about to start bawling all over again from fear, the sicko maid interjected on my behalf. Her assistance was…unexpected. *So it looks like even the weirdo maid has some common sense.* Just as that flashed through my mind, the Empress tossed her head back and laughed. "Only joking!" she trilled, trotting back over to her throne and sitting down. Joking. Great. Just great.

"I like to get verbal consent; it's just the way I roll. So I won't fondle the goods until you say so."

"You already kissed me without consent…"

"Hmm!"

The Empress looked taken aback for just a moment.

"…Wa-ha-ha! Fascinating, simply fascinating! You didn't even call me 'Your Majesty'! Why, it's almost as if we've been best friends for a decade or so already! I like it!"

Friends? I've never had a friend in my life.

Ignoring my blank expression, the Empress crossed her legs daintily before speaking again.

"You know, you're really so much like your mother. I mean, your vibe is sorta different, but chatting with you kinda takes me back!"

"What…really?"

"Mm. You've got the same beautiful face as her. Yulinne Gandes-blood was a real siren, a true beauty back in the day, and you've got the exact same facial features. It's uncanny, it actually gives me the shivers! Ah, Yulinne, how I hoped to make you mine one day, but that rogue Armand stole you away with his man-charms… Oh my! That pendant around your dainty neck—it's Yulinne's, is it not?"

"Er..."

I cringed back as the Empress's eyes bore into my neck.

Now I was completely mute and frozen. She chortled breezily. "Sorry, my bad!" she said, waving her hand.

"None of my business really, is it? Anyway, Terakomari Gandes-blood. You are about to join the Crimson Lords. Are you feeling prepared?"

"Sure."

Not in the slightest.

"Because if you're feeling apprehensive, I find a nice juicy smooch often helps..."

"Y'know what? I think I do feel pretty confident..."

"Come on, let's smooch! It'll give you a real boost!"

"N-no thanks! I feel confident! Super-confident! Paws off!"

"Ah-ha-ha! You really are a fascinating little thing!"

Fascinating?! How?!

But the Horny Empress was obviously deaf to my internal screaming.

"Well, that's enough jokes for now. Let's get back to the topic at hand. With you all set to join the Crimson Lords, there's a few things I need to warn you about."

"...Warn me?"

"Yeah. You're actually super weak, aren't you?"

I twitched.

But there was no real reason for me to hide it. My complete lack of any combat skills would be immediately apparent to anyone who did even the slightest bit of digging into my personal background.

"So what if am? Oh, are you saying I'm too frail to join the Crimson Lords after all? I totally get that. So I think the best thing for me would be to return home at once, and—"

"Fear not. My kiss is the only seal of approval needed for your appointment as a Crimson Lord."

Drat.

"The issue is whether you can do the job or not. You probably know this already, but being a Crimson Lord and supreme commander is a very important role. If you can't manage to slay the enemy commander, your wages will just continue to decrease and decrease."

"So you mean…if I do a poor job, I'll get…fired?"

"Yeah. Fired right into the sky. BOOM!"

Oh great. Just when I was thinking I'd actually managed to find a tiny shred of hope.

"Anyway, that's what I expect of you. Now, are you prepared to slay the enemy commanders?"

The Empress's gaze grew solemn.

But I refused to be rattled this time.

"Just so you know, I happen to possess a rare scholarly intellect."

The Empress folded her arms, eyebrows rising. "Aha," she said. "I've heard all about that from Armand…I mean, your father. Apparently, what you lack in physical prowess, you more than compensate for with your quick mind."

"Precisely. The amount of knowledge I've managed to amass in a mere fifteen years of life is enough to put the average grown-up to absolute shame. So even if I lack prowess on the battlefield, I have enough knowledge of warfare and tactics to direct an army to victory. Why, I've read every volume of *The Andronos Chronicles*, I'll have you know. You're probably familiar already, but that series has fourteen volumes, and each volume is over four hundred pages. I've memorized every single battle plan that appears across the entire series. It's all up here. I'll make an amazing supreme commander. I don't need practical battle skills, not even the tiniest little bit."

Right. The reason I agreed to go along with joining the army as a Crimson Lord in the end was because I was confident I wouldn't need to do any actual fighting. If I had been ordered to become a regular soldier instead, I would surely have thrown my dignity out the window and got down on my knees to beg for clemency. That would have been my only option. Yup. I mean, nope.

"Lady Komari, that just sounds a bit too…"

For some reason, the pervert maid was looking at me with sympathy.

The Empress, however, was grinning with amusement. What did I say that was so funny?

"…Very well. Let's assume that you are as talented a commander as you say. Nevertheless, are you confident your subordinates will accept a weakling's orders? Strength is everything in vampire society, after all."

"What, you think my subordinates are going to force me to do push-ups or something?"

"No, I think they're going to mutiny against you and overthrow you."

I felt a huge lump in my throat as the Empress continued.

"The previous leader of your unit, your direct Crimson Lord predecessor, was sadly overthrown and killed. All because he happened to be weaker than the people he was supposed to command."

"Just…just hang on a second! And you just let them get away with that?!"

"Not officially. But it happens a lot, you know; mutiny in the ranks. The vampires responsible for murdering the previous commander are all still members of the army in good standing. Why waste good soldiers? I have no plans to punish them at this time."

"So your point is…?"

"Ah, yes. Should your subordinates find out how weak you really are, they will no doubt beat you to death. You know our kind—we all strive for domination, don't we?"

"Domination…"

A bead of cold sweat slid down my back. I could hear my pulse throbbing in my ears.

"…You can't just let that happen to me! Dying like that has gotta really, really hurt! Worse than trapping your finger in a desk drawer!"

"Oh, you loathe the thought of expiring that much?"

"Obviously!!!"

"But if you die, you can go back to being a shut-in again."

"Agh…"

Thanks to the power of the Dark Core, we vampires can regenerate over and over after death. It's basic vampirology, something every kid grows up knowing. So theoretically, if my unit ended up murdering me, and I was forced to retire from my position in the army, that would solve all my problems, right? But…I didn't want that to happen.

"I don't wanna kick the bucket. Besides, Daddy worked hard to get me this opportunity. I have to see it through. Failure is…not an option."

The Empress gave me a hard, piercing stare for a few moments, before her cheeks crinkled into a smile.

"Then you'll just have to hide your true nature, won't you? No matter what happens, you need to pretend to be brave and strong as long as your subordinates' eyes are on you. That maid standing beside you will support you every step of the way."

"You can count on me, Lady Terakomari. Together we'll pull the wool over the eyes of every last one of them!"

"Why does that not make me feel better?"

I had been given no fixed term for serving in the Crimson Lords as a unit commander. My options were either to keep fighting in the wars indefinitely, get overthrown, or achieve the rank of Empress Heir Apparent. I had no other avenues of escape. My seemingly endless tour of duty was about to commence.

"Vill…*you* won't mutiny against me, will you?"

"Never. I love you more than anyone else in the universe, Lady Terakomari."

You filthy liar. You've only just met me.

At the Mulnite Palace's Bloody Hall, located in the Crimson Tower, the vampires assigned to the nascent Commander Komari were all lined up in a row. All wore crimson-colored attire and looked most fearsome. Their bloodshot eyes rolled around as they awaited the arrival of their new commander. However…

"Hurry up! What are you *doing*, Commander?!"

A golden-haired youth stamped his foot in unrestrained frustration. His name was Yohann Helders. A rookie genius who specialized in fire magic.

"Look, it's five minutes past the time we were supposed to meet her! This tardy slacker is supposed to be our new leader? Seriously? I'm not having it! We should march to the Empress and demand that she fire this new Crimson Lord immediately!"

Yohann looked around at the other vampires, seeking agreement.

Some nodded along, but they were all sycophants who agreed with whatever left his lips. The majority of the vampires were actually against him.

"Seriously? Doesn't it piss the rest of you off? Basic timekeeping is, like, rule number one of adulting!"

"Be quiet, you annoying gnat. We are to fulfill the commander's orders. It's not our place to voice complaints."

A low voice rumbled across the room. It belonged to a large man with the head of a wolf who was leaning against a wall, arms crossed. This was Bellius Hund Cerbero.

Shooting a look of hatred at Bellius, Yohann spat, "What's that you say, dog-head? You want to be sent back to the beast-folk kingdom in a crate, hmm?!"

"Excuse me, maggot? What did you just say to me? Someone ought to cut out that flapping tongue of yours, you impudent little brat."

"Excuse *me*? Who are you calling a brat? I'm twenty years old!"

"With a mental age of three. We should inform the local kindergarten that you've escaped from the sandbox."

All of a sudden, there was a loud snapping sound.

It was Yohann. He'd snapped.

"I'm gonna freakin' kill ya!!!"

With a silent spell, Yohann conjured the flames of hell and launched himself across the room with floor-shaking might. Now he was a mere sixteen feet away from his opponent. Close enough to punch him in the kisser in the space of a second.

"Quick to anger, I see, like all brats are."

Bellius readied his hatchet. The rubberneckers all cheered in approval, and flames licked the ceiling as the two immediately launched into an all-out attack. But just at that moment…

CLANG! Yohann slammed into an invisible wall, before ricocheting off backward.

Sprawled on his back, the vampire scrambled to get back to his feet and regain his dignity. His eyes were darting all around. That was when he spotted another man, right hand still outstretched.

"Caostel! Don't interfere!"

"Comrades fighting among themselves…pitiful. Sheathe your weapons, the both of you."

"Pah!"

But the man simply smiled, in a "that puts an end to that" type of way.

His name was Caostel Conto. He was as tall and imposing as a stark, branchless tree. Of the vampires present, he was undoubtedly the most evenly matched magic user with Yohann.

As Yohann gnashed his teeth in frustration, he felt someone pat him on the back.

He whirled around.

Before him stood a flashy-looking man, flipping him off with both hands.

"The name's Mellaconcey, check this sexuality! Little brat from the sandbox, you ain't no match for me! Who's the greatest? Mella-concey! DIG IT!"

Infuriated, Yohann jabbed him right in the face.

Why was this unit composed solely of the most irritating specimens?

"…Ahem. Let's put an end to these silly quarrels, shall we? The new commander is on her way, and we don't want her to see us behaving so shamefully now, do we?"

"I agree. We should wait patiently for her to arrive."

"Dig it! Kindergarten brat, don't know how to wait and see? Let's get lit and bust it up, then lay it down real freaky!"

This back-and-forth between the three of them was nothing new to the rest of the unit.

Infuriated, Yohann made a leap toward Mellaconcey, but this time his sycophants all intervened and grabbed him, holding him back.

Caostel crossed his arms, casting a sideways glance over at the struggling golden-haired rookie.

"Still, I do understand your sentiments, Yohann. None of us knows anything about this young lady, this 'Terakomari Gandesblood' who has been appointed to the Crimson Lords. She's a complete stranger to us."

Bellius snorted air through his nose.

"Lady Terakomari's mother was in the previous generation of Crimson Lords. And the Gandesbloods are one of the Mulnite Empire's finest families. I'd hardly call her a stranger."

"Dig it! Gandesblood, Empire, aristocrats, yeah! Bellius the Imperial dog is barkin' everywhere!"

Mellaconcey went flying after being decked again. Courtesy of Bellius this time.

Caostel rolled his eyes and sighed.

"I wonder if this Terakomari girl has the slightest hope at all of leading a bunch of wild and uncouth misfits..."

"If not...then it's gonna happen again, isn't it?"

"Oh yeah. And who will do the honors this time? Bellius?"

"If the situation called for it, I would. I'm not as hasty as half the idiots in the Seventh Unit, though. It's thanks to the unfettered actions of those morons that we're saddled with this 'Blood-Smeared Unit' reputation after all."

"Man, this revolving door of commanders is a serious pain in the ass."

"Then why don't you assume command, hmm?"

"Not me. The Empress hates me, and all of us guys here."

The Seventh Unit of the Mulnite Imperial Army.

It was a ragtag bunch, consisting of misfits who hadn't managed to fit in elsewhere. Half of the vampires in this squad of five hundred had been demoted from more important teams following incidents of rule-breaking and troublemaking. The other groups in the Imperial Army looked down on the Seventh Unit and regarded them as nothing more than a motley crew of uncouth, undisciplined, rowdy losers.

Mutinies and uprisings were common throughout its history.

"I do hope the commander manages to hang on for longer this time, though. We can't very well go to war without a leader in charge. Ah, speak of the devil—it sounds like she's arrived!"

Bellius turned his head to where Caostel was looking.

The great doors of the Bloody Hall opened with a *bang.*

From the corner of the room, someone sprang forward.

"*En garde!* I don't know where you came from, but you're crazy to think you'll ever stand in charge of ME!"

It was Yohann. His sycophants all scrambled to stop him, begging him to stand down, but he silenced them with wildly swung punches then dashed forward with fireballs streaking from both of his outstretched fists.

"…Huh. Should we stop him?"

"Nah, let's see how this plays out. We can gauge the capabilities of the Crimson Lord."

Caostel smirked wickedly.

☆ (Let's go back a bit, shall we?)

After the audience with the Empress came the first meeting with the subordinates.

I followed Vill as she escorted me to the East Tower, accessible to all high-ranking Imperial Army personnel. It was otherwise known as the Crimson Tower. According to Vill, the tower was a fairly subdued part of the palace complex. And indeed, its thick white walls gave off a sturdy, military aura, without a hint of luxury. It was hardly the kind of place one would expect to find someone with such a superlative mind like myself.

Vill dragged me excitedly to a dressing room.

"Here, change into this."

She handed me a Mulnite Imperial Army uniform. It was pretty stylish, but as I stared at it, I couldn't help wondering all over again how I'd ended up here changing into something worn for combat.

"I'll help you undress. Arms up."

"N-no thanks. I can do it myself."

"Nonsense. I am your attending maid, Lady Komari. It is my duty to undress you."

"No it's not! You just stand over there! And don't move!"

"If you insist. Then I shall simply stand here and observe your strip-tease, Lady Komari."

"No! Don't look!"

Was it my imagination, or was she getting more depraved by the minute? If I didn't do something about her soon, I got the feeling I'd end up on the receiving end of a serious personal space violation. Feeling awkward and exposed, I changed as quickly as possible. Then I checked myself out in the full-length mirror. Hmm, not bad. The Mulnite uniform was pretty chic. Military officers certainly made waves when they were spotted about town.

"That looks wonderful on you, Lady Komari."

"D-does it? Well, I *am* a knockout beauty after all, I guess. I'd probably look good in anything."

"Yes, you look amazing. Adorably adorable. Once we get home, I'd love it if you would give me a fashion show… I'll prepare a variety of period costumes for you to model. It will be such fun. You'd look amazing in formal wear, I bet, but also very pretty in something more coquettish… Perhaps a nice party dress, or even a Gothic Lolita ensemble…"

"When hell freezes over!"

I rolled my eyes. The last thing I wanted to do was indulge the sicko maid's perverted dress-up doll fantasies. Taking the initiative, I swept out of the dressing room even though I knew there was nowhere to escape to. It would be better to just get this meeting over with.

"Amazing… You look just like a real Crimson Lord."

"Well, I am about to become one. Against my will, of course, but here we are."

Examining myself in the uniform had caused a heavy feeling of resignation to wash over me. My heart was still thumping like crazy, and I was afraid that my knees and hands would start shaking if I didn't keep myself distracted.

We strolled through the building for several minutes, passing quite a few vampires, who stopped and bowed before me with a strange sense of reverence. Then, at last, we reached the door to our destination. This was the "Bloody Hall," where my subordinates were waiting to greet me. Curious about the weird name, I asked Vill about it. "Oh, there was a murder in there once," she told me. If that was meant to be a joke, I didn't find it particularly funny.

Taking a deep breath, I placed a trembling hand on the door to push it open. But it wouldn't budge.

Sheesh, this is heavy! What was with these giant double doors? Not exactly friendly to elderly or disabled visitors, were they?

"Guh! How much does this entrance weigh, a million tons?!"

"Nonsense. Any vampire of average strength could open them."

"Oh, well, ex-CUSE me for not being of average strength! Ex-CUSE me for being feeble!"

Grumbling, I began slamming my body weight against the doors. I really wanted to make a dramatic entrance by flinging open both of them at the same time, but if I actually had that amount of physical strength, I really would have used it to subdue the sicko maid and run home to the safety of my bedroom instead. *Oh, I think it budged a little.*

"You can do it, Lady Komari."

"Don't just stand there! Help me!"

Vill just placidly ignored me. I was furious. Beyond incensed. But anger wasn't going to serve me in this situation. Trembling with fatigue, I managed to scrape one of the doors open about halfway. Yes! Entrance! Then, just as I was about to step triumphantly through…

"Die, Commander Scum!!!"

"...Huh?"

Through the crack in the door, I saw it.

A demented golden-haired youth, barreling toward me with murder in his eyes.

"Wait, what the—?!!!"

"Hyah-ha-ha! My flame attack will burn that shining mane of yours to a crisp! Taste the wrath of my...GAH!!!"

There came a thick, heavy boom, followed by a juicy crunch.

I *think* it was the sound of the door closing?

I wasn't exactly sure what made it, 'cause I wasn't looking. As soon as I clapped eyes on that psycho running in my direction, I instantly went into tactical retreat mode. I released my grip on the door, leaped behind Vill, and adopted the brace position as a strategic means of... Oh, all right, then. I ran away in terror and hid behind the skirts of a maid. I mean, I had no idea what was going on! What was wrong with that lunatic back there?! He was shouting about killing me! Someone contact the authorities!

"Are you all right, Lady Komari?"

"Y-y-yeah, I th-think s-s-o..."

"There, there. Good girl."

Vill hugged me gently as I crouched there trembling.

I was so totally overwhelmed. That crazy dude back there must have been one of my subordinates, right? Why was he trying to take me out?! Surely they at least wanted to *meet* me first before mutinying against me? Were they all just brain-dead morons? And while this hug from Vill was nice and all, did she really have to be kneading my butt and boobs with her palms? Gosh, she really was lecherous, wasn't she?

"What...what should I do, Vill? Maybe they've already found out about what a weakling I am..."

"Fear not, Lady Komari. You have already proven victorious over the lawless traitor."

"Er, what?"

I gazed at her in confusion before I followed her eyes to see what she was staring at.

Then I thought my jaw was going to drop clean off.

The golden-haired youth was sandwiched between the two portals, and he wasn't moving.

"Vill…Is he…"

"He's dead."

"He's dead?!"

There was a murder in the Bloody Hall all right! And I was the perpetrator!

"That was wonderful! You took out a vampire without employing weapons, magic, or physical force at all. Such skill! You truly are an unmatched genius, and the rightful Crimson Lord and Unit Commander, Terakomari Gandesblood!"

"Stop clapping! Shit, why did this have to happen to me?!"

I quickly hurried over to the dead guy trapped in the doors. Thanks to the Dark Core, no one really expires in the Mulnite Empire territory, at least not during their natural lifespan. Even this dude would regenerate good as new in a few days. Still, killing a person, however temporarily, made me feel pretty bad about myself.

"Oh dear…I feel like I should lay flowers or something…"

"Flowers? Just spit on the body and step over it. Besides, we have more important matters to attend to. Your subordinates await within!"

Vill scoffed then slammed her palms on the doors and swung them open with ease. It made my pathetic huffing and puffing from earlier seem even more shameful in hindsight. I suddenly felt too small and insignificant to reply. Saying a silent prayer over the body of the fallen man with golden locks, I quickly hurried after my maid.

The next instant, an overwhelming wave of dread washed over me.

The vast hall was filled with vampires, all lined up waiting for me. But these were no ordinary creatures of the night. Though clad in military attire, they appeared disheveled and rough. And all of them had their eyes fixed on me.

Ah, nope. Can't do this.

I turned to flee, but Vill grabbed my arm straightaway. After seeing how she pushed open those heavy doors, I knew I had no chance of shaking her off. I was done for.

"Terakomari Gandesblood. We've been expecting you."

One of the soldiers stepped forward. He was tall, like a stark, leafless tree, and clad in a crimson uniform. Obviously a vampire. I was so nervous, I thought I was gonna die, and when he dropped to his knee in front of me, I was sure I was going to go into cardiac arrest.

"It is an honor to make your acquaintance. I am Caostel Conto, First Lieutenant of the Mulnite Imperial Army's Seventh Unit. May your tenure with us be long and fruitful."

"Oh, uh, thank you..."

Caostel beamed, gazing up at me as I stammered out a basic response.

"Supreme Commander, I am extremely impressed. To have slain the bloodthirstiest member of our troop, Yohann Helders, in a single blow...I can scarcely believe it."

He must have been talking about that blond kid. But I didn't *mean* to kill him. I mean... *Oh, wait. This might be my lucky break. I should try to affect an air of confidence, without being arrogant about it.*

"Hmph. I could kill a weakling vampire like that with only my pinky finger."

The crowd all began to murmur with excitement.

Uh-oh. Maybe the pinky finger bit was overdoing it a little? But it was too late to back down now. I would have to push through. Caostel was staring me right in the eye, one eyebrow arched.

"Your...your *little* finger, did you say?"

"Yup. This one here."

"But...Yohann is a highly trained vampire soldier..."

"I, too, am highly trained! You all don't know much about me, that's clear, but those who are aware never even make so much as a pinky promise with me, lest they wish to have their finger snapped clean off!"

"Oh my..."

I was pushing it, for sure, but they all seemed to believe me somehow. But yikes, I sure was playing with fire. I resolved not to come out with any further rash, boasting claims. If they found out I was lying, I would be destined for a painful demise. *I should adopt a more laid-back persona and rely on my tone of voice and body language to convey confidence.* Yeah, I could do that. With my rare scholarly intellect and all.

"Actually, Lady Komari killed a hundred vampires in her youth using her pinky finger alone. If she wanted to, she could eviscerate every vampire present in this hall within the span of a mere five seconds."

Excuse me, sicko maid?!

I couldn't believe what she was saying. And no one else would believe insane claims like that, either! Wait, why was she shooting me a thumbs-up?! Did you seriously think I'd actually be pleased to have you "back me up" like that?!!!

"Furthermore, Lieutenant Conto, your tone is completely inappropriate. If you truly wish to pledge fealty to Lady Komari, then you had better get down on the floor and lick her shoe."

Ack! Shut up! Lick my what?! Yikes, he's gonna kill you for that! Eek, look at his eyes! There's bloodlust in them! There's... Oh, wait, not so much...?

"I apologize for my lack of decorum. Supreme Commander, may I have permission to lick your shoe?"

"No! No way! Ewww!"

I yelped by pure reflex, but then I instantly regretted it. What if he felt rejected and got violent? But no, Caostel was already prostrating himself on the floor before me with lightning rapidity.

"Please, forgive me. It is just as you say. A lowly wretch such as I should have never deigned to touch the feet of one so exalted as you, Supreme Commander. I ought to be thrown into the dungeon for even suggesting it."

I felt my skin crawl.

Yes, the groveling was pathetic. But it was enough to finally convince me that this man truly meant no harm. Feeling a little bit less frazzled now, I composed myself and spoke in a calm tone of voice.

"Now, now…lift your head. Enough of the introductions—hadn't we better get on to the speech?"

"Yes, Supreme Commander! Right away! The members of the Seventh Unit…I mean, the Komari Unit…are all waiting to hear you speak!"

Komari Unit? How embarrassing.

Well, whatever. I had more important things to worry about. I would let it slide, along with the pinky finger thing. If I didn't keep pushing forward, I was going to have a full-on emotional meltdown.

I glanced around the room, trying to stand tall even as I trembled. Just then, all five hundred of the rough-looking vampire soldiers took a knee in unison. Now I was so terrified that I was certain I would break out in tears before this was through. But I couldn't run. I had to stand firm. I had to get through this. I took a deep breath, then let it out. Deep breath…and let it out. Okay… Go for it, Komari!

"Friends, vampires, countrymen!"

Oh, yikes, that sounded far less cheesy in my head… Still, no time to dwell on the cringe. I had my whole speech planned out, and I'd been practicing it over and over on the way here. Now was the time to say it aloud. *Just say it. Say it!*

"I am the newest member of the Crimson Lords, Terakomari Gandesblood! Now that I am your commander, the slacking off slops here!"

…Did I just say "slops" instead of "stops"? The silence in the great hall was deafening. I could hear myself gulp. Save me, Vill.

"Lady Komari is a little nervous and has muddled her words! Isn't she adorable?!"

You're just making it worse!!!

Turning to the sicko maid for help was an exercise in futility; that much was clear. Trying desperately to start over, I resumed my speech.

"The slacking off *stops* here! From now on, every day is war! Not a moment will pass without bloodshed! The rivers will run red! But you are not to fear! Just follow me, and victory will be yours! Put all thoughts of mutiny and uprisings out of mind, and simply accept the orders of your new leader, the brilliant, arresting Terakomari Gandesblood! As long as you continue to fight loyally under my command, I swear to you that every day will be like a never-ending party!"

The crowd all murmured appreciatively at this.

Gosh, what nonsense was I spewing, though?

War? Slaughter? Blood? I hadn't the slightest bit of interest in any of those things.

"Yes, absolutely! I am the vampire who will conquer the world! As long as I exist in this realm, I shall hold sway over all! For I am a mighty warrior! With the skill and power to win a hundred battles! I've got the brains! I've got the magic! Indeed! All you people need to do is follow me and believe in my might! Always be obedient, faithful, with all inclinations of mutiny erased from your minds, as you put your faith in me and lend me your protection! Do you heed me, most noble and beloved soldiers?! The future is as bright as fresh crimson blood spurting from the necks of our enemies!"

They were all staring straight at me. Yikes. I felt like I was gonna hurl. Why did I have to make my speech so wordy and rambling? This is what reading too many novels does to a person.

"Now is the hour! Take up your arms! Are we all on board? Is everyone ready to follow me? No stabbing me in the back, now! If ever the thought of rebellion should cross your minds, I promise that you will meet the same fate as that golden-haired young man I just painted the floor with! I'll choke you out with my bare hands without a second's hesitation, so be warned! Got that? Do you? Good! Now, all those who wish to follow me may stay. The others know where the exit is! Are you ready to taste true glory under the steady hand of Terakomari Gandesblood? That is all you need to ask yourself! Period!"

With my speech concluded, I clamped my lips together and shut my eyes tight.

I said everything I wanted to say, I think. But the last part was totally ad-libbed, to be honest. Still, not bad for someone who'd never had a public speaking engagement in her life. Talk big, and the people will be fooled. This ragtag bunch of soldiers would certainly swallow it all, hook, line, and sinker. Right?

…I wished my knees weren't trembling so much.

Unable to bear the silence any longer, I cracked open my eyelids and peeked out at the crowd.

Just then…

"HAAAAAAIIIIILLLLL!!!!"

They all suddenly began cheering, loud enough to shake the great hall to its very foundations.

"Wh-what? What's going on?"

As I stood there flummoxed, the vampires began to cheer and chant my name in a frenzy, as if they were high on some kind of illicit substance. My ears rang with the sound of *"KO-MA-RIN, KO-MA-RIN!"* I could feel my cheeks burning with embarrassment. Komarin? They had a pet name for me now? What was I, a pop star?

I looked over at Vill, who dropped me a sassy wink.

"Congratulations. The people love you, Lady Komari."

They *love* me?

Wasn't it all a bit too easy, though? I thought winning them over would be a much…lengthier process.

"Anyway, it looks like you've got them right where you want them. All that's left is to keep your true self squirreled away for the foreseeable future."

"Yeah, that's the whole problem…"

My spirits sank just as I realized that several of my new subordinates were approaching me. Oh gosh, could these ones be…*in*subordinates?! I felt myself getting ready to dash, but what they ended up saying sent me stiffening instead.

"Supreme Commander! May I have permission to lick your shoe?"

"Supreme Commander! Please! Step on me!"

"Supreme Commander, Supreme Commander! Would you crush me like you did Yohann?"

Now I wanted to turn tail for entirely different reasons.

What was wrong with this unit? Were all of them this messed up? And that last guy... If he wants to die so bad, fine, but don't get me involved!

Eh, not that it mattered much to me. My job was the same, whether these guys were the sickest perverts in the land or not. I just had to keep playing the tough girl, so they didn't rebel and try to kill me. I managed to get through my speech, full of lies as it was, but now the hard work of keeping those lies rolling was about to begin.

Just thinking about the grueling, difficult, and terrifying days ahead made me heave a huge sigh.

I wished I could go home and dive into the safety of my bed.

※

How had Terakomari Gandesblood come to receive so much support?

To find out, we need only ask the vampires of the Seventh Unit, aka the Komari Unit.

"Oh, the commander? Well, she's freakin' cute, isn't she?"

"I fell in love with her at first sight."

"She's like a beautiful flower blossoming in the dirt of military life. Let me tell ya, my little soldier is primed and ready for action with her anytime!"

"For me, it was when I saw her slay that annoying brat while barely even lifting a finger. That's when I started to think she had what it takes to be Supreme Commander. I honestly don't know how good she is on the battlefield, but she has to be better than the last one. I'll be observing her closely."

"Komarin really is supreme!"

"I want her to step on me."

"I wanna lick her like an ice cream cone."

"I wanna suck her blood!"

"Dig it! Supreme Commander, ain't no one grander, got the book smarts and the magic arts, all the respect, ya gotta hand her!"

"She's got a cute voice. It's so...*squee*! It makes me tingle!"

"I wanna hear my name on her lips..."

"To tell you the frank and honest truth, she made a big impression on me from the start. Her iron will, the way she dealt with an unruly subordinate like that with zero hesitation. She's a genius, and she looks like an actual angel. Now that's the kind of woman I want to serve. I'd be happy to lick her shoes...or preferably her bare feet...*ahem!* At any rate, I look forward to seeing her in action. Especially her patented pinky finger murder technique. I'd really like to witness that up close."

The fact that the last commander of this unit had been your typical crusty middle-aged man probably worked in Komari's favor. Half of the unit had already completely lost their heads over this adorable young girl who'd come to lead them. They might have been a ragtag bunch of uncouth misfits, but they still had a little romance in their hearts.

Or perhaps they were just like all men...driven by their carnal desires.

In her innocence and naïveté, Komari would never notice that, though.

Now, let's go back to where we left off in the prologue.

The Mulnite Empire, domain of the vampires.

The Lapelico Kingdom, domain of the beast-folk.

The Enchanted Lands, domain of the Immortals.

The Gerra-Aruka Republic, domain of the Warblades.

The Haku-Goku Commonwealth, domain of the Sapphires.

The Heavenly Paradise, domain of the Peace Spirits.

Each of the Six Nations of this world has their own customs regarding the Dark Core.

The Dark Core is a source of never-ending magical power, an unholy font of sorts. Many say the current magical society was built upon the regenerative powers it bestows.

Take the Mulnite Empire, for example. New vampires who are born into the Empire undergo a special ritual two weeks after birth. In this rite, they offer up their blood to the Dark Core. This serves to pledge the infant's soul to the Empire forevermore in a blood pact, but it also fulfills a far grander purpose. Through mixing their blood with the Dark Core, the vampire child accepts it as part of themselves and gains an unholy blessing. In other words, the vampire is reborn, as a part of the Core itself.

Then what happens? The answer is simple.

The Dark Core releases nigh-ending magical power, including that of infinite regeneration. Since the vampire has become a part of the Core, they share its abilities. All the folk of this world can use magic without limits (although the specific strengths of the individual dictate what kinds they can use), thanks to the energy of the Dark Core. As long as they remain within a certain range of the Core's true source, known as a Dark Core Zone, they will arise good as new following a short period of death, regardless of how gravely injured they might have been.

In this world, war is not a matter of life and death.

Instead, modern combat is more like a demonstration of power. Lands do battle with one another to assert dominance, to show off their prowess, or simply for the fun of it. Warfare is their primary source of entertainment.

As a director of war, the commander was responsible for projecting a good image for their country. A Crimson Lord suffering a humiliating public defeat would be the same as publicly smearing mud on the face of the Empress.

Although personally, after stealing my first kiss from me, I think the Empress deserved a face full of dirt. No, something worse than that...

I got the feeling my impending explosion would only be hastened if I actually spread mud or whatever on her, though.

"This whole situation is completely insane."

I sighed and gazed upward.

We were right in the center of the world, the heart of the Dark Core Zone.

Actually, this area was where the six countries' Dark Core ranges overlapped, so it was the perfect place to duke it out.

Today had been a fine slaughter. The land was awash with blood.

The Eastern Army, composed of brawny beast-folk. The Royal Army of Lapelico.

The Western Army, composed of a select vampire elite. The Imperial Army of Mulnite.

It was only yesterday that I had been looking my subordinates in the face for the first time. I'd been planning to stay shut up in my room alone today to think and ponder, but then my sicko maid suddenly appeared and dragged me out to the battle. Apparently, the previous commander had scheduled this battle before being usurped, so I was duty-bound to take over. Thanks a lot, ex-Commander. Get wrecked. Oh, I guess you already did.

"Battle report! Battle report! Lieutenant Bellius has felled the enemy commander! I repeat! Lieutenant Bellius has felled the enemy commander! We've won!"

I felt all the tension drain out of my body as the battle reporter bellowed this message of victory.

Oh, what a relief! Now there would be no need for me to step into the fray and expose myself.

"Ah, ah-ha-ha. Good work, ol' Bellius. He can have a treat later."

I couldn't remember which one he was.

"Ack! But we were just about to see the commander in action!"

"Way to spoil everyone's fun, Bellius. Thanks for that."

"Wait, a treat? From the supreme commander? I'll kill that mutt!"

"I'm gonna put pins in his boots! That'll learn him!"

Wait, aren't you supposed to be his buddies?

"Congratulations on your first victory, Supreme Commander. Victory is ours."

Caostel bowed his head low before me as I sat there grinning weakly over my troops' banter. It seemed that he was the only one who could reliably keep the others in line.

"W-well, of course we did! This is *my* unit, after all!"

"Amazing, Supreme Commander. While it is a shame that we did not get to see your skills in action, there will be other opportunities. I look forward to it."

"Oh, please don't. All this praise is embarrassing me, tee-hee."

"No, I am desperate to witness it. Let us build upon this victory and progress to the next bout. Our next opponent is the Gerra-Aruka Republic, as I recall."

Please, no more. I've had enough. I need at least three months alone in my room to recharge. That's what I wanted to say, but I knew doing so would look suspicious and lead to my doom. Just then, my maid leaned in to whisper to me.

"…Lady Komari. This is your cue to smile and nod."

"Eugh…"

I clutched at my temples. There wasn't a single soul here who understood me. I felt so lonely all of a sudden. It sucked so bad.

"Come, Supreme Commander! We must return to the Crimson Tower and begin forming a battle strategy for the upcoming fight! There's no time to hesitate! After all, you are the commander who will conquer the world!"

Hang on, I never said anything about wanting to conquer the world! …Did I?

Though I scowled internally, I pasted on a bland smile outwardly. There was no way out of this. That much was clear.

"Y-yeah, you're right! Okay, good job, everyone! But there's no time to loll about enjoying victory! I promised you a life drenched in the blood of your enemies! We return to the Mulnite Palace at once! No dawdling! No stragglers! Or I'll turn you into fertilizer! Got that?!"

Before I could even finish speaking...

"HAAAIIILLL!!!"

They began yelling and cheering for me like they were demented again.

I wanted to die. They were just like sheep. Sheeple!

"Um, excuse me, may I say something?!"

Just as I was seriously contemplating wringing my own neck, a high voice rang out. It was such an odd voice to hear in a setting like this, so I looked around in surprise.

The voice belonged to a young girl holding a pen, a notepad, and a camera. She was smiling over at me. Her skin was as white as snow, which made me immediately guess that she was a Sapphire, from the Haku-Goku Commonwealth.

"Hi, I'm Melka Tiano from Six Nations News! Can you just confirm for me that you're Terakomari Gandesblood, the new Crimson Lord of the Mulnite Empire? I'd love to get an interview if possible!"

Whoa, she was standing way too close all of a sudden. Her face was practically smushed up against mine. *Wow, what long eyelashes. No, no, forget about that right now, Komari!*

What was up with this pushy reporter? To be completely honest, I kinda hate perky girls like her...

Troubled, I chanced a peek behind me.

Vill was gazing at me in silence. Caostel nodded, grinning away.

What? He wanted me to do the interview? Oh, all right, then!

"F-fine. You can ask me anything. Just...take a few steps back first."

"Thank you! Whoops!"

Yikes! Don't cling! Ouch! We just bumped noses!

"I was having a lot of trouble with my story, actually, because I had no idea what you were like at all, Lady Terakomari! So please let me ask some questions. To start, allow me to just jump right in and ask how you were able to become a Crimson Lord? And is it true that you're one of the famous Gandesbloods?! What is your relationship with the Empress like?! What's your favorite food?! What's your favorite animal?! Where have you been all our lives?! Is it true you killed a hundred vampires using just your pinky finger?! What are your future battle plans?! Do you have a lover?! When was your first kiss...?"

Oh my gosh! Shut *up*!

"Just...get off me, will you?!"

"Yeek!"

Gathering up my courage, I shoved the reporter away from me by pure reflex.

"A truly strong warrior doesn't boast of their exploits! But I see that you need assistance. You're a reporter. It's your job to write stuff. So very well, I'll tell you a little. My future battle plans? Simple. Complete world domination! I, Terakomari Gandesblood, will slay all five of the enemy commanders and spread the influence of the Mulnite Empire across the globe! Did you get that? Oh, and by the way! My favorite food is omelet rice! Komari out!"

Exhaustion washed over me as I finished reeling off this little speech.

But could you blame me? So much had happened since yesterday. Dragged out of my safe and comfy room by a perverted maid, worshiped like a goddess by a scary bunch of soldiers, then forced right into conducting a battle. This was all too much for a weakling vampire like me to handle!

But it was odd. The people around me didn't seem to see me that way at all.

"W-wow!"

The reporter girl's jaw was hanging as if it had become detached. What was there to be wowed about? I'd just rattled off whatever came to mind, something that would sound good in a newspaper.

My subordinates, who had been observing all of this, began to murmur among themselves.

"Now, that's what I call a true Crimson Lord." "She really is a perfect specimen of the vampire race." "Has there ever been a commander with

such zest for battle before?" "This will go down in the history books." "I totally agree with you." "This is a legend being born." "I'm so glad I get to walk these lands at the same time as the supreme commander." "We owe the gods our thanks for her," and so on. Give me a break!

Still, it's better to be overly worshiped than the alternative. I mean, if they all found out what a weakling I was, they'd rip me to shreds for sure.

At this rate, though, I was liable to drop dead from stress before they even had the chance to do that.

Just thinking about the days, weeks, and months ahead made me heave a sigh that was almost a scream.

2 Komari's Charming Comrades

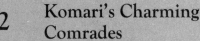

The following morning. In my room. In my bed.

I awoke from a horrible nightmare.

A vision that terrified me half to death.

In the dream, the soldiers found out about my physical weaknesses and killed me. They dropped me into a big pot of boiling water as I screamed and wailed. They were *so* mad at me. After all that worshiping, they felt as though I'd betrayed them. After boiling me for about ten minutes, they crisped me up in hot oil and served me as fried chicken at the dinner table. I saw a pretty girl licking her lips as I was served, and I'm pretty sure it was Vill. That sicko maid, who ignores every one of my orders... With a smirk on her face, she skewered me with a fork and gulped me down into her belly...

"Good morning, Lady Komari."

"Whaaat?!"

I whirled around in terror to find something that totally shocked me.

Vill had burrowed her way into my blankets.

Though I tried to scramble away from her, she locked her arms around my midsection and held me tight.

"Wh-what the heck are you doing here?!"

"Don't you remember? You asked me to sleep on the floor beside your bed. Ah, just remembering how we tussled last night sets my loins ablaze!"

"I don't recall asking any such thing!"

"Ooh my!"

As I leaped out of bed, backing the deviant maid against the wall by her neck, as mad as a hissing cat, I suddenly realized she was stark naked! Agh! She really was a sicko!

"You... What have you been doing to me?!"

Vill gave me an impish smile.

"Thank you. It was *most* delicious."

I felt a chill go down my spine. I would rather have been turned into fried chicken than this.

"Oh dear, you're shivering. I can warm you up if you'd like..."

"N-no thanks! Put some clothes on! You'll catch a cold!"

"Aren't you interested in girls?"

"Girls? Yeah, sure. But why are you asking that now...?"

"Oh, you do? I'm so glad."

Vill smiled, seeming pleased about something. I got the feeling we were totally misunderstanding each other in ways that could prove dangerous, but I didn't want to think about it anymore. It was probably just my imagination anyway.

She jumped back on the bed then did a quick twirl. All at once, she was dressed in her maid outfit again, like a magic trick.

"So answer. What are you doing here?"

Vill jumped off the bed with a flounce.

"I came to share the act of love with you, Lady Komari..."

"Enough of that already!"

"I came to have sex with you, Lady Komari..."

"I wasn't asking you to remove the euphemism!"

It was far too early in the morning for such bawdy talk. Having to chastise her was also pretty draining.

Anyway, I just wanted to move past this.

"Answer me. What are you doing in my room?"

"I have two reasons."

Vill put up two fingers.

"The first is because I *am* your personal maid, Lady Komari. Waiting on you hand and foot morning, noon, and night is my job."

"You really don't need to bother."

"The second reason is because I'm desperate to learn all I can about you, Lady Komari! The article in this morning's paper was very enlightening, and I couldn't wait to see you. So I broke down your door to get inside."

"You...broke down the door?!"

Looking over at the entrance to my room, I noticed for the first time that the doorframe was empty and the door itself was lying in several pieces on the floor. This was a blatant case of breaking and entering! That was a crime! Okay, I wasn't going to think of her as a sicko maid anymore. She was getting an upgrade. Now I was going to think of her as a sicko, criminal maid.

"Lady Komari, never mind the door. Take a look at the newspaper. See, there's a photo from yesterday."

"Are you insane?! Who cares about that when—"

As my eye fell on the newspaper that Vill was holding out to me, the door completely left my mind. I couldn't comprehend this. It was unbelievable. I was on the front page. It was my beautiful face, the same one I saw in the mirror every morning. And the article itself read...

NEWEST CRIMSON LORD SPEAKS: "I'LL TURN THE ENTIRE WORLD INTO OMELET RICE"

The newest Crimson Lord of the Mulnite Empire, Terakomari Gandesblood, pulled off a stunning victory as supreme commander during the battle against our neighbors of the Lapelico Kingdom on the eighth day of this month. Gandesblood inherited her position on the seventh day of this month from her predecessor, Augus Nuppaiyer, who was himself slain on the second day of this month… **Blah, blah, blah…** The defeated commander of the Lapelico Kingdom's forces, Commander Hades Molekikki, had this to say when we caught up with him: "I do not accept this defeat. She'd better be watching her back." According to our sources, a revenge match has already been discussed. In her victory speech, Commander Gandesblood said the following: "I love omelet rice. I'm going to wipe out all the commanders of the other five countries, and then spread ketchup all over the world as if it were a giant omelet all for me!" Her choice of words speaks to a bloodthirsty nature, which… **Blah, blah, that's enough reading.**

This was dreadful reporting! This was…this was FAKE NEWS!

What was wrong with that demented journalist?! I only said that bit about liking omelets over rice as a favor to her, an extra tidbit of Komari info! That wasn't some kind of coded message! Way to jump to conclusions!

"How photogenic you are, Lady Komari. You look like a very naughty Empress."

"That article is a disaster! It makes it sound like I've declared war on all the other countries!"

"Indeed, it does. You had better watch out for that chimpanzee fellow. After all, this is a national paper. And you basically announced that you have evil intentions toward everyone."

"Aaagh!!!"

Clutching my head, I flopped back onto the bed. The heck?! Just when I was starting to think I would be able to enjoy three sweet months of quality shut-in time…that blasted rag! Now all the other countries would be vying for my blood and declaring war! Ugh! The press SUCKS!

"Don't worry, Lady Komari. I shall guard your chastity."

"You're more of a threat to my chastity than anyone else is!"

Vill had somehow wormed her way back onto the bed beside me. I gave her the mightiest shove I could muster and managed to push her off. Then I pulled the blankets over my head and tried to dissociate

from reality. I was *not* going to participate in any more wars. I'd made up my mind, and nobody could force me. I was just going to stay here in my little blanket fort and shut out the world forever.

"Lady Komari, about today's schedule…"

"Can't hear you! Can't hear a thing! Today's my day off!"

"Just because there are no battles planned doesn't mean you get a day off. A Crimson Lord must be on call day in and day out."

"Tell them I'm sick."

"This is not school, Lady Komari. If you plan to stay wrapped up in that blanket all day, well…I have plans of my own in that case."

"Hmph. Don't go getting violent and trying to drag me out. If you take even one step closer, I'll set off my personal safety alarm and start screaming, I warn you!"

"The formula for strawberry milk…"

"…"

All of a sudden, I froze.

Wait a minute, wasn't that…

"I want a love that's as sweet as strawberry milk…"

"…"

"Sweet and creamy, oh so soft on the tongue…no sharpness, no bitterness, just smooth and warm like the sun…I want a love like that…"

"…Wait…"

"You may say I've read too many fairy tales… You may laugh and say such love doesn't exist…and I thought so, too, at first. But ever since I met you, my world has been tinged as pink as strawberry milk…"

"CUT IT OUT!!!"

A roar bubbled up inside me and spewed from my mouth.

I leaped out of bed without even realizing what I was doing and flew at the sicko maid. But I was powerless against her superior arm strength, and before I knew it, she had me in a wrestling hold.

She moved her face right up to mine, grinning. I could feel her breath.

"Your heartfelt work is most inspired, Lady Komari."

"Gahhh!"

My cheeks felt as hot as magma.

After desperately flapping my lips for a few moments, I managed to speak.

"Where did you find it?"

"It was written on a scrap of paper in the wastepaper basket here in your room."

"…"

"What was it, a trashed manuscript draft? I made a copy for my own personal use, just in case."

"…"

"I was very surprised to discover that you write romance novels. You don't seem to have had much experience with relationships."

"…"

"By the way, if you still insist on shirking your duties, I'll make copies of your manuscript and post them up all over the palace. Don't worry, I'll make sure you're properly credited."

"…"

"Hmm? Lady Komari? Are you listening? Lady Komari?"

I grabbed Vill by the collar. More like I was hanging off it.

Then I pleaded with her through tightly clenched teeth.

"I'll do anything you say…*anything!* But please! Don't tell a soul!"

…*Splurt!*

For some reason, a fountain of blood came spurting out of the sicko maid's nose…

Now it's time for a little contemplation. It seemed my biggest issue at present was the fact that the sicko maid had dirt she could use against me. Things would go out of control very quickly if I allowed her to get the upper hand. If she threatened to blab about my romance writing, I might lose the ability to fend her off if she tried any freaky stuff on me. That would be bad. Very, very bad. I needed a plan, and fast.

Plan 1: Get ahold of the copies of the novel excerpts she has and burn them. Ah, no, that won't work. Vill has probably already memorized them word for word and could rewrite them at any time. Pointless.

Plan 2: Find a way to erase the weirdo maid's memories… Ah, no, that won't work. I can't use memory-obliterating magic, and I feel as if punching her in the head in the hopes of inducing amnesia would be a touch too cruel. Besides, I don't have enough arm strength for that.

Plan 3: Find her weakness and use it against her. Ah, yes. This was the only thing that came to mind right now that would work. If I could get a juicy scoop on her, something that made my novel writing look insignificant by comparison, then I could flip the situation to my advantage. Okay, so what I needed to do was monitor Vill closely, around the clock. Even by sleeping in the same room, if possible. I'd start my observations now. Stare mode activate…

"L-Lady Komari…don't stare so much. You'll make me blush, ahhh!"

"Enough with the erotic moans!"

Darn it! She was always two steps ahead.

I definitely needed to find out the weirdo maid's shortcomings ASAP, but right now I did have a more pressing issue to attend to.

The issue of work, that is.

By this time, we'd relocated to the Crimson Tower office.

Each of the Seven Crimson Lords of the Mulnite Empire had their own private office. My quarters, located on the top floor of the Crimson Tower, were crazy big and luxurious. If I peered out the windows, I could see the whole city spread out below. But I had no time to enjoy the view. As much as I hated it, I was going to have to engage in the act of labor.

"So what's on the table?"

"Ah, right. Well, Lady Komari, you're about to have a meeting with your subordinates."

I scowled reflexively. Didn't I just have a meeting with them the other day? But Vill shook her head, interpreting my expression with embarrassing ease.

"The purpose of today's conference is for you to get to know the higher-ranked officers, the top brass. Those good-for-nothing hooligans are going to be your right-hand men, so it's better to get off on the right foot with them by having a friendly introduction, don't you think?"

"Did you just say 'good-for-nothing hooligans'…? Isn't a hooligan a bad thing?"

"'Hooligans' is the most accurate description. They're mercenary and self-serving, so they won't hesitate to overthrow you in an instant."

"I see, I see. Excuse me, potty break."

She grabbed me by the shoulders.

"Let gooo! I don't wanna die yet!"

"STRAWBERRY. MILK."

I sat down.

Vill began detailing the day's schedule in a brisk and official manner.

"Besides me, there are four other officials who will be attending with you. Oh, but one's dead right now, so they won't be able to make the conference."

"Wish they were all dead."

"Ahem. Your main order of business today, Lady Komari, is to chat with the other three officers and develop a strategy for going forward. Simple, right?"

"There's nothing simple about any of this."

I scowled. If I made even the tiniest error here, I'd end up crispier than fried chicken.

Anyway, what did people usually talk about in gatherings? And what was this "strategy for going forward"? I had no idea what that even meant. Since I had no knowledge of military stuff (besides theoretical battle strategy), my plan was to say as little as possible. In fact, I had already decided that was how I would approach everything from now on.

"Don't fret, Lady Komari. All you need to do is sit there and say 'Mm-hmm,' and 'I see,' and 'Indeed' at regular intervals. Or I guess you could just nod along; that would also work. The others will take care of everything else, you see."

"Are you sure that's going to be okay? If they figure I'm clueless about military stuff, they're gonna overthrow me..."

"If you're that worried about it... Hmm, yes...the best thing to do would be to compliment them; butter them up as much as possible. Win over their hearts, and then you'll be safe."

"But what would please them?"

"Well, in my case...a hug as a reward for all I do would go such a long way..."

"We're not talking about you right now."

I planned to just go with "I really respect all your hard work, guys!" and leave it at that. Logically, everyone wants the boss to appreciate them, right? I just hoped they operated from positions of reason...

"Now, here are the individuals you'll be meeting with today..."

Vill pulled three documents out of a folder and spread them out on the table. They looked like résumés.

"First, please familiarize yourself with their backgrounds. That will make the conversation go more smoothly."

"I see... Hey, wait, Vill. This guy's a dog!"

Attached to one of the files was a picture of a canine head. Ha-ha, it looked like a dog's résumé! But I remembered this guy. He was the one who took out the Chimpanzee during yesterday's battle. Thanks to him, I didn't have to go out onto the battlefield. So I guess he saved my life. All right, he gets one point for being a very, very good boy.

"That's Lieutenant Bellius Hund Cerbero. He used to be in the Sixth Unit, but he murdered someone and got demoted."

"Oh my gosh! Are you sure he's safe?!"

I was shocked. Bad dog! Very bad dog!

But wait a minute. It seemed clear that my squad, the Seventh Unit, got all the troublemakers and outlaws from the other groups. So did that mean...

"Wh-what about this guy?"

"Ah, Lieutenant Caostel Conto? He was demoted on suspicion of kidnapping a little girl."

"Goodness! That's a terrible crime!"

"And this one is Captain Mellaconcey. He was demoted after a failed terrorist plot to blow up the palace."

"A terrorist? Why is he walking around free?!"

My head was spinning.

What kind of place had I entered employment into?!

Pale in the face, I sank down onto the (very gorgeous, ornate, and fancy) chair. Then I felt a hand plop down my head. Vill was patting it in a soothing manner. *Stop that!*

"There's no need to be anxious. If anyone bothers you at all, Lady Komari, I will turn them into charcoal."

"Vill, you—"

"Now, let us begin preparations for the meeting. Please don't be afraid. I'll be with you the entire time."

She dropped me a saucy wink. I felt a little relieved and a little impressed. She may have been a pervert, but I felt I could count on her to do her job and support me fully in this.

Maybe I should say something nice to her. To express my gratitude.

"Th-thanks, Vi—"

"*Snurrrf!* Lady Komari! Your hair smells so *good!* Oh, this is so much better than simply sniffing your pillow! Mmm, this sweet, strawberry-milk-like scent could send me right to heaven! *Snurrrf!*"

"You're the most disgusting person I've ever met!!!"

At some point, she stopped stroking my hair and started sniffing it. Huffing on it.

Forget the gratitude. Ugh!!!

Ten minutes later, the other three officers of the Seventh Unit arrived at my office on Vill's summons. As they slunk in, the atmosphere in the room grew heavy and oppressive. I felt like I'd been locked in a cage with hungry carnivorous animals. Oh gosh, they were seriously scary. Wish I'd gone for that potty break.

I checked out the three men in front of me as subtly as I could.

On the right, Caostel Conto. Tall and stringy like a bare winter tree, one of those unsmiling weirdos.

In the center, Bellius Hund Cerbero. A dog's head and a muscly body. A convicted murderer!

On the left, Mellaconcey. A terrorist and rapper with a flashy persona.

Any one of these dudes could spell my end.

"Greetings, Commander. What business have you with us today?"

Caostel grinned at me. Oh, he *totally* kidnapped that little girl. I wasn't a kid anymore so I was probably safe, but I would have to be on high alert around him. I nodded, trying hard to seem relaxed and confident.

"Please, just take a seat."

"..."

"What's wrong? There's no need to stand on ceremony. Please, sit down."

But my subordinates remained completely still.

I gazed at them in confusion until Bellius finally spoke. "Commander," he said, "there are no chairs."

We forgot the chairs?! Aaargh!!!

This would leave a terrible impression of the new commander, aka me! Sitting in this fancy seat while my subordinates hunkered down on the floor before me?! No one does that anymore! It was totally a human rights violation!

"Nonsense, Bellius! The commander has told you to sit, so your job is to sit, chair be damned! If she tells you to place your posterior on a roaring campfire, you sit! If she tells you to settle down on a bed of nails, you sit! And if she orders you to sit in her lap...*hee!* You SIT! Got that?"

"Check it! A mutt's gotta sit if he wants ta be legit! Wanna bone? Got no throne? That don't matter, dude, just park it!"

©riichu

"Who are you calling a mutt?!"

A big fist suddenly collided with Mellaconcey's nose, sending spittle and snot flying. A moment later, Bellius dropped to a knee in front of me in a bow of contrition, rubbing his knuckles.

"I apologize for that, Supreme Commander! I shall sit on the floor with gratitude!"

The three of them hunkered down on the ground.

Yikes.

Double yikes!

Infinite yikes!!! That brutal act of random violence had me freaked out so bad that the chair snafu now seemed totally insignificant. But I couldn't wimp out yet. Not as a proud Crimson Lord. Pulling myself together, I cleared my throat to speak.

"Uh, anyway! Thank you for taking the time to attend this conference today. I know this is sudden, but I hoped to have our first strategy meeting. Let's discuss where to take the Seventh Unit, starting with the overall direction of our operations henceforth!"

"A tactics meeting? I like the sound of that! Seems so official!"

Caostel was beaming. Bellius and Mellaconcey seemed interested, too. Okay. Things were going well so far.

"Let's dive right in. Here's my question… What direction were you all leaning toward?"

"Constant, all-out war," answered Bellius.

"I'd love to see *you* in action, Supreme Commander," replied Caostel.

"I wanna rap battle with the Supe-Com! Dig it!" responded Mellaconcey.

I wasn't really sure what the last one was talking about, but eh.

Still, it was clear as day that the Seventh Unit was chock-full of battle-hungry berserkers.

"I…I see. So fighting is the way to go, eh?"

"You got it."

Caostel shrugged.

"You're well aware, right, Commander? The Seventh Unit is all made up of people like us, troublemakers and extremists who screwed up in our previous posts and got lumped together here. Well, most of our problems came from our insatiable need to throw down and rumble. For instance, a major battle got called off this one time because of a typhoon. But we couldn't deal with it, so we hit up a town and went a little crazy to let off steam. Some of us even got so mad at the enemy side, who canceled the engagement, that we went over there to assassinate their commander anyway. Stuff like that, you know."

Yeah, and also, you kidnapped a little girl.

But I wasn't about to bring that up to his face. If what Caostel was saying was true, then the Seventh Unit was more of a band of radicals than a military unit. Going around assassinating people isn't really in the martial spirit after all. That's got to breach, like, a bunch of international treaties.

"Okay, I think I get the picture. You guys wanna throw hands more than anything else in the world, right?"

"Yes, Commander."

"Okay, okay, noted. I can dig that. I mean, I'm a warrior, too, y'know. I've tasted the thrill of imminent battle, known the bloodlust that comes over you all of a sudden and makes you wanna rip off an enemy head or two."

That was obviously total bluff by the way. However…

"In that case, Commander, might I ask you to spar with me tomorrow?"

The dog-man gazed at me with expectant eyes.

I froze up for a second. But then…

"Goodness, what utter barefaced cheek! You think you deserve to go up against me? If you want to duel me so bad, then let it be after you've first slain the enemy commander! If you still have the will to fight afterward, I'll indulge you!"

"I see…"

His canine ears flicked and lay back against his head. It was kinda cute… Wait, no! Stop it! He's not a real dog! He doesn't play fetch or shake paws—he's a ferocious wolf-beast with murder on the brain!

"Dig it! Mutt gets rejected, now he's all dejected! Supreme Commander, his attitude's corrected!"

The ridiculous rapper received another fist smash to the face and went flying across the room. Those two were *such* an odd couple.

Steadying my nerves, I cleared my throat.

"Uh, anyway! It seems you're already set on how to proceed! That makes this conference pretty superfluous! So war it is! We'll war as much as your fearsome hearts desire!"

But I had to add a single caveat.

"However! I, personally, do not stoop to boring engagements! Yes, it's good to rack up the numbers, but I feel quality matters more than quantity! Thus, if it's the kind of fight that won't satisfy my bloodlust, I shall not partake. I shall simply remain at HQ and direct the battle."

"B-but, Supreme Commander!"

"Don't be disappointed, Caostel. I simply won't participate in conflicts that are beneath me... It's just my personal philosophy. There will be plenty of conflicts, rest assured, but you'll be doing the fighting yourselves for the most part."

"I...I understand."

Caostel looked like he had more to say on the subject, but the other two had no strong reaction to what I was saying. Ah, yes, I was playing this perfectly. These fellows would be satisfied with plenty of chances to slake their bloodlust.

But then Vill stepped in front of me and cleared her throat.

"Now then, I will take over the arrangements regarding future operations. If you have any opinions, I do intend to take them on board, so please notify me of them. Thank you."

She lifted up her skirts and curtsied. Slightly impressed, I raised an eyebrow. I had assumed she was nothing more than a dirty perv, but it appeared she could be businesslike when she really tried.

So I guess that concluded the meeting... It wasn't anywhere near as bad as I'd been expecting. I felt silly now for being so trepidatious about it! Okay, time to head back and maybe do a little more novel writing...

"Finally, I believe it's time for Supreme Commander Terakomari to dole out some special rewards for a job well done the other day. The commander was very pleased with the performance against the Lapelico Kingdom and has decided to offer special tokens of her gratitude to say thank you. You may request anything, so long as it has nothing to do with military matters or strategies. Please, take this opportunity to state your heart's desire."

"Wait, wait, *what*?"

I dragged Vill quickly to a corner of the room and scrunched my face up against hers in a frenzy.

"Special rewards?! Can't we just go home already?!"

"I already mentioned this. Praising and providing for your subordinates will decrease the likelihood of them revolting against you."

"Yeah, but...I get it, but..."

"Please, don't fret. You're the leader of that bunch of punks...*and* you're a Crimson Lord! They won't ask you anything crazy. And if they do ask something like, *Let me smell you!* or *Let me squeeze your boobs!*, all you have to do is have them executed."

"Why don't I just have *you* beheaded?"

"I have a special exemption when it comes to you, Lady Komari."

"I don't remember exempting you from anything! You know, you—"

"Supreme Commander!"

I whirled around. Caostel was looking this way, grinning widely.

"Wh-what is it, Caostel?"

"Ah, I have to say, what a generous commander you are! To gift us whatever we desire."

I wasn't the one who'd put it out there, but I couldn't exactly go retracting the offer now.

"...Uh, yeah. Well, hard work mustn't go unrewarded, and all that."

"Splendid! Has there ever been a Crimson Lord who has shown such care for her subordinates?! You are truly the most supreme of supreme commanders who ever commanded...supremely!"

What the heck was he on about?

"So I would love to have my request granted, if I may...?"

Still grinning, Caostel began casting magic. I stiffened, terrified that he was about to do me in, but he was merely casting an advanced-level magic spell called the *Gates of Hell*. It allowed one to temporarily store objects in another dimension and retrieve them at will. It was very handy, and very advanced. Even in the Imperial Court, only a few magicians could pull it off. This stripped-tree-like fellow wasn't just your average weirdo after all.

I gulped, trying to relax as Caostel reached into the void and retrieved an object. It was a…camera?

"I'd love to photograph you! Say cheese, Commander!"

"Um, what? What for?"

Flash. He just took my picture. *Hey, you're supposed to ask permission first!*

"Ah, yes, I do love that stern expression on you! But a smile is what I'm after. Supreme Commander, I do apologize, but would you mind unclenching a little?"

"Hey, hold on! What are you taking pictures of me for anyhow?!"

"For my request. I get one request, right?"

"…"

"Now, now, don't worry. I won't use these photos for any nefarious purposes. But we've had a huge drop in new recruits to the Mulnite Imperial Army… After mulling over the issue, I realized that you would be an excellent draw to entice people to sign up! With these pictures, I plan to make a bunch of merch, like posters, calendars, and so on, to sell! It's good business *and* good PR for the army. See what a beautiful…I mean, what an excellent commander we have here! It'll really bring in the loli— I mean, budding heroes who are yet to join! But that's not all. With your merch circulating on the streets of town, the army's image will get a major boost! So you see, my request really is quite philanthropic and not at all self-serving! These pics won't be for personal use, cross my heart!"

While Caostel was delivering this speech, he continued to snap pics of me. *Flash. Flash. Flash.*

"You only get one request! You're taking tons of photos…"

"No, my request wasn't for a photo; it was for a *photo shoot!*"

What a greedy snake! Vill, can we get an execution order for this one?

"Let's have a series of wardrobe changes for Lady Komari's photo shoot! I just so happen to have a maid costume here, plus swimsuits, and even a kindergarten uniform!"

"One execution order, coming up! No, make that *two!*"

Furious over being betrayed in this way, I bolted for the door. Before I could reach it, the maid grabbed me by the arm and shoved me into a headlock. "Strawberry miiilk…," she hissed in my ear, and I went limp. Ah, yeah, I was too hasty. I needed to stay my rage, at least until I had some good dirt on the sicko maid that I could use to manipulate her. I couldn't take much more of this.

"Cut the crap! There's no way I'm agreeing to this!"

"But Lady Komari, you must open yourself up to your subordinates; otherwise you'll lose their support. Maybe they'll even rise up against you. Are you truly willing to take that risk?"

"Guhhh!"

"No, no, it wouldn't do to lose their favor. Now, be a good girl and get changed. I have *so* many naughty and sexy outfits for you, and I want you to try them *all.*"

"You…you…PERVERTED MAID!"

I was powerless to resist as she dragged me off to get changed.

Thus began the fashion show from hell.

"If I have to wear a costume, couldn't it at least be something normal…?"

But my reasonable request fell on deaf ears. All the outfits were either drowning in frills, or were so skimpy, they left nothing to the imagination. Still, I had no say in what I wore as the camera flashed away. By the time I was finally released, the sun resembled a red fireball as it dipped down past the horizon.

I felt utterly ashamed. Now I could never be a bride. I'd have to return home and lock myself in my room for the rest of my life.

But my path was blocked by…

"Check it! Rap battle!"

"…What?"

"Rap battle!"

Despair overwhelmed me.

I'd forgotten that I had requests from three people to answer to that day. But a rap battle? Was he stupid? *What's that, Vill? He's the scariest of the bunch, so I'd better do what he says? Darn it! Okay, you terrorist scum, let's do this.*

I think I was probably delirious from everything I'd been through and what was going on.

"Check it! Commander, what's your thrill? Is it going for the kill? A billion red poppies bloomin' on a hill? As for me, you can see, I ain't got no mercy! I'm the rappin', happenin', killin' machine, Mella-concey! When I sing, they be like, 'Dude, my ears!' But I ain't what I appears! You and me, Komari, let's go slay a whole army!"

"Yo! Yo! It's me, Komari, havin' a heck of a time! I don't know how to rap, but I know how to rhyme! I'm the commander, take a gander, check this pinky finger on my hand here! A heaven-sent soldier to the Mulnite Empire, but that don't mean I'm ya regular vampire. Rhymin' stuff is really tough, I think I've had enough, rap ain't my forte, I gotta say, but Komari, she, uh, she slay!"

The rap battle ended up lasting an entire hour.

By the time we were done, it was full dark outside. I was exhausted, but Mellaconcey was grinning, positively vibrating with happiness. That was good at least. As soon as our verbal bout finally ended, I accidentally made eye contact with Bellius. At first I was scared he was gonna make me do something else weird, but he just declared: "I'll postpone my request until a later date." Wow, at least the dog was a gentleman. Who knew?

So at last, my first meeting with my officers was over.

But what the heck kind of conference was that anyway?

I mean, an impromptu photo shoot? A rap battle? This was supposed to be a gathering, not a variety show!

And Vill, curse her...

"Today's meeting was a big success. You showed magnanimity to your subordinates, and you managed to procure their loyalty! Your work today will pay dividends later, and I think you'll see the benefits of it very soon!"

I just stared at her blankly.

Whatever. I was so done. All I wanted to do was go home and sleep.

2.5 A Fox Face in the Dead of Night

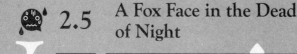

"Hmm, I don't know about her."

After the meeting with the top brass…

Bellius Hund Cerbero muttered under his breath as he walked down the corridor of the Crimson Tower.

It was past eight p.m. The sun had long set, and the view outside the windows was of the Mulnite Empire dyed inky blue in the darkness. The country always seemed most itself after dark.

"You don't know what about her? Her cup size?"

"What nonsense are you prattling on about now?"

From the perspective of an outsider, Caostel was indeed talking nonsense. Though he had combat smarts, it sometimes seemed like he had a screw loose.

"Well, what are *you* talking about?"

"Supreme Commander Terakomari. She's got charisma, sure. But there's too much she keeps hidden. Take a guy like you—all it takes is a glance to realize you're a sicko."

"So we need to find out more about her."

"Right. Her choice of words sometimes lets her young age show, but her overall demeanor is just…strange. It's hard to explain. She seems on edge, even just during normal conversation. Like she's always intimidated, or up against someone she finds awe-inspiring or terrifying…"

"Hmm. Speaking of which, the commander hasn't demonstrated any magic ability at all. It's almost as if she doesn't have any... That's odd, right?"

Caostel stroked his camera, one side of his mouth rising in a lop-sided grin. The sooner this guy got put behind bars, the safer the world and its people would be.

"So what? She's still the commander. And a commander's what we need. What do we care? She's going to give us tons of engagements to participate in, so what are we complaining about exactly?"

"You've got a point there..."

Still, Bellius couldn't fight his very natural desire to know more about Komari before he gave her his trust. His instincts were sharp and rarely led him astray. The rest of the Seventh Unit—ninety percent of them, in fact—never used their brains. They would just blindly follow and worship her. Hold on, they were *already* doing that.

"Still, I understand your reservations. I actually did a little digging into the commander's background..."

"How?"

"I checked some government records. Real sneaky, like."

"...That's illegal."

"Now, now, let's just ignore that. Anyway, what I found out is this... Terakomari Gandesblood is an absolute...enigma."

"What do you mean?"

"Part of her personal record is baffling. Until the age of twelve, she attended a regular school and studied magic like any other girl her age. But from that age onward, there's a gap...a three-year gap, in fact, with zero information on her at all."

"Maybe she just didn't do anything of note during that time frame?"

"I thought the same at first. Or I figured maybe the records were wrong."

As he spoke, Caostel handed over a document. It was made of parchment and covered in spidery handwriting. Bellius couldn't read, so it would probably take him a long time just to figure out what he was even looking at.

"What's this, then?"

"A confidential document from the Imperial Court."

Bellius almost fainted in shock. What was Caostel doing with something like that?

"The file details an incident that occurred three years ago. Though it's not public knowledge, of course. The whole thing was a huge hassle for the government after all."

"So what does that have to do with the commander?"

"She caused the incident."

"What?"

"The Imperial Academy raid incident. Thirty staff members were murdered. Of the troops sent in to break up the raid, seventy were killed. She slaughtered *all* of them using only her pinky finger."

Even Bellius, who knew little of the world, had heard of the event. A bloodbath that had taken place at the Academy three years prior. Apparently, the culprit was a student there. The newspapers and the weekly magazines had eaten the story up with a spoon. It was a total press sensation. But...

"Wait. The ringleader of that operation was already identified. It wasn't her."

"She had a fall guy. It was Terakomari Gandesblood who planned it all, but she had a totally innocent patsy called Millicent Bluenight take the blame for her. Although some people say this Millicent Bluenight character never actually existed at all..."

"I don't understand."

"Me neither. All I know is that Terakomari Gandesblood was involved in a horrific crime three years ago, a transgression for the ages."

Bellius felt a shiver go down his spine.

If this were all true...then what the heck was going on?

"No one knows why she plotted it. But after the incident, she naturally dropped out of the Academy, then disappeared."

"Where to?"

"No one knows. The records don't say. Or they were erased...maybe prison, or juvenile detention. If you really want to know, why don't you try asking the commander yourself...?"

"..."

Bellius was silent. He was speechless.

All he could do was keep pacing, arms crossed pensively. Just who was this girl anyway? For some reason he couldn't stop shivering, despite the mildness of the evening.

"Well, there's always the possibility that this confidential document is a fake, though. Hmm..."

Caostel suddenly stopped in his tracks.

They had just exited the Crimson Tower's gate. The indigo-blue-tinted gardens looked the same as they ever did, and yet beside the fountain, there stood the shadowy form of a person, almost ethereal to behold.

The individual was of middling height and was draped in a black cloak.

They also wore a fox mask.

Clearly, they were highly suspicious.

Caostel crossed his arms and launched into a lecture.

"Naughty, naughty. You've concealed your face, yes, but it's clear you're a female underneath those robes. But not a child. You're fifteen, maybe sixteen. Not yet seventeen, I'd wager. I can tell from your scent. You smell sweet like flowers, with just a hint of tartness."

It looked like the interloper wasn't the only sketchy character present in the gardens that night. But we needn't be concerned about him right now.

Bellius scowled threateningly at the suspicious fox.

"You, over there. Woman. The Imperial Court is off-limits to outsiders. Leave at once if you don't want to be killed."

The fox-girl observed him in silence for maybe ten seconds before speaking.

Her voice was syrupy sweet, incredibly grating to the human ear.

"I'm surprised by how well guarded the Imperial Palace is. I was thinking about sneaking into the Empress's bedroom and doing her in, but I couldn't get past the magical boundary that's in place."

Suddenly, the atmosphere grew leaden with tension. Bellius found himself instinctively reaching for his ax.

Plans to kill the Empress... They were often heard around the palace. The Mulnite Empire was rife with attempted mutinies and uprisings. This was exacerbated by the fact that the Empress herself was generally extremely lenient toward her subjects, on top of being so totally secure in her own position that she never took threats seriously anyway.

But the words spilling from the lips of the fox-faced girl had an ominous edge.

There was no reason to be alarmed. And yet Bellius's beast senses were tingling.

His instincts warned him that this fox-faced girl was dangerous.

"You're pursuing the Empress, are you?"

He could sense that she was smiling beneath her mask.

"I'll kill her one way or another. But now is not that time."

"Huh. So then why did you come here?"

"No real reason. Just to confirm a few things for myself. I read in the newspaper that Terakomari Gandesblood has become the new Crimson Lord. Is that true?"

Bellius drew his ax without any further hesitation. He could ask questions after this fox-faced demon was dead. Instantly, he sprung forward. At the same time, Caostel cast the *Dimensional Blade* incantation and sent a magical sword slicing through the air.

"*Pfft.* Such amateur magic."

She laughed as she cast an elementary-level light spell, *Magic Bullet*, to easily deflect the blade and send it clattering to the ground. Bellius raised his ax, determined to chop the smugness right off her face... but just as he was about to bring it down with all his might, he noticed something odd.

The fox-girl had suddenly disappeared.

"…Above!" Caostel yelled, and Bellius looked up.

Bellius's jaw dropped. The fox-girl was floating in the air, silhouetted against the moon. He dodged back out of attack range, but she made no move to strike against him. Instead, she simply looked down in silence, grinning.

"Hmm. Based on the evidence, it seems the one mentioned in the newspaper is indeed the real Terakomari herself."

Bellius bared his fangs at the fox-girl. It hardly mattered under the circumstances, but he couldn't help noticing how he could see right up her robe and even up the miniskirt she was wearing underneath. Casting levitation magic while wearing such a skimpy, revealing outfit…it had to be deliberate. That made her an exhibitionist, a deviant.

"Who the hell are you?"

"What business is it of yours who I am? This is between me and her. It's got nothing to do with a mangy dog and a sleazy vampire."

"What did you just say, wench?!"

"You won't get away with saying that. Who are you calling a sleazy vampire anyhow?!"

The fox-girl threw back her head. "Ah-ha-ha-ha!" she cackled. "It's clear you'll be no obstacle to my plans. I'm glad I learned that much from this little visit. Well, say hello to Terakomari for me."

"Hey! Get back here!"

But they were powerless to stop her.

As Bellius flung his ax into the sky, the fox-girl vanished like a flame being snuffed out. His weapon flew through the air, unimpeded by its absent target, and disappeared against the starry indigo blue sky. It appeared she'd used teleportation magic. Pursuit would be impossible.

The two remaining figures in the garden exchanged glances, the night air thick and silent around them.

"She's after the commander. What should we do?"

"There's only one thing to do: track her down and deal with her."

"You're right, of course…but shouldn't we warn the commander?"

Caostel grinned.

"If she learns of this, then she'll track down Foxy and obliterate her before the next sundown with her inimitable skills. Then we won't get any of the glory. We need to act of our own accord and track down that wench ourselves. Then we'll win Komari's favor and the right to lick her shoes."

"But—"

"But nothing. Troubling the commander with trifles such as these... that would bring shame upon us. Our job is to keep things running smoothly so that she can focus on tactics, right?"

Bellius had to agree.

The Seventh Unit didn't care for following military protocol at the best of times.

And so while it remained unbeknownst to her, another source of trouble was hurtling Komari's way...

3   A Mutinous Uprising

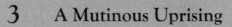

The following morning, I awoke to find the sicko maid standing by my bedside, dressed in an apron and…nothing else.

"Good morning, Lady Komari."

"Good mor—the heck are you wearing?!"

A second too late, my personal safety alarm bells started ringing in my head, and I leaped up. Recently my pervert sensors had been going into overdrive. Every time this weirdo came near me, my hair stood on end, and my heart started hammering.

I backed up to the safety of the wall then glared at her.

"How can you walk around dressed like that? Have you no shame?!"

"Nope."

"What am I supposed to say to that?!"

"Never mind. Breakfast is ready. Today's your favorite, Lady Komari—French toast! I really put a lot of effort into making it, so please, enjoy!"

"Wait, really? Woo!"

I sat down at the little table I had in my room and gazed at the plate Vill had brought. A delicious, sweet scent was wafting into the air. It looked super yummy.

"Can I go ahead and eat?"

"Please do."

"Okay, time to dig in!"

Nervously, I placed a forkful into my mouth. Oh, so fluffy. Oh, so sweet. It put me in the mood to stay in my room all day and shut out the world.

It had been arranged that Vill would prepare all of my meals. She told me it was the "basic duty of a lady's maid," and to be honest, she was a pretty sweet cook. I sometimes baked cookies and stuff, but I could never make anything that came close to what she could whip up.

"Thanks, that was amazing!"

Within ten minutes I'd cleared my plate. I was super full. I wanted to keep the good vibes going by heading back to bed for another snooze. Oh, but first I had to brush my teeth.

As I poured milk into my cup and hummed to myself, Vill spoke up in a cold, clear voice.

"All right, then, now that you've eaten, it's time to get to work, Lady Komari."

"Splurt!"

Milk came shooting out of my nose.

Curse her! What a sneaky, underhanded play!

"Hold on just a minute! Yesterday I worked myself half to death! Now I have to do that again today?!"

"Obviously. What do you think working is anyhow? Now come on, change into your uniform. Off with your jammies. Arms up! Show me those pits!"

"I'll show them to you…in hell!"

Stubbornly, I zipped back to bed and wrapped the blankets around me. Work again today? When I had just toiled yesterday? Was she crazy? Why couldn't the weekend last seven days a week? Why were the fates so cruel?

"Lady Komari, about today's business…"

"Don't care! Tell them all I'm sick!"

"I don't think that would be such a good idea. Besides, are you sure you want to miss today? You're going to meet your very own personal mount."

"…Huh?"

I popped my head out of my blanket roll and looked right at Vill.

"Mount? By 'mount,' you mean…to ride?"

"Yes, by 'mount,' I mean to ride. Since the days of old, every great commander has had their own great horse. Oh, it's not always a horse, of course. But anyway, it's going to be your very own, very important partner from now on. And today you are going to visit it."

"Mount…"

If that was the case, then…surely I could step out for a few minutes, couldn't I?

"Now, let's get you dressed. Today, I absolutely insist on helping you out of those pajamas."

"…Hey, Vill. Am I really getting my own ride?"

"Yes, the Empress has signed off on it. Now, hands to the sky."

"Oh, okay… Wow, the Empress sure is generous, isn't she? By the way, where do we go for me to pick my mount? A ranch or somewhere?"

"There's a special stable near the Crimson Tower. That's where we're heading. Oh, Lady Komari, you really do have the most beautiful pale skin. I could gaze upon it for eternity…"

I see, I see…a special stable, eh. Interesting. Hee-hee-hee. Actually, I've always really wanted to have my own steed. The protagonist in *The Andronos Chronicles* rides a magnificent mount. And I had the feeling I could bond better with an animal of my very own than I could with any person.

"Everything has been so awful since I became a Crimson Lord, but this is an unexpected treat! Don't you think so, Vill?"

"Indeed. I, too, am beyond excited to see you ride your noble steed, Lady Komari. Oh, it's time for the pajama pants to come off. Could you turn that way for me?"

"Oh, sure."

Ooh, I just couldn't wait! I wondered what my mount would be like.

Oh…but I'd never ridden before, so would I be any good at it? Surely someone would be able to teach me the basics? And practicing would be half the fun! Wow, how long had it been since I was this excited to go out? Hurry up, Vill!

I let my guard down. While I was distracted with exciting thoughts of my mount, the deviant maid had succeeded in getting me undressed. If I'd been in my right mind, this would have been my cue to rebuke her with the fury of a thousand cats, but right now, I was in such a good mood that I decided to allow it.

"I've been expecting you, Lady Gandesblood. Now, please…this way."

At the stables, we were met by a polite, well-mannered silver fox of a vampire. He was the official stablemaster, appointed by the Empress herself. When he spoke about the beasts in his stable, his eyes seemed to sparkle. I was relieved to have met someone new who wasn't a complete freakshow for once.

"The beasts, they can see into a person's heart. If someone has wicked intentions, they'll spot them right away. It's important to keep your thoughts and feelings pure while you're interacting with them."

"I…I see… Pure thoughts, pure thoughts…"

As I stepped tentatively into the stable, my nostrils suddenly filled with the distinctive smell of the countless beasts who lived there. But I was so excited, I barely even minded.

"Wow, there's a ton!"

The Empress's stable was filled with so many creatures that, even to a layperson like me, it was obvious they were the finest animals money could buy. On top of that, there were many different kinds… Some resembled horses in form, while others resembled reptiles. I approached a serpentine dragon nearby and nervously reached my hand out to it. It seemed accustomed to people and allowed me to stroke its head. It even narrowed its eyes in pleasure. *Oh, how cute!*

"Do you like this one? It's a Mizuchi from the Enchanted Lands.

They're one of the more mild-mannered beasts but are capable of quickly covering wide distances."

"Huh…"

I went along the rows of stalls, peeking in at all the creatures as I listened to the stablemaster's explanations. They were all such splendid mounts. I felt like their magnificence would only be wasted on someone like me.

"Well then, have you decided?"

I hesitated. In truth, I didn't even know where to begin. They all looked so amazing. Deliberating, I paced up and down the aisles. At the far end of the stables, a certain beast caught my eye. It was a dragon-type creature, with incredibly luxurious fur and an impressive aura. The proud way it stood with its head held high drew me in, as if magnetically attracted…

"Stablemaster. What's this beast here?"

"That one?"

The stablemaster frowned.

"That's one of the rarest types of Mizuchi there is, a Crimson Mizuchi. We only have one of its kind in our stable. It is peerless in its bravery, strength, and agility. But I don't think…"

From the way the stablemaster was chewing his lip and trailing off, I realized there was some baggage attached to this animal.

But it was too late. I had already fallen for the Crimson Mizuchi. Its aura of aloofness and detachment reminded me of myself. As I approached the stall, I tried to keep my heart as pure as possible. "Come here," I whispered.

"No, Lady Gandesblood! It's dangerous!"

"What's dangerous about it? This beast and I are kindred spirits, can't you see? There, there."

At first, the dragon seemed wary of me. But gradually, it seemed to recognize my peaceful soul, and it began to approach me. I reached out to stroke its soft white fur. It felt cool and pleasant to the touch. When I scratched its chin and neck, the Crimson Mizuchi seemed to relax, trumpeting through its nostrils with pleasure.

"I…I can't believe it…"

"Heh, surprised? I bet you were about to tell me that this beast is a troublemaker who can't get along with people. Right? But see, this one and I are on the same wavelength. Our souls are aligned."

There was a sad light in the Mizuchi's blue eyes. I felt that it was the light of a wise soul, a misunderstood spirit who couldn't form close connections with anyone. Its unusual white fur must have set it apart from the others, leading it to spend its days alone and misunderstood. I could relate. Boy, could I.

After a few more minutes of stroking and petting, the Crimson Mizuchi had completely opened its heart to me. Crooning quietly, it suddenly huffed air from its nose as it began rubbing its face against my chest. "Whoa! That tickles! Hee-hee-hee! Cut it out!"

"…Excuse me. What's the deal with this creature?"

"Ah, Miss Villhaze… Many military commanders have attempted to tame this beast, but all have failed. The Crimson Mizuchi has a strong preference for little girls and will open its heart to no one else. Of the schoolchildren who come to visit the stables on trips, it singles out the tiniest girl among them for attention."

"I see. That makes sense, I think."

"As I said, beasts are skilled at reading people's hearts. The problem is, people aren't skilled at reading the hearts of beasts."

I was dimly aware of Vill and the stablemaster discussing something behind me, but I wasn't paying attention. Since I was so delighted to have made a new friend, I couldn't care less about anything else. And I think the Crimson Mizuchi felt the same way. It kept nuzzling its soft nose against me as if greatly excited.

"All right! I've chosen!"

I turned to Vill and the stablemaster, my eyes shining.

"I'm making this Crimson Mizuchi my loyal steed! Stablemaster, may I?"

"Are…are you sure that's really what you want?"

©riichu

"I've never been more sure of anything! We're kindred spirits! Like one heart, residing in two bodies... Right, Bucephalus?"

The Crimson Mizuchi nodded its head vigorously as if agreeing with me. I just came up with the name on the spur of the moment, but it really suited him! All right...from this day forth, I would ride out on my noble mount for all to know his name...Bucephalus!

"If it is your wish, Lady Gandesblood, then I have no objection, only..."

"I'd give up if I were you. Lady Komari only looks frail. In truth, she's incredibly stubborn."

What better time than the present to take a first ride on my new steed, Bucephalus? A great commander should have a loyal mount or two that she can hop onto when she feels the need for speed, after all! Hey, Bucephalus! Don't put your nose there! That tickles! Ha-ha-ha! Nooo! Don't lick my neck!

After that, I had my first riding practice.

It was all so new to me. I struggled at first, crouching above the saddle, but with the stablemaster's instruction and Vill's words of support, I managed to relax and sit nicely on my new friend. Yikes, it was really high up, though. Too high. Ten times higher than I'd been expecting. I've always wished I were taller and forced down glasses of milk every day hoping to grow, but being this far off the ground didn't actually feel so good. Every time I looked down, I felt my head start to get dizzy...izzy...izzy...

"Are...are you all right? Your expression..."

"Wh-what?! I'm simply trembling with...excitement!"

"That's right, Beastmaster. A Crimson Lord of the commander's pedigree would never shake over something as basic as riding. She may look like she's quivering like a leaf, about to burst into tears, but don't be mistaken."

"Y-yes, of course. Now then, shall we try walking? Go for it, Lady Gandesblood."

Following the stablemaster's gentle instructions, I squeezed my mount's sides with my heels. Bucephalus responded obligingly. Wow! I was actually riding!

"Wonderful, Lady Komari. What a spectacle... You're so splendid, I can barely stand it!"

"Wah-ha-ha! Right? *Right?* Giddyup, Bucephalus! Let's become one with the wind! Let's ride off the edge of the world!"

Bucephalus neighed shrilly. He seemed to have picked up on my exhilaration, and it spurred him on. Wow, wow! Had I been a secret riding master all along?! All right! *Now, let's take a turn around the palace gardens, and... Huh? Whoa!*

"Slow down, Bucephalus. You're going too fast. All that stuff I said about going off the edge of the world, that was just bluster. Can you stop now? Please? Ple—WHOA!"

All of a sudden, we were galloping like the wind.

I couldn't process what was happening. It was as if Bucephalus was streaking across the ground as fast as lightning. The scenery around me was a blur. We were going so fast, I couldn't focus. I tried yelling at my mount, but he refused to slow. Yikes. This was bad. Very, very bad!

"STOPPP!"

"Lady Gandesblood! Draw back on the reins!"

The stablemaster was shouting something at me, but I couldn't hear him. I was frozen in fear, my throat suddenly paralyzed. Bucephalus seemed oblivious to my discomfort. He had lost himself in the thrill of flight.

Yohann Helders was very annoyed.

It was magic practice time at the Mulnite Imperial Palace, and the Seventh Unit was sparring on Training Ground Number 7...

They may have been a bunch of wild outlaws, but the Seventh Unit still went through drills diligently. Even when there were no battles in the offing, they still practiced. Today the training area was filled with vampires engaged in mock combat.

The brawl between Bellius and Mellaconcey was a sight to behold in particular. The earth had been scarred from impact, and the air was thick with explosions, which rained sparks down on the spectators. Several got killed while watching.

But Yohann did not share their fighting spirit. He sat cross-legged on a bench in the shade of a tree, gnawing on his lunch, which consisted of a leg of meat on the bone, trying to suppress a wave of powerful emotions.

He was angry. So, so angry.

The object of his rage was Terakomari Gandesblood herself. That little strumpet had snagged the spot of Crimson Lord and unit commander right out of his hands with her family connections.

But no, that wasn't all. That alone he could have dealt with. The military was rampant with nepotism. Many a skilled soldier got passed over for those of better status.

The thing that really ground Yohann's gears was the fact that the bitch had embarrassed him. Publicly.

Just thinking about it made him shudder violently.

Just a few days earlier, Terakomari Gandesblood had attempted to make her entrance to the Bloody Hall. Yohann had launched his attack against her. If she really had what it took to be a Crimson Lord, then she would have been able to deflect his attack effortlessly. That was the logic behind his actions.

But she'd made Yohann look like a fool.

In front of everyone, she had closed the doors on his neck and ended his life in an instant. They all ignored him for two days after that, and he hadn't even been able to take part in the battle against the Lapelico Kingdom.

Never before had he been so humiliated.

"I'll have my revenge, mark my words..."

The bone in his leg of meat suddenly snapped. Yohann's sycophants squealed girlishly in surprise, but he didn't have time to care about them. His mind was racing a mile a minute.

He needed to track down the commander and beat her to death. No, no, simply killing her, that was too boring. Yes, he would execute her publicly, that was a given, but first he needed to concoct a good plan to make sure she suffered as much as he had. First, he would burn off all her hair. Then her clothes. And then...

"Now, now, revenge is hardly in the spirit of peace, is it?"

Someone called out behind him. It was the stripped-tree man, looming over him. Caostel Conto, the head vampire of the Seventh Unit.

"What do you want? I'm not in a good mood right now."

"You never are. That's why you're always making dumb mistakes. Too distracted by your fits of ill temper."

"Did you come here to fight?"

Yohann glowered up at Caostel. The stripped-tree man chuckled.

"You've been sitting there muttering about revenge for a while now..."

"What of it?"

"Could it possibly be revenge against...the supreme commander?"

"Who else?"

Caostel shrugged.

"Well, you ought to know better than anyone else that Terakomari Gandesblood's power is not of the standard variety. But who would expect anything less of the noble daughter of the exalted Gandesblood family?"

"Don't spout that horseshit! That was just an accident! There's no way I would ever lose against a coquette like her! Why, I caused that famous prison riot and massacre; don't forget about that!"

"Yeah, but you still died, though."

"I just told you! It was an accident! Pure coincidence! You've all completely lost your minds! That stunted wench doesn't have any powers! When I flew at her, she went as white as a sheet and turned to flee! It was only by happenstance that I got wedged between the doors like that!"

"Suppose that's true, then. In that case, what do you make of yesterday…?"

"Yesterday? What are you talking about?"

"The battle against the Lapelico Kingdom. You missed it, so probably you wouldn't know, but the commander was incredible at directing the battle. She was like one of the great generals the history books tell of."

"Can you be more specific?"

"Her orders, they were so succinct, so perfect. 'Kill 'em all,' she shouted."

"…"

"I mean, for a bunch of bloodthirsty meatheads like us, what better command could there be? And it was only her second day at her post. In that tiny span of time, she had the Seventh Unit all figured out. I tip my hat to her."

"Even a chimpanzee could develop tactics like those! She's nothing more than an incompetent rich kid who got promoted to the Crimson Lord position through family connections. Nothing more!"

"Now, now, settle down…"

No matter how shrewd Yohann's take on the situation was, Caostel seemed determined to dismiss him, rolling his eyes and calling him a brat. Aware that Caostel outranked him, all Yohann could do was gnash his teeth in fury and scowl at the stupid, stripped-tree fellow.

"Watch how you look down on me. If you don't wanna end up bald."

"I'd like to see you try. In fact, I was just looking for a sparring partner. Perfect timing."

"Ha-ha! All right. Let's do it."

Suddenly, a fireball sparked up in Yohann's cupped hands with a *whump* sound. Just as he geared up to blast Caostel in the face with it, the other vampire suddenly gasped, as if noticing something.

"Ah, stop, Yohann…"

"What? Now you're punking out? Nuh-uh. Prepare yourself! Here comes my hair-singeing attack!"

"Aaargh!!! MOVE, MOVE, MOVE! MOOOVE!"

"What the—GAH?!"

Something hard struck him on the back of the head.

Yohann had no idea what was happening.

Before he could even begin to feel the pain of the blow, his eyes rolled back in his head. Blood poured from the wound. Then everything went black.

Yohann had been killed. Again.

☆

Around that same time, I was fearing for my life.

Bucephalus continued to fly across the ground as if he were really heading to the edge of the world. By this point, I had given up on trying to focus on the blurred scenery around me. In fact, I had given up on thinking at all.

It was hopeless, and I was powerless. I could see my grandfather waving a greeting to me from the afterlife…

Just as I was mentally resigning myself to the grave, there was a gigantic bump and I found myself tumbling. I was rocketing through the air, and my steed was nowhere in sight.

Apparently, I had been flung from Bucephalus's saddle.

Everything suddenly went into slow motion.

As I went spinning through the air, nausea overtook me. But even in my panic, I recognized the faces of the people standing nearby. Caostel, standing as tall and skinny as a winter tree. Bellius, with his dog head. And the permanently rapping Mellaconcey. I'd reached the Mulnite Imperial Army's training grounds. Most of my subordinate troops were there, too. Everyone was staring at me with looks of surprise on their faces.

I mean, I get it. I'd be surprised, too.

And I'd also be pretty shocked if I saw my commander come hurtling off her mount like an uncoordinated sack of potatoes.

Ah, here we go. This is where the mutiny starts. Will they do me in, too, for good measure?

That is, if falling off my steed didn't kill me first, of course.

Perhaps I had enough time to compose a short death poem for myself? Yes, I had just about accepted my fate. At that moment, my face made contact—not with the hard ground I'd been expecting, but with the soft lace and ruffles of a warm body in a maid outfit. Wait… maid outfit?

"Oh, Lady Komari. What a dynamic dismount. How many times have I asked you to alight in the usual fashion? Please consider the feelings of your poor Vill. Your daredevil antics are terrible for my blood pressure!"

Slowly, I gazed up.

A familiar girl was smiling down at me.

That's when I realized I was being cradled in the arms of the sicko maid, bridal carry style.

What the… How had she managed to catch up with Bucephalus after he'd bolted? Magic? Or perhaps she just had incredibly muscular legs for sprinting? Had she—*whoa! Creepy maid! Quit trying to cop a feel! Pervert!*

"I'm n-not gonna th-thank you."

"Oh dear, you're delirious from shock."

"Sh-shut up. And let me down."

"Certainly."

Vill gently lowered me to the ground. I felt my head spin. But for all her faults, Vill…held my hand until I managed to steady myself. *Darn it.* She'd earn no brownie points with me.

"If it isn't our supreme commander! That was some entrance!"

I tottered across the grass, feeling like a heavy drunk on her third pub crawl stop of the night. Caostel approached me, grinning. *Ah, crap. Not now.*

"Caostel. How are you?"

"Ah, I'm doing well, thank you. Your troops are training hard again today, Commander Komari."

"I see. That's good."

"Indeed. It would be splendid if you would join the practice session, Commander."

"Wah-ha-ha! Don't be silly. If I joined, I'd TKO everyone in the space of five seconds."

My soldiers all gasped in awe. Why were they so dumb?!

"Hmm, indeed. And look, that moron is once again dead, before he could even engage you in battle this time."

The dog-headed Bellius flashed me a cynical smile.

Moron? Dead? What was he talking about?

I turned around, confused, and immediately spotted the figure of a blond-haired young man sprawled on the grass with the whites of his eyes showing. I felt my lower lip start to tremble. Wasn't that...?

"Yes, Lady Komari. It appears you kicked him in the head when you dismounted your steed."

Whaaat?!!!

I killed someone again! The same someone as last time!!! Oh, he's gonna be sooo pissed at me! I better not go out alone at night if I don't wanna get shanked! And where the heck did Bucephalus go? Did he really head to the edge of the world without me? Stupid Mizuchi!

I stood there clutching my head in horror as my subordinates began to roar and chant: *"All hail the commander!" "Glory to the Slayer!" "Purge the betrayer!"* and so on. But just then—

"I'm not dead yet, you filthy nepotistic scuuum!!!"

A sudden wave of heat sent my back tingling.

I turned again to find the blond youth, who had ostensibly died, standing there glaring at me, his body engulfed in flames. I was so scared, I almost peed myself. *He survived?!*

The blond youth roared at me, his face contorted with deep resentment. "Supreme Commander, isn't launching a sneak attack like that sort of...cowardly?!!!"

My throat nearly closed from fear. But I had to say something.

"Oh, cram it. Your fault for not dodging."

"Hah, is that so? Well, if I kill you now, that'll be fair, right? No complaints!"

The blond-haired youth came barreling at me, fireball in hand.

Uh-oh, this is where I die.

But just at that moment, Vill finally released me after she'd been helping me to stay upright for the past few minutes. Then a miracle occurred. Still dizzy from my fall, I suddenly lost my balance and toppled over, dropping out of range of Blondie, who'd charged at me like an enraged boar, only to end up tripping over me and cartwheeling across the grass.

"Wow!" "What a dodge!" "Nice move, Supreme Commander!" "Just like a bullfighter!" "Seeing the commander in action puts me in the mood, if ya know what I'm sayin'!"

Oh, shut up. Morons.

But never mind them. I had to do something about the blond-haired youth before—

"This is where your luck runs out! Prepare to die!"

The blond-haired youth had gotten to his feet and was coming at me again. I had to make a break for it, or he was going to wipe me out. Somehow I got my legs to cooperate. But I was still so dizzy. Curses! Three years of being a shut-in had left me as weak as a kitten.

"Ha-ha! Burn, burn, Supreme Commander! Burn in—GLURP!"

"Yeeek!"

I went flying.

The sky and the ground switched places again. Unable to figure out what was happening, I froze up. I'd gone soaring again; that much was clear. But why wasn't I feeling any pain...?

"GYAAAHHH!!!"

Just then, I heard an earsplitting scream. I looked down, and my jaw dropped—the blond-haired youth was between my legs. I was sitting astride him like he was a pony! On top of that, it seemed I'd poked him in the eye with my right pointer finger. Hence the scream.

"Amazing, Lady Komari! You swept your enemy's feet from under him, mounted him to show dominance, and went for the eyeball in one swift movement! Exerting the maximum amount of damage while conserving as much energy as possible...that's the distinctive art of Komarism!"

Thanks for clarifying that, Vill. But what the heck is Komarism?

Ah, but that hardly mattered right now! I removed my finger from the eye with a schlorping sound and scrambled off the guy in a hurry. He was rolling back and forth on the ground, screaming, "My eye! My eye!" I glanced around me, trying to casually take stock of the environment. My subordinates were all sighing and nodding in awe. Several were weeping tears of blood, and one was loudly wailing "I wish I was him!" ...Goodness, what a freak.

What was I supposed to do next?

Maybe I should follow this up with a little speech for the masses? To show dominance?

Inhaling a deep breath and taking care not to stutter, I launched into a little speech.

"You see? Do you see what happens when you attempt to rise against me? Your eyeballs aren't the only balls you people will have to worry about if you cross me!"

"HAAAIIILLL!!!"

The roar of approval from the crowd made my ears ring painfully.

I despised this job. So much. How much longer did I have to do this for? I guess quitting was out of the question. I felt so...caged and impotent. I would have to take my anger out on the weirdo maid later. That would soothe me.

Just as I began dreaming up ways to psychologically torture my maid, Blondie stopped rolling around. Then he rose to his feet, yelling.

"N-nice trick! But you won't get away with this!"

Pressing his palm to his right eye, he snarled threateningly in my direction. I trembled, wondering just what he was planning.

Meanwhile, he started rummaging around in the pocket of his uniform. He produced what seemed like a bit of cloth and threw it at me.

On closer inspection, it turned out to be a badly burned glove.

Was he throwing it away? It still looked usable...

What a waste, I thought to myself before realizing that the atmosphere had suddenly become tense.

My subordinates were all grinning, eyes shining as if entertained by the blond youth's sudden move. Caostel in particular was grinning demonically, looking every bit the criminal he was.

What? What was the meaning of this?

I turned back to Blondie. He gave me a beastlike smirk.

"Terakomari Gandesblood...I challenge you to a duel!"

A jewel? But I left all my good jewels at home because I was going riding. Why did he want...

Wait...DUEL?!

"Now, hold on just a—"

"Ha-ha, ha-ha-ha! Yes, yes...I should have just done it this way from the start! I'm clearly the superior warrior here! In a fair fight, on a fair and neutral battlefield, I will crush you! But what's this, Commander? Surely you don't intend to decline my challenge?"

He was sneering at me like a shark.

I looked around, scanning the faces of the crowd.

Vill was there, giving me a thumbs-up. Caostel was flashing me the ol' thumbs, too. Bellius, by contrast, was standing stock-still, arms crossed. Mellaconcey was ducking and weaving, waving his arms as if keeping tune with inaudible music. The others were all gazing at me with shining eyes.

Nobody was going to come to my aid.

Well, yeah. Stupid to expect that.

Taking a few steps forward, I stooped then picked up the charred glove from where it lay on the grass.

Then I turned to Blondie again and smiled with as much fake confidence as I could muster.

"All right. I accept your challenge. But I warn you, I will give you no quarter. You will look back upon this folly with the deepest regret."

☆

"AAAAAAAAAAAAAAAAAAAAAA!!!"

Back in my room, I flung myself onto the bed, overcome with regret.

I couldn't believe I'd actually gone and done it—agreed to a duel with that blond dude…Yohann Helders, I mean! He was going to roast me like a pig at a barbecue in front of everyone, and that would be the end of the short life of Terakomari Gandesblood.

"Lady Komari, you seem overjoyed with your successful showing today!"

"I am not!!!"

I whirled around to peer over my shoulder at Vill. She looked as unruffled and carefree as ever. Had she no sense of danger? But actually, why would she? I was the one who was going to end up in the ground. Shit!!!

"Ugh…what am I gonna do? I could flee the country…but where would I go? Lapelico? No, no, the Chimpanzee would have me executed…"

"Lady Komari, look at me."

I had buried my face in my pillow, snuffling back tears as Vill hovered behind me, her voice low and soft. What did she want now? I lifted my head to glare at her sideways.

"What do you want, creep? Leave me alone!"

"Now, now, there's no need to be rude. But I understand how you feel, Lady Komari. If you go ahead with this, there's no way you're getting out of it alive."

"Right! My life is over! In the literal sense! Ohhh!!! There was so much I still wanted to do! I wanted to publish a novel! I wanted to try making a gingerbread castle, at least once! Also, I wanted…"

"Yes…?"

"I wanted to swim in a pool of honey."

Vill sniggered. Darn it. The fear of my impending mortality had loosened my tongue and made me spill my most deeply held aspirations. Now I would never live this down! Well, I wouldn't have to *live* it down very long at least. Since I was gonna be dead soon. Real dead.

But Vill merely smiled. "Aw, it's okay," she consoled. "Have you forgotten? Even if you get done in, it's not like you'll stay dead. The Mulnite Empire has the power of the Dark Core to draw on, right?"

"I know that! But it's gonna hurt! It's gonna *burn*!"

"Still, there's no need to worry. As long as I'm around, you'll never succumb in some silly duel. I know that for certain."

My brain sputtered to a halt. What was she saying now?

I gazed at her blankly as she smiled with pride, drew herself up to her full height, and raised her chin.

"I am Special Lieutenant Villhaze, of the Mulnite Imperial Army's Third Division, specialist in secret intelligence and covert ops! I will ensure your victory, Lady Komari!"

After that, the day of the duel came around in the blink of an eye.

The Mulnite Imperial Palace grounds had a full-size battle arena. It apparently did double duty for pop star concerts and end-of-year death fights. But thanks to my influence as one of the Crimson Lords, I'd been able to secure it for my duel. Lucky me, right? Crap.

"Lady Komari! Look this way, Lady Komari!" "Supreme Commander! Make mincemeat out of Yohann, okay?" "Ko-ma-rin! Ko-ma-rin! Ko-ma-rin!" "Ah! Ahh! Ahhh! Komari-baby!"

The spectator seats were packed. Everyone was staring down at me, screaming and cheering as if they were on some kind of intoxicating substance. And the majority of the crowd was actually composed of people *besides* Seventh Unit soldiers. In addition to officers from other units, even civvies who came from all over the city just to watch were in attendance. They comprised seventy percent of the crowd. News of my impending duel had spread across the Imperial Capital. It was obvious who'd leaked the info—the Komari Unit. My own merry band of idiot subordinates.

Thanks to them, I was half dead with embarrassment before the duel even started.

...Agh, I was hoping for less public humiliation. If I had to have an audience, why couldn't it be limited to the five hundred soldiers from my squad? I wasn't expecting this...circus. It was like...like the kind of crowd you get at a pop concert! What did these people expect from me?!

"*Lady Komari, how are you feeling?*"

I could hear the sicko maid's voice crackling in my ear. She'd fitted me with a magic earpiece before I left for the arena.

"How am I feeling? Like crap obviously..."

"*Do your best. This is the time to show your mettle!*"

"I don't wanna! I wanna go HOME!"

"*Once this is all over, I'll give you a special reward.*"

"A reward?"

"*Five tickets, each redeemable for one night spent sleeping beside a beautiful maid.*"

"I don't want them!!!"

"*Ten tickets?*"

"It's not a question of how many tickets!!!"

"*Incidentally, you'll be dressed as the maid in this scenario.*"

"Say what now?!"

"*The reward is your share of the revenue for the tickets. We're sold out.*"

"What are you, my pimp??!!"

"*Don't worry, I bought all of the tickets myself. I wasn't about to let you sleep next to some stinky, dirty old man. But you know what, why don't we dispense with the tickets, and I'll just pay you directly for a tumble in the sheets instead?*"

"You're the dirty old man in this scenario!!!"

My last shreds of motivation were fading away. Why, when I was just about to embark upon a horrific battle, did I still have to deal with this creepy maid's perversions?

"Vill, can we be serious for a second?"

"Go ahead."

"Am I…really going to make it back alive?"

I heard her chuckling through the earpiece. But only for a second. Then she was back to speaking in her usual smooth and steady voice.

"Don't fret. I am your faithful servant, Lady Komari. No matter what happens, I won't ever abandon you. Ah, it seems your opponent has arrived."

The arena erupted in a roar of excitement.

I looked up expectantly at the gates directly opposite me through which my opponent would enter. They opened with a dull scrape. I swallowed hard. It was almost time. My duel was about to start. How was Vill—cursed Vill—planning to keep me alive through this? I wasn't sure I could withstand even a single blow. My body was as fragile as a peach. As a shadow emerged from the gate, I chewed my lip with anxiety.

"T-Terakomari! T-today I will b-b-burn you to a cruh-cruh-crisp!"

It was Yohann Helders.

But something was wrong with him. He was white as a sheet, wobbling along on unsteady legs. Clutching his midsection as if trying to hold back a torrent of diarrhea. Oof, he just fell down. Wow, he looked really sick. Wait, hold on a minute. Could it be that he—

"I poisoned him, just a little."

"You did that?"

Poisoning?! That was so…sneaky!

"Just doing my duty. Lieutenant Helders takes his meals every day in the cafeteria. And he always eats the same thing—meat on the bone. So I injected a slow-acting poison into every cut of meat in the cafeteria."

"Into...*every* cut of meat?!"

"*I needed to make sure that he ingested the poison. There was no other way. Okay, so around twenty to thirty other people will probably die, but that's a small price to pay. We can't quibble over a little collateral damage, you know.*"

She was nothing more than a terrorist! Her methods were far too out of line! Of course, it was nice than she was helping me, but did she have to take it to the extreme?!

Yohann turned his wild gaze on me. He looked like a starving beast.

"H-heh-heh! Wh-what's wrong, Commander? It's too late to turn on the wuh-wuh-waterworks and try to worm your way out of this n-now! I'm gonna in-in-incinerate you and send you s-straight to the inf-inf-infirmary!"

"Er, I think you're the one who needs to go to the infirmary."

"What you say?! D-d-don't look down your nose at me! I'll buh-burn off all your hair!"

Yikes, threats aside, he really did look worse for wear. And what did he mean, burn off my hair?

Just as I was feeling super conflicted, a gigantic *clang* rang out. It was the gong marking the start of the match. The roar of the crowd reached fever pitch, and I could hear people starting to yell things like, "Kill him!" and "Die, pig!" ...It was almost loud enough to pierce my eardrums.

"I'm gonna kuh-kuh-kill you!!! Nnng! BLURGH!!!"

"Eeeeeeek!!!"

He was approaching me now, puke spurting from his mouth and... something else...spurting from the other end. It was splattering everywhere.

And yikes, he was shambling so slowly. He looked like an old man who was having a senior moment. Or maybe a zombie.

"Vill! Do something! Children shouldn't be witnessing this! It's like a horror movie!"

"In that case, Lady Komari, please use your magic."

"Whaaat?! If I could use magic, I wouldn't be in this mess in the first place!"

"It's okay, just pretend to be casting it. When I give the signal, just snap your fingers. Make it showy, so the audience sees it. Ready? Five, four, three, two...now!"

SNAP.

...All I did was snap my fingers, as instructed.

Instantly, Yohann vanished with a *fwump*. No, he didn't vanish. He descended. All of a sudden, a massive hole opened in the ground. *What?*

"Wooow!!!" "What a spell!" "She just opened up a hole at her enemy's feet!" "Such precision!" "Such power!" "That's advanced magic, all right! It's called the Kingdom Cracker!" "But I didn't sense her casting any spell at all..." "Which means the commander can cast magic invisibly! Incredible!" "Ah, I see! She must have used the advanced-level spell Lacquered Wings!" "Wow! She really is supreme!" "Amazing, Commander!"

The crowd was going wild. I could hear Vill in my ear.

"I dug a hole in the arena floor last night."

"You did what now?!"

"Yeah, and I filled the bottom of the hole with bamboo spears. Lieutenant Helders ought to be nicely skewered right now, like a shish kebab."

Gosh, that was sick! But hold on... There was a major hole in her plan, pun intended. Where was the guarantee that Helders would be the one to trigger her pit trap? It could have been me! Did that thought not even cross her crazy mind?!

"Don't worry. Just stay still. I wanted to make sure I got him, so I actually dug a whole bunch of holes all over the arena. That way, he was bound to fall in no matter which direction he took."

"..."

Was I in hell? Trembling from the danger I could sense all around me, I gazed up blankly at the crowd. For some reason, they had all gotten to their feet in excitement. Confused, I turned to see a bloody Yohann crawling his way out of the pit. So he was still alive, then.

"Ha-ha-ha! You call that magic? Gimme a break! You…imposter!"

Guilty as charged. I watched silently as Yohann crawled his way out of the pit, his entire head stained crimson. Staggering to his feet, he conjured two fireballs as his eyes burned into mine.

"You set that little trap up last night, didn't you? Can't win if it's a fair fight, can you?"

Nope. Sorry.

"What a rude little man. Lady Komari, hit him with some smack talk!"

Ugh, I'd rather not. But I needed to play the tough guy, or I would meet a very sticky end.

So…

"Ha-ha-ha! Very amusing! As if a warrior of my caliber would need to resort to traps! Nonsense! Ludicrous! You're a dim-witted fool, Yohann Helders! An insect! I'll kill you just as easily as swatting a fly! Then I'll blend you up like a smoothie and sip on you while relaxing after my evening bath! Hah!"

""""OOOOHHH!""""

The crowd frothed in excitement. Then, Yohann seemed to completely snap.

"Let's see you try it, you duplicitous wench! Yaaaargh!!!"

"Vill! Help! He's really mad!"

"You shouldn't have incensed him. But leave it to me. Ah, but one snag—there aren't actually any more pitfall traps between his current position and yours."

"What?! I thought you dug a whole bunch of them?"

"Just the bad luck of the draw. What else do you want me to say?"

"You…idiot!!!"

Just then, a flaming fireball streaked past, almost singeing my ear. Shocked, I whirled around to face Yohann. He was pelting fireballs in my direction furiously, his whole body dripping with blood. Even his eyeballs were scarlet.

"Hyah-ha-ha! Burn, burn, you wench!!!"

"Whoa! T-time out..."

He was like some kind of horrible fire demon, shambling his way toward me and leaving flaming drops of blood in his wake. The fireballs he'd been chucking in all directions had landed and continued to burn. The arena was starting to heat up, and a ring of fire had formed all around us. Though he seemed to have little control over his aim, he was narrowing in on me. It was only a matter of time before one of his fireballs made contact. After all...I couldn't move.

"Vill! Should I snap my fingers again...?"

"Nah, too late."

"Too late?! You mean...my time's up? Give me a freakin'..."

...Break, I was about to say. But before I could finish, there was an immense explosion.

It felt like my eyes were about to fly from their sockets.

A blast of hot air hit me like a truck. It was all I could do to stay on my feet. The blast seemed to have come from the position where Yohann had just been standing. Unable to process what was happening, I covered my face with my arms. In my magic earpiece, I heard Vill's cool, calm tones.

"Ah, that'll be the land mine."

What...? A land mine?

"He must have stepped on one. It was about time he did. I buried about ninety-six of them all throughout the stadium."

"This arena is a total deathtrap because of you!!!"

How much prep had Vill actually done?!

Had she been out here all night, tinkering with her little tricks and traps? All to save my life, I guess?

"Well, that's the end of Lieutenant Helders. You win, Lady Komari."

"I mean...I guess so..."

The billowing clouds of smoke were starting to dissipate. What had happened to Yohann? Had he been reduced to a pile of charred body parts? I didn't really want to find out...

Suddenly, the crowd gasped.

I blinked in complete disbelief.

Yohann Helders was still alive! Alive, but crawling, bit by bit, like a caterpillar. Crawling toward...me!

Even though he was a complete mess, he still refused to give up...

For a moment, I found myself overwhelmed with respect for him, but then—

"Hee! Hee! Good...trick, you...wench! Gonna capture you... Burn off all your clothes... Expose you in front of everyone... Make you do a fire dance buck naked... Hee!"

Terror hit me like a sledgehammer.

But it was too late for that.

Yohann continued to slither and crawl his way right up to my feet.

I considered fleeing, but I couldn't move an inch. Vill's booby traps were all around me, remember? But I needn't have worried. Out of nowhere, Yohan's strength seemed to have depleted, even as he grasped for me with a clawlike hand.

He wasn't moving anymore. This time he was dead for sure.

Oh, what a relief! Ah, but I felt bad rejoicing over someone's demise.

Still, the winner of a duel has the right to rejoice in their victory. I placed my foot on top of his head (gently, of course) and raised my arms high in the air as I prepared to give my victory speech.

"The mutinous wretch has been exterminated!!"

"HAAAIIILLL!!!"

The crowd went nuts. My Seventh Unit soldiers completely lost their heads in the excitement and stormed the arena. Fools! This whole place was one gigantic booby trap!

I cringed as explosions started to pop off all over the arena, but at the same time, I was overcome by a strange emotion.

I was happy I'd survived, of course, but I felt sort of terrible about Yohann. He'd suffered so many wounds. You couldn't even call this self-defense. It went way beyond that. And some of the tricks we'd used were really, really unsportsmanlike. Despite all that, my subordinates were chanting *"Komarin! Komarin!"* (Even as several of them went up in smoke from stepping on land mines…). Yeah, I just felt kind of… crappy about everything.

"Hey, Vill…I kinda feel like we're deceiving everyone…"

"We're totally deceiving everyone. Duh."

"Gah! I know, I know, you're right…"

"You're far too good a person, Lady Komari. A Crimson Lord should be more cutthroat. Please try to work on that."

"Okay…"

Well, no point dwelling on things.

I gazed out across the stadium. Land mines were still going off here and there. *BOOM, BOOM.* I heaved a sigh. Whoa! That was a close one! *Ack! Body parts!*

And so I managed to narrowly cheat death.

By the way, all of the wounded, Yohann included, were taken to the infirmary straight after the duel. I say infirmary, but it's more like a morgue. Like a warehouse for storing bodies securely until the Dark Core can do its work and revive them. If this place were a hotel, it would have negative five stars.

But I digress.

I arrived back home exhausted, but I needed to take a bath. My hair and clothes were drenched in blood, and I was covered in sweat. I didn't even know whose blood it was. I needed to wash up before hitting the hay. Otherwise, I knew I'd have bad dreams all night.

So I headed off to the dressing room. But then…

"Hey, you. I was just about to take a bath."

"All right. I'll prepare you a change of clothes."

"…"

"Is something wrong?"

"What are you going to be doing while I'm in the bath?"

"My duties, of course."

"..."

"Enjoy your bath."

Vill left with a smile.

Suspicious. Highly suspicious. What was suspicious? I wasn't sure myself. All I knew was that it was suspicious.

I mean, this was the sicko maid we were talking about. How many times had I been subjected to her groping? And we're not talking subtle touches. We're talking manhandling the goods. Repeatedly.

"...Whatever."

I was probably just overthinking things.

I mean, take yesterday, for example. Nothing weird happened yesterday, right? Or the night before. So I should just put Vill out of mind. Reading too far into things was only going to lead to excess stress building up in my body.

I shook my head and slapped my cheeks briskly. Then I got undressed and stepped into the bathing area. I don't know what kinda bathtubs they've got in normal people houses, but I have the feeling ours is exceptionally large. You could swim laps in it if you wanted. By the way, I can't swim.

After washing my hair and body over at the wall showers, I dipped a toe into the steaming hot bathtub.

Then I sank in right up to my shoulders and heaved a humongous sigh.

"Ahhhh! I can't *believe* I survived today!"

I was still reflecting on the afternoon's duel.

The blond guy...Yohann Helders...he seemed to really despise me. I guess it made sense, though. Anyone would hate it if a rich aristocrat's daughter with zero credentials showed up as their new boss. In fact, it was the other guys—the ones who worshiped me like some kind of goddess—who were the weirdos.

Yeah, Yohann had my number all right.

If the others found out about my true character, they'd turn on and usurp me just as he had.

I'd managed to eke out a victory at today's duel, thanks to Vill, but the next time I was called upon to defend my honor, I'd end up on the morgue slab for sure…

"…"

Darn, when I thought of it like that, Vill was my only ally in all this…

And she never once criticized me for being me.

She always seemed to just…accept me. Weaknesses and all.

And how many times had she come to my rescue…?

"I should probably thank her…"

"I appreciate the sentiment very much. But perhaps instead of a verbal expression of gratitude, you could express it with…your body?"

"I knew it!!!"

I'd been expecting this, you see. The second I heard her voice, I scrambled. But I forgot about my lack of strength and coordination. And the fact it's hard to run through water also slipped my mind. I splashed and floundered for about five steps before Vill came bounding through the water like a human grasshopper, cutting off my exit.

"Damn it! Why are you here?! You said you were doing work!"

"Yeah, that was a lie."

"Ugh! I should never have trusted you! Wait…don't squeeze those… Yeeek!!!"

I looked down at Vill's fingers, interlocked around my midsection, and saw that they were red and swollen with multiple nasty-looking cuts.

Whoa, hold on…

"Now then, Lady Komari, shall we…soak together?"

"You're injured!!!"

"…!"

I felt like time froze for a few moments.

The next second, the sicko maid jumped away from me with a huge splash. I raised an eyebrow, slightly tickled that I'd rattled her for once. But never mind that now! Vill was composing her expression, hiding her hands behind her back.

©riichu

"It's just blisters. They'll be all healed up by tomorrow. Dark Core and all."

"But they look super painful!"

"Pain is fleeting. Besides, they're only superficial wounds."

That was beside the point. I wasn't backing down on this.

"Tell me how you got those wounds."

"No."

"That's an order. Tell me at once."

Vill chewed her lip for a second, looking torn. I stared her down until she sighed and finally started talking.

"Remember the pitfall traps I set up to kill Yohann Helders?"

"Yeah."

"I dug them all by hand. With a shovel."

"You did all that landscaping work by yourself?!"

"The only magic skills I have involve poisoning..."

"I...I see..."

"..."

We gazed at each other silently for a few moments.

The sicko maid's cheeks were cherry red.

But she wasn't blushing because we were both buck naked. She was embarrassed that I'd pointed out her injuries. What a strange girl she was...

"I apologize. I'd rather you hadn't seen that. It's shameful."

Vill hung her head, wearing an expression of remorse. Her usual aura of perversion seemed to have vanished into the steamy air. What a fool she was!

"It's not shameful at all."

I gathered my courage and slid over to Vill in the water. Before I could reach her, though, a wave of embarrassment washed over me, so I could go no farther. Instead, I plopped down on my butt.

Clutching my knees to my chest under the water, I cleared my throat several times.

"You really worked hard for me, didn't you, Vill? If it weren't for you, I would be dead by now. I really...I really appreciate what you've done. So, um...you don't have to hide the wounds you got helping me. I mean...this might sound a bit sappy, but...I feel like I should have been there to share the burden with you, to share the pain..."

I was stumbling over my sentences. Words really are inadequate when it comes to expressing the true feelings of the heart, huh. This wasn't what I wanted to express to her at all. I mean, I didn't even know what I wanted to convey myself...

"Um, anyway, what I mean to say is...thank you. That's all. Do you get that?"

Who could understand this gibberish? I thought. But...

"I do."

"Huh? You do?"

"I understand that you love me, Lady Komari."

"..."

Oh, uh, that's not really what I meant. But whatever.

"Lady Komari?"

"Yeah?"

"You're always the same old Lady Komari...aren't you?"

I turned my head to look at her. To my surprise, she was smiling.

"I'm just an average, nondescript vampire, you know? Not a weirdo like you and the rest of the unit..."

"No, that's not what I meant..."

But she trailed off, as if she'd changed her mind about what she was going to say. I waited for a few moments, but then I decided it probably wasn't important anyway. I'd just drop it.

Instead, I brought up something that had been worrying me a little.

"Hey, are you having an okay time with me? It must be quite grueling trying to keep a useless weakling of a vampire like me alive all the time..."

"Not at all. I have my special ability to rely on."

"You mean your poisoning magic?"

"Core Implosion."

What was *that*?

"It's another type of power, distinct from magic. It's a little hard to wield it, but...anyway, it's nothing for you to worry about, Lady Komari. All you need to know is that it's not a burden for me to look after you. No trouble at all."

I didn't get it.

"...Okay... But why are you so attached to me anyhow? It's a little creepy, you know."

"It's because you're a total knockout beauty. That's why."

"Yeah, I know that already. But that's not what I mean. It feels like there's some kind of special reason why you're so attached to me."

Vill sighed a little.

She paused for a long time before speaking up again.

"I committed a crime, you know."

"I'm aware of that, too."

"What? You've heard about that?"

"Yeah, sexual harassment. On me. Multiple counts by now."

Vill pouted then grinned. Don't get too comfortable, though, deviant maid. If I wanted to, I could pull up your criminal record using my government connections anytime... Wait! I could get some dirt on her like this! Then I would be free from the curse of the strawberry milk!!!

"It's not the kind of offense you'd ever guess, Lady Komari. It was terribly serious."

"Terribly serious? Did you grope me while I was sleeping or something?!"

"Oh, I do that every night. I'm talking about something that happened in the past...the reason I was sent down to work as a maid. My punishment. One day I'll tell you all about it. When the time's right."

"Oh, okay... Huh?"

I felt like there was a part of that sentence I should have been more concerned about, but Vill looked so peaceful and happy right now that I didn't have the heart to chastise her.

A grave infraction. Terribly serious...based on how solemn Vill seemed about it, I guessed it wasn't something on the level of simple perversion.

I was curious, of course, but I didn't intend to press her about it. I could wait until she was ready to tell me herself.

For a while after that, we just chilled out together and enjoyed a nice bath.

What was weird, though, was that Vill didn't make any further attempts to grope me.

It felt kind of...lonely...I mean, no no no! Wake up, Komari! She's got you addicted to her pervert schtick!!!

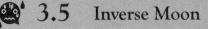

Vexations

Yohann Helders sat at the counter of a bar in the Imperial Capital's downtown area, nursing a glass of blood-and-wine. The joint was called The Gates of Dawn, and hardly ever got many customers.

A week had passed since the duel.

In that time, Yohann's life had been completely upended.

After losing to Terakomari, the military kicked him out of his unit. Yohann had already screwed up once by committing arson, which was how he landed himself in the Seventh Unit in the first place. Switching to Units 1 through 6 wasn't in the cards anymore. He had no choice now but to drop out of the military altogether.

How far he'd fallen from his days as a genius rookie, mastermind behind the prison massacre incident. He'd possessed such ambition that he'd been determined to get that coveted Crimson Lord position and command his own unit one day. But thanks to that stunted strumpet, all his plans had turned to dust.

"Ah, life is pain. Barkeep, another glass."

"You've had enough."

"What's it to you? I can pay."

"That's not the problem."

But he poured Yohann another glass anyway.

The barkeep owned the establishment and was also a foreigner, which was a pretty unusual sight in the Mulnite Empire. His dark skin identified him as a former resident of the Gerra-Arruka Republic, which meant he was currently too far away from his country's Dark Core to revive upon death. The fact he'd moved so far from his own nation to set up a business here meant that he was either a crazy fool, had issues back home, or was just extremely confident.

Yohann fixed his doleful eyes on him.

"Hey, barkeep. You heard of that Terakomari Gandesblood?"

"The new Crimson Lord, yes. I heard she's made quite a name for herself as a commander, despite her young age."

"Yeah. But she has no power! No abilities! I would have been a much better choice for the Crimson Lords! She stole the position that should have been rightfully mine!"

"Oh dear, that's terrible."

"It *is* terrible. The entire history of the Mulnite Empire is gonna shift because of this. I had plans to lead the Seventh Unit to victory by burning all the other countries to ashes…"

The barkeep sighed in disgust, but Yohann barely noticed. He could think of nothing but Terakomari. How could he get to her and burn her to a crisp? How could he yank the Crimson Lord's chair out from under her? That was all that had been on his mind since his humiliating defeat during their duel.

But this obsession of his was about to bear fruit in the most horrid of ways.

"That's an interesting tale you've got there."

There came a sickly sweet voice.

Yohann looked over in surprise to find a young girl sitting beside him at the counter, pouring herself a glass of wine. A fox mask obscured her face.

"Hey…how long have you been there…?"

"Oh my, a little tipsy, are we? I've been here from the start," tittered the girl.

He couldn't make out her face beneath the mask. *You don't encounter many folks as suspicious as this*, Yohann mused. Pensively, the girl picked up her glass and swilled its contents around.

"Lieutenant Yohann Helders of the Imperial Army, I presume?"

"…How do you know my name?"

"Well, you're famous. Prison slaughter mastermind, that's you."

Yohann frowned. Was she mocking him? He didn't want to talk to this wench. She was putting him off his drink. Besides, it was getting late. But just as he slipped off the barstool to head home…

"Terakomari Gandesblood."

"?!"

"You hate her, don't you?"

Yohann swallowed hard. The girl had a weird, dark aura about her, and he felt almost as though it were sucking him in. A bead of cold sweat slid down his back.

"Who are you?"

The girl giggled.

"I'm Millicent. Member of the incredible, amazing Inverse Moon."

Yohann froze. She'd dropped that name so casually…the name of a terrorist organization that had sowed so much tension and fear in the Six Nations over the past few years. The group had this weird slogan: *Life in the Shadow of Death Is Mankind's Long-Cherished Desire.* They'd been parading around trying to destroy the Dark Cores of the world's nations. Total lunatics.

"Don't mess with me, wench. You'll find I can't be fooled so easily."

"I don't really care if you don't believe me. But what I have to say could be of great interest to you."

She lifted her glass and sipped her wine. Correction. She *tried* to sip her wine.

Instead, the glass merely clinked against her fox mask. She froze.

"…I think you're the one who's drunk here."

Though her face was still obscured, Yohann could see that her ears were bright red.

"I don't really care if you don't believe me. But what I have to say could be of great interest to you."

"Um…excuse me? Did we just skip back in time?"

"Don't be ridiculous! You really must be hammered!"

Then the girl removed her mask.

She had a beautiful face, with striking eyes that were long and slanted. This time, she managed to sip her wine. But upon closer inspection, it wasn't alcohol at all. It was grape juice. She was a minor.

The girl put her glass down and turned to stare at Yohann.

Her eyes burned with a twisted kind of ambition.

"You're with the Mulnite Army, right?"

"Huh? Uh, yeah…for now, I guess…"

"The Imperial Palace has a magical boundary spell placed on it. But someone like you could get inside, right?"

Yohann wasn't following.

Millicent leaned in to whisper in a harsh, demonic voice as he froze.

"Why don't you and I team up? I, too, have a personal grudge against that little wench…"

Recently, I'd been starting to think that I was seriously fated to die.

Sure, there were plenty of hairy moments when I had to interact with my charming subordinates, but I'm not talking about meeting my end through violence. More like expiring from stress or overwork.

In the past month, I'd worked nonstop, without even a single day off.

It was all that newspaper's fault. My false declaration of all-out war had spread throughout the Six Nations, so the enemy commanders were all vying for my blood. They'd even drawn up their own official declarations of war.

First off, we'd had a rematch against the Lapelico Kingdom five days after my duel. Commander Molekikki (the chimpanzee) had been determined to make up for last time by humiliating and torturing me to death. His assault had been several magnitudes more aggressive than before. In the final stages of the engagement, the Chimpanzee himself managed to infiltrate our stronghold and lob a stinkbomb right at me! If it hadn't been for Mellaconcey grabbing it in the nick of time, I would have been a goner.

Anyway, after that, it had been battle after battle.

The day after the Lapelico fight, we'd gone up against the Gerra-Aruka Republic. Then the Haku-Goku Commonwealth after that. Followed by a bout with The Heavenly Paradise. Luckily, we always managed to eke out a victory just as it was looking like I'd have to step in. It was kind of a miracle that we'd managed to win all those battles.

Then, a new source of stress popped up for me to deal with.

News of the Seventh Unit's victories had the Mulnite citizens all riled up. They were in full-on party mode, even those who didn't care or pay attention to politics. According to Vill, my name was on the lips of everyone at the Imperial Court. Curious to see for myself, I started reading the newspapers. Not a single day went by without at least one article on me. The Seventh Unit and the battles were barely mentioned; it was all stuff about my personal, private life. Reading the articles made me feel antsy and exposed. It was such an invasion of my privacy. Stuff about what I'd been doing with my life before now, my favorite foods, what I liked to do on my days off…it was all such a huge source of psychological stress for me.

But there were other things giving my mental health a beating, too.

Take the banquet parties, for instance. My charming subordinates had completely lost their heads, drunk on victory, and would use any excuse as a pretext to throw a lavish shindig. Just this month, there had already been about twenty parties. I loathed each and every minute of them. I've always been terrible with big groups and being in public, so every time there was a celebration, I spent it painfully aware that the slightest misstep could mean blowing my cover. Plus, a lot of them devolved into drunken bingo games, or even impromptu rap battles. A considerable number ended with fights to the death. For my part, I spent most of the time hiding in the bathrooms.

And that wasn't all, either.

Throughout this whole thing, I'd still had to keep on buttering up my subordinates to stave them off from rising up and overthrowing me. I'd started baking sweets and handing them out to all the troops. This actually worked really well. You should have seen the looks on their faces when I came around with my goodies and treats. *"You really spoil us, Supreme Commander! You're a true angel!"* They would applaud, openly weeping over the cookies and the cakes. It certainly made all that time slaving over a hot oven seem worth it.

Anyway, all this time spent schmoozing the soldiers outside of battle was to my benefit, since it kept my approval ratings up high. But the closer I got to my subordinates, the more frequently new dilemmas popped up out of nowhere, like bamboo after heavy rain.

Feeling close to me, their kindly leader, my troops had started to increasingly seek me out, swinging by my office all the time and engaging me in idle chitchat. At first, it was innocent enough stuff like them asking about my hobbies and favorite foods, but then they started oversharing about their personal problems. *"I have doubts about my future career path, Commander..." "I just can't make myself wake up early in the mornings, Commander..." "My magic skills have been a little sluggish lately, and I don't know why, Commander..." "I wanted to talk to you about my love life, Commander..."* All superheavy, super-personal stuff. *"This is my office, not your therapy room!"* I wanted to scream, but I had to keep making nice with them. So on top of my other duties, I also had to become a de facto agony aunt for five hundred weirdos.

Nevertheless, I tried to draw on all of my life experiences (not that there were many) to give the best advice (that I could come up with at the time) to people twice my age. I was worried that some of my recommendations would cause offense, but they seemed genuinely pleased. It got to the point where there would be a long line of soldiers outside the door to my office every day, and the other Crimson Lords had started up a running gag about Dr. Gandesblood's therapist rates and qualifications.

So what I'm saying here is that I hadn't gotten any time off in ages.

I guess I reached my breaking point.

"I'm not doing it and that's that!!!" I shouted, slamming my hands down on my desk with a colossal *THUD*. Vill arched an eyebrow as she observed my outburst with cool detachment.

"What's wrong with you? The signing event is just about to begin."

"Why do I have to do that anyway?! That's not the work of a commander! Look at the other Crimson Lords! You don't see any of them signing autographs, do you??!!"

We were in the Mulnite Palace's Grand Hall.

My charming sicko maid had bundled me into my uniform with much manhandling and cajoling and had forced me to sit down on a fancy chair. Spitting with all the fury of an enraged cat, I'd demanded she tell me what was going on. That was when she'd replied, *"It's your autograph-signing event, Lady Komari."*

I could understand being forced to wage war (I mean, I couldn't really understand it, but I'd grown to accept it), but there was no reason for me to perform like some kind of idol for these people! …Maybe it was because I was a total knockout beauty?

"It's supply and demand, Lady Komari. The other members of the Crimson Lords are all stuffy old men, while you're a beautiful young girl, sweet and angelic. Everyone wants a piece of you."

"But there's other stuff I could be doing! I need to study up on magic books so I can recommend a good one to Marco. I need to finalize my cookie recipe because I promised Teressa I'd share it with her. Danilo's best friend is getting married, and he has to give the speech, so I need to write it for him. And I haven't even started concocting schemes Loran could use to patch things up with his wife yet. Oh, and Pekolle…"

"It's amazing the lengths you go to for your subordinates. Simply splendid."

"Splendid?! Give me some freakin' time off!!"

"But I have. Today's been written down on the books as paid vacation."

"This is corporate oppression!"

"Now, now, Lady Komari, your adoring public is about to arrive."

"But…wait, I…"

Before I could process the unfairness of it all, the doors to the Grand Hall opened and a river of vampires spilled in. I immediately pasted on a smile. *All right, then! It looks like we're doing this! Signatures for all!* But even as I tried to switch up my attitude, I couldn't ignore my quickening heartbeat. Oh, I wanted to puke. I'd been expecting an audience of mostly girls my own age, but there were an overwhelming number of men, too. It was…kinda scary.

"Wow! It's the supreme commander in the flesh!" "Her aura is so…distinct!" "Wow, no wonder she's one of the youngest Crimson Lords ever." "But she's so much smaller than I was expecting." "That just makes her success that much more impressive."

The organizers shepherded my fans (fans?) this way. I wished I could slap the one who'd called me small. After all, I drank pints and pints of milk every day hoping to grow. It wasn't *my* fault. But I had to let it slide. I needed to put on my mighty commander persona.

"Erm, erm, my name's Rakuna! I'm your biggest fan, Supreme Commander! P-please, may I have your autograph?!"

The first in line was a young man with a bright red face. He was so nervous that he seemed like he might explode any second. Well, it made sense. I *was* a member of the Crimson Lords after all. Practically royalty, right? But his trembling approach actually put me at ease a little. A dweeb like this dude didn't warrant pulling out the tough girl act.

Taking the colored sheet of paper from his hands, I quickly signed my name with a flourish. I'd been practicing my autograph for a while now, anticipating the book signings I would hold as a published author. Just as I was about to hand the slip back to the young man, I quickly changed my mind. Simply scrawling my name and handing it back seemed a little curt; rude even. I looked up at him and manufactured my biggest, warmest smile.

"Thank you, Rakuna. I'll do my best during the next battle, and when I leap into the fray, I'll think of you."

"?!"

The young man accepted the sheet, lips flapping wordlessly like he was trying to say something in response.

Um, was he okay? His ears looked like they were about to pop from too much blood flow.

"What's wrong, Rakuna? Do you have a fever?"

"Ah, n-no… Thank you!!! Good-bye!"

As I watched him scuttle away like a fleeing crab, I felt a nagging sense of unease. Vill leaned in, her expression sour, and spoke right into my ear.

"Lady Komari. Try not to tease your fans."

"Tease? I wasn't… Did I do something wrong?"

"For crying out…" But Vill trailed off, shutting her eyes for a second. Then her usual composed expression returned. "At any rate, please refrain from excessive friendliness with the guests. Next!"

I must have been signing autographs for hours. It sucked so badly. I couldn't even drum up any excitement about it, like I'm sure I would have if I were signing copies of a novel I'd penned myself. Just more ridiculous supreme commander busywork. I hated it!

Despite that, at least the fans were nice. Most of them said things like, *"We're rooting for you!"* and *"Do your best!"* but then a lot of them made weird demands that I didn't quite understand, like, *"Please make me miso soup every morning,"* and *"Please enjoy my miso soup every morning."* Still, my interactions with them were surprisingly pleasant, which was a relief.

"Supreme Commander! Would you like to go for a drink with me after—GACK!!!"

Toward the end of the event, Vill suddenly sprang at one of the fans and seemed determined to wring the life out of him. That had been kinda weird. But apart from that, there had been no major incidents. Then, at last, the autograph session was over. By the time we were finished, it was already evening. After watching the very last customer exit the Grand Hall, I collapsed across my desk.

"I'm done. Finished. Wanna go home."

"Well done today, Lady Komari. You have no further duties today, so you're free to return home. Let's take a bath together. I'll scrub you in all sorts of hard-to-reach places…"

"Yeah, sure… Wait, I didn't mean that! I wasn't paying attention!"

Sheesh, I couldn't let my guard down around her for even a second. But actually, she hadn't intruded on my bath again since the evening of my duel with Yohann. The day after that, she'd tried it, but I'd told her straight up: *"If you don't quit the sexual harassment, you're going to seriously lose my favor!"* And surprisingly, this had worked. Vill had gotten all quiet and had simply withdrawn. I wasn't sure why, but I was glad putting my foot down seemed effective. Just as I was making up my mind to be a lot firmer with her in the future, I heard a familiar voice.

"Hello, Komari. You're working hard, it seems."

"Daddy?"

I turned to see a tall vampire standing there, dressed in a black cloak.

"What are you doing here? What about work?"

"I just happened to drop by on my way home. I had a little chat with the Empress. Also"—he grinned in a satisfied sort of way—"the signing event seems to have been a huge success. The public's got Komari Fever, and that's no overstatement. At this rate, you just might be able to end up on the Empress's throne, Komari."

Oh shoot, I'd forgotten all about my becoming Empress one day.

"Cut it out, Daddy. I have no intention of ending up in charge…"

"Now, now, Komari. Even if you don't think that way now, you'll change your mind later on. Besides, the Empress holds your abilities in high esteem, I'll have you know."

"That perv—I mean, the Empress does?"

"Indeed. But there's been a lot of hoo-haa and to-do over terrorism lately. You know that group Inverse Moon? Well, having strong Crimson Lords in place is a very good deterrent for threats of that nature."

"Er, yeah, but I'm not strong at all…"

"That hardly matters. After all, you—" But then Daddy suddenly paused. "Ah, never mind that. More importantly, Komari, you have a special invitation from your so-called pervert Empress herself."

He reached into his chest pocket and withdrew an envelope, which he handed to me. I was immediately struck with a sense of deadly foreboding.

"It's a party invitation! For you!"

○

Do I get paid overtime for official military parties? What's that? I don't? Not even a bean? Well, do I get to take a half day off in compensation? I don't? Oh, okay. I get it.

…SCREW EVERYTHING!!!

But my scream was internal. Shouting out loud wouldn't change my situation after all.

A day after the autograph session, I was standing in the Mulnite Palace's Hall of Applause.

The Empress herself had forced me to attend this buffet gala. Scrumptious dishes covered the tables littering the hall, and the various Mulnite aristocrats were having a grand old time stuffing their faces and guffawing loudly together as they heaped their plates high with meat.

Meanwhile, I was cowering in a corner trying to blend into the wallpaper.

Beside me, as ever, was my creepy maid, Vill.

But to my other side stood the murderous dog, Bellius Hund Cerbero. Why was he here? Why was Vill? Well, the invitation from the Empress stipulated that I should bring two guests. I should have brought Mellaconcey, really, since he was the most highborn of my officers, but I was afraid he would break out into an embarrassing rap. There was no way I could deal with that. After much contemplation, I chose Bellius instead by a process of elimination. Even though he was a murderer, he was still the least risky choice of party guest.

I'd put on something extremely fancy (or to be accurate, I had been forced into an exquisite dress), and as soon as we'd arrived at the party venue, I'd scuttled to the safety of a far corner and nervously sipped a glass of milk as I cowered behind my two guards. The possibility of schmoozing or making small talk with the other guests petrified me.

"Supreme Commander, what do you want us to do?"

Bellius frowned, at a loss. I drained my glass of milk in one big gulp and shot him a look from under my bangs.

"You don't like sophisticated get-togethers?"

"…No, I don't, to be honest. I've always tried to keep my distance from all that aristocrat stuff."

I recalled reading on his résumé that he was from a lower-class area. Bellius tutted with annoyance.

"These nobles, they only think of themselves. They see the rest of us commoners as little more than insects. Oh, I'm not including you in this, of course, Commander."

Hmm, sounds like there's some background there.

"Well, don't worry. If anyone comes over here and tries to talk smack about you, I'll chase them off. My family is actually one of the finest bloodlines in the Empire. All I have to do is drop the Gandesblood name, and those lower-level aristocrats will run off with their tails between their legs."

"Oh no, I'd hate to trouble you, Commander…"

"Now, now, no need for courtesy. I'm your leader after all. Besides, I wouldn't want you to debase yourself. Why, your efforts thus far have brought you all the way here; you joined the Imperial Army, distinguished yourself in battle in the Seventh Unit, and now you've even been invited to one of the Empress's parties. Most normal vampires couldn't achieve half as much. You should feel proud of yourself."

"Oh…Commander…"

Bellius gazed down at me, his eyes filled with emotion. I felt a little scummy for sounding so pompous just then, but he seemed to appreciate the sentiment.

"Anyway, let's distract ourselves from the awkwardness by filling up on some of this food. Although we may get caught up in small talk by

the buffet tables. Oh, why don't we chat instead? No one will interrupt us then."

"Very well, Lady Komari. Where are your erogenous zones? Mine are right below the navel, and—"

"Pipe down, you! Someone might overhear!"

"All right, I'll ask you that question later, when we're alone…"

"Enough! Right now, I am speaking with Bellius, not you!"

I turned my back on Vill and faced Bellius once more. Now, to have a nice conversation, so I didn't look like an awkward loner at this party. I felt like I could talk to him. I mean, he was like a dog, wasn't he? Like a pet.

"…What is it you wanted to…'chat' about?"

"Anything. The weather forecast. Stuff you're into lately. Your favorite snacks."

"In that case, I'd like to ask you your opinion on the current balance of political power among the Six Nations."

"P-political power?"

"Especially the Gerra-Aruka Republic, which has been heating up as of late."

"Oh…Gerra-Aruka, eh? Yeah. I heard they have really great fried shrimp over there."

"That's not the sort of discussion I had in mind…"

Bellius looked like he had something he wanted to say, but just then I heard a high, tinkling female voice.

"If it isn't the delectable Komari! Are you enjoying the party?"

With a sinking feeling in my chest, I reluctantly turned around. There she stood, utterly gorgeous, with shining silvery hair and eyes, the color of moonlight. She was dressed in a luxurious gown, with her boobs prominently on display. And she was about my height. By which I mean, unusually short.

It was her, the stealer of my first kiss…the perverted ruler of the Mulnite Empire.

Vill and Bellius immediately dropped to a knee. I quickly attempted a curtsy myself, but the Empress shot her hands out to grab my shoulders and prevent me from doing so.

"Now now, no need for formalities. Besides, you and I are friends, Komari! I do grow weary of being treated with such reverence all the time."

"Er...really?"

"Oh, sure, sure! In fact, I'd love it if you'd call me Len."

Whoa. Back off. Too close, Len! And why are you massaging my shoulders? I've got goose bumps!

Though I turned my head to and fro in search of help, Bellius was just standing there in attendance, like a faithful hound. Vill, on the other hand, was trembling, her face twisted as if she were sucking on a lemon. Wait, was she jealous?

"By the by, Komari...how's the Crimson Lord life going?"

"It's...going."

"Oh dear, that bad, huh? But you don't give yourself enough credit. Why, since your tenure began, you've smashed four countries in battle! That's all of them, except for the Enchanted Lands! You're a natural! I've never seen a Crimson Lord do so well!"

But that was all just luck.

"I invited you here today to praise you for your excellent work, you know. Now come, come, eat and drink as much as you like! Shall I fix you a plate? See here, we've got summer vegetables with hemoglobin sauce, crocodile simmered in blood, one-hundred percent blood juice, oh, I forgot you don't like blood... In that case, let us head to that table over there! It's got plenty of plasma-free dishes. Come, come!"

Grabbing my arm, the Empress hauled me off with incredible grip strength. We cut through the crowd of laughing aristocrats and headed to a table across the room. I hadn't seen the Empress in a while, but she was just as weird and eccentric as I remembered. To be honest, I didn't really like her. And why did she have such enormous...assets? They were jiggling and pressing against my arm as we walked. Goodness, what had this woman eaten to make them that big? It must have been blood, right? ...Curses!

"Hee-hee-hee. Actually, to be honest, I'm quite relieved."

The Empress lowered her voice as she piled sausages onto a plate.

"You've been a shut-in for three whole years. I was worried you wouldn't be able to rejoin society if your hermitage went on much longer. That bet with your father ended up working out after all."

"…Bet?"

"Yeah. We wagered on whether we could get you out of your room and into the Seven Crimson Lords. It was risky, though. A lot of shut-ins tend to protest if you try to drag them back out into society. They scream, wail, throw tantrums, and sometimes even murder their own parents…but you managed the transition just fine!"

Well, yeah. What would be the point of crying or throwing a tantrum? The mark of our contract had been seared into my belly. Plus, the threat of spontaneous combustion for shirking my duties as a Crimson Lord was hanging over my head. And who did I have to blame for all of that? That's right. This busty gal right here.

"Do you hate me for forcing you into a contract? Your father asked me to do it, you know. And how could I turn down an offer in the tens of millions?"

So! An under-the-table deal, was it?! What corruption!!!

I shivered at the depths of their subterfuge as the Empress broke into a smile.

"No, you don't despise me… I see that red light in your eyes, the same scarlet hue of Mulnite's sunsets… This new lifestyle of yours… you're actually enjoying it."

"Er…"

She reached out and pressed her hand against my lower belly for some reason. Then she began to pat and stroke it through my clothes.

"You're not alone anymore, Komari. Do you understand what I mean?"

Er, no. Enlighten me.

"You have so many subordinates who you can trust and rely on. Ah, and not just your soldiers. The whole of the Empire adores you.

Everyone's turned into hardcore Komarists! Why, tonight's guests were all talking about how desperate they were to share a few words with you. But decorum dictates that none should approach you before I had my chance, so they all refrained."

Hold on. The heck are Komarists? They sound insane.

But never mind that now…

"I'm really not on my own?"

"Of course not. You never have been, but now you have so many people who love you! There's no need to be afraid! Just open wide and have some of this."

As I chewed on the sausage she'd just popped into my mouth, I couldn't hide my befuddlement.

Swallowing my mouthful of meat with difficulty, I spoke again.

"Why are you so concerned about me anyhow?"

The Empress blinked.

"Ah-ha-ha. That's a good question. All right, I'll tell you something astonishing. The reason I'm so attached to you? It's 'cause you're the child of my ex-lover."

My jaw fell open. But the Empress quickly shook her head.

"Don't misunderstand me, I'm not talking about your father here, just so we're clear?"

"So you mean…"

"Many years ago, your mother and I were betrothed…"

"…"

Er, what? What were you doing, Mommy?!

"But then, that blasted Armand…I mean, your father…stole her away, right from under my nose! Ah, Yulinne, you never did have any taste. How could you have allowed that man to bewitch you when you had me?"

Yuck, I did *not* want to hear about my parents' past romances.

"But whenever I look at you, Komari, I see Yulinne. Once you grow up a bit, you'll be a beauty to rival your mother, I bet. Oh, I just can't wait to see you blossom!"

The Empress slid her hands around lasciviously to knead my buttocks. She truly was on a level of perversion that put even Vill to shame.

Just as I was starting to sweat, the Empress suddenly released me and held her palms up innocently. "Just joking!" She giggled.

"As I said, I always like to get verbal consent. That tale about kissing you in your bed, that was actually a lie. I didn't do a thing to you. There are other ways to seal a contract, you see."

Then she turned to leave, addressing me over her shoulder.

"Anyway, what I wanted to tell you is that you aren't alone. You have many supporters, myself included. So make sure you don't give up and sink into despair…like you did three years ago. Now, enjoy the party, my dear."

And with that, the Empress floated gracefully away across the room.

I had no time to contemplate the meaning behind what she'd just told me. The other aristocrats, who'd been watching our conversation intently, now started to crowd around me as if unable to delay gratification for even one more second. *"Good evening, Supreme Commander!" "What an honor it is to meet you!" "Would you consider our son for the Seventh Unit?" "Would you consider meeting* our *son about marriage…?"*

As they all crowded around me, I cringed out of awkwardness and embarrassment.

It certainly seemed true that everyone here had taken an interest in me. But that was because they believed I was this superstrong Crimson Lord. They were just like my Seventh Unit and all the fans I had in town…completely convinced I was something that I wasn't.

The Empress had told me I wasn't alone.

But if the truth about Terakomari Gandesblood came out, how many vampires would remain by my side?

At that moment, however, I wondered why I even cared.

What had happened to the old Terakomari Gandesblood? I'd been a lone wolf, an artist. The only thing I'd needed out of life was curling up to write and read books. So who cared what the others thought of me? Mutiny aside, that is.

That's right… I knew who I was. I was a shut-in vampire princess.

That was how I'd always been, ever since that day three years ago. And I remained one to this day.

"Terakomari, may I speak with you as well?"

I flinched. Who was this, addressing me by my full first name?

She was wearing a fox mask, the girl who'd just spoken to me. And she was staring straight at me.

What was her deal? This wasn't a masquerade ball. Didn't she get the memo?

"Um, yes…? Who are you?"

"Just a passing aristocrat. Do you have a problem with that?"

"Er, no, not especially…"

Why was she being so combative? Excuse me for noticing how obviously fishy she was. But this gala was under the protection of a boundary spell, so if she'd been able to waltz in here, that had to mean she was safe, right?

Still, I switched instantly into commander mode.

"Hmm. All right. So you want to chat, eh? Go ahead, then. Don't be shy. This is a soiree after all. We're supposed to mingle and make small talk." Why did I sound so stiff?

The fox-faced girl threw her head back and cackled. *"Ha-ha-ha!"* I blinked, taken aback.

"Fascinating. Just fascinating. You're really pretending to be carefree and relaxed, aren't you? Just like I'd heard. But your subordinates are making you look good, eh? Winning all those engagements for you."

"Huh…? I mean…I guess you're right."

"But do you really trust your troops so much? That band of freaks?"

"My confidence in them has nothing to do with how they do their job. They're crazy about war. All I have to do is release them, and they storm the battlefield to rack up hundreds of kills."

"Even while you do nothing?"

I nodded absentmindedly before catching myself. "Ah…no… Of

course, if I joined them in combat, it would all be over in a matter of seconds, so where's the fun in that?"

She snorted with amusement.

"Wow, you've got it all figured out. But it is true that battles these days are little more than a show of force. Entertainment for the masses. So as you say, it's best to keep the circus going. If you leaped into the fray and started, uh, 'slaughtering' left and right, well, that would be no fun at all."

"Yeah, yeah, totally. That would never do. Even though I'd much rather be lopping off heads than dealing with the public, heh-heh."

"But of course… Still, in my opinion, these silly conflicts, which are good for nothing other than political pissing contests, make a total mockery of the sacred art of war."

…*Er, what?* What were we even talking about here?

"Ah, well, yes…I suppose that's one way of viewing it…"

"Right, and the one besmirching it most of all is…*you*, Terakomari."

"Excuse me?"

"I neither like you nor what you represent. How can you stand as a member of the Seven Crimson Lords, behaving as you do? How can you even show your face in public? Do you really enjoy everyone pampering you so much?"

Er. What?

"It's because of people like you that society is going down the drain. I was like that once. If it wasn't for you…if it wasn't for you, I wouldn't be… But no, never mind that. I'm happy with my lot in life. Breaking with my country and joining Inverse Moon was always my destiny."

The heck was this fox face saying…?

"Uh, excuse me, but—"

"Ah, sorry! My name is…*Millicent Bluenight.* I've come to collect what you owe me, after what happened three years ago."

Then she whipped off her mask.

Revealing a face that, as much as I wished otherwise, I could never erase from my memory.

Millicent. The reason why I'd wound up becoming a shut-in.

Her blue skirts flipped up and she took a step forward, even as I stiffened in surprise. Clutched in her right hand was a shining silver dagger.

"Commander!"

Someone tackled me from the side and sent me flying. I hurtled across a nearby table, getting drenched in meat sauce. Spaghetti hung from my ears. Scrambling to my feet, I whirled around to see a scene that I could barely even process.

The girl had buried her knife into Bellius's stomach.

"Oh dear. I missed."

"Guh! Ahhh!"

Blood spurted from the wound and splashed across the floor, forming a big puddle. The other guests were screaming. I was in a total panic. What just happened? How could there have been so much blood? So much bright, scarlet blood?

"Lady Komari! Get back!" Vill screamed.

Then, with clearly advanced magic power, she conjured a multitude of throwing knives and sent them zooming through the air. Millicent grinned and bent down to pluck the knife out of Bellius's chest before she jumped away like a monkey. The throwing daggers missed their target and thunked into the tables and the fleshy bodies of the other guests. Purple, poisoned blood began to pour from their wounds. The party was in pandemonium, with guests screaming and scrambling in panic, slipping on the fallen plates of food. I cowered where I stood, my eyes filling with tears of terror.

"Whoa, watch out, maid! Those daggers almost hit me!"

"Next time I won't miss!"

"Give it up. I'm far stronger than you."

The girl grinned. A smug, knowing, sarcastic sort of grin.

The heck was happening?!

She just tried to gut me...? But Bellius took the hit for me...?

"S-someone grab her!" "She's an intruder!" "What happened to security?!" "This has never happened before!" "What is to become of us?!"

The hall was filled with the screams of the hysterical aristocrats. But the intruder remained calm, still beaming smugly.

I was frozen, completely paralyzed by fear.

Millicent hadn't changed a bit since three years ago. She still thought nothing of inflicting pain on others and never dropped her smirk, even under the harshest moral criticism.

She was completely wicked.

"You! Commoner! How dare you destroy my lovely gala? I hope you're ready to die for this!"

"Be quiet, Empress. I didn't mean to ruin the stupid party. I just… Yeah, actually, my plan was to dispatch you, Armand Gandesblood, and then Terakomari, trembling over there. Then I'd be satisfied."

Millicent turned to me.

It felt like she was rummaging around inside my mind.

Those eyes of hers… Clouded, like a muddy swamp. Because of her, I'd spent the past three years…

"You're too stupid to bother addressing. Killing you is the only way. Now die!" shouted the Empress.

Flames sprung up from her fingertips. Millicent cackled and shot high in the air, landing beside me. As she leered at me, snakelike, I froze like a terrified rabbit.

"Lady Komari!"

"Pfft…some hostage. You're such a sniveling coward."

Vill and the Empress were standing helplessly as Millicent pressed her blade to my neck.

"Boring. You're no fun like this. Where's the joy in taking your life now? I want to execute you while you're actually fighting back."

"Wh-what do you mean?"

"Like you could ever understand how I feel. Anyway, I'll be back, Terakomari. Next time, I'll kill you. I'll show you the taste of true death—when there's no chance of revival.

"Enjoy…"

Millicent hissed that final word in my ear, grinning, as she reached

out to cast magic with her left hand. But it wasn't attacking magic she was casting. I realized that a moment too late.

"She's opening the void! You're not gonna escape that easy, you fox-faced wench!"

But Millicent disappeared into thin air even as the Empress's thunderbolt zipped through the air toward her. It continued along its trajectory and smashed into the wall of the party venue. Several guests died in the ensuing rubble, but that couldn't be helped. Collateral damage and all.

Looking uncharacteristically distraught, Vill flew to my side.

"Lady Komari! Are you hurt?"

"N-no…I'm fine. But Bellius…"

The dog-headed beast-man was lying unconscious on the floor. But Vill simply grinned.

"Oh, don't worry about him. He'll be right as rain in a few hours. Dark Core and all, remember?"

"Yeah, but…"

I'll be back, Terakomari.

I continued to tremble in terror, the strands of spaghetti jiggling as they dangled from my ears.

This felt like the start. The start of my life going completely off track.

Millicent Bluenight.

Why? Why was she here? I hadn't done anything wrong. Why had she come back to torment me again? Why?

"Lady Komari…?"

I couldn't respond. There was a door in my mind. A door I'd kept sealed up tight for three years, too afraid ever to open. But it was opening now. With an ominous, creaking sound.

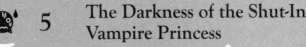

"We need to destroy Inverse Moon! Right now!"

The sicko maid, Villhaze, sighed internally as she gazed down at the fist that had just slammed into the desk.

The location? Commander Gandesblood's office, in the Crimson Tower.

The commander herself? Absent.

Villhaze and Caostel Conto stared at each other across the polished black table. No one else was in the room. But the hallway outside was crammed with Seventh Unit soldiers, who were clamoring and yelling out of deep concern for their commander. It sounded like the doors to the office would break at any moment.

Caostel was deeply agitated himself.

"They're criminals who seek to damage the Mulnite Empire! They should be punished!"

"But we still haven't been able to locate their hideout. Even with all Six Nations working together over the past few years."

"So we should find it ourselves. What are you suggesting, that we just sit around until they strike again? Are we fools?!"

A week had passed since the girl calling herself Millicent Bluenight had infiltrated the Empress's party, attacked Komari, and stabbed her chief officer, Bellius, sending him into a coma.

That's right, a coma.

Typically, the power of the Dark Core would regenerate someone killed or gravely injured within a short span of time, but a week had passed without Bellius regaining consciousness. Plus, the knife wound didn't seem to be healing at all.

The busty blond Empress explained it like this:

"She used some kind of cursed knife to do it. Something with the power to cancel out the Dark Core's influence. Something with enough strength to rival that of the Dark Core itself. The only way to help your wolfy friend is to find some way to revive him ourselves. The Dark Core will be of no use here."

Years ago, back before the Dark Core existed, there were people called "Doctors," who were very highly regarded in society. But once the era of the Dark Core began, wounds started to heal themselves automatically, so the "Doctor" profession died out. As a result, not a single one remained in the Empire. Sure, there were a few who dabbled with the old trade as a curiosity, but their skills were lackluster, so they would not be able to revive Bellius.

Caostel seemed to want to avenge Bellius, of course. But he also seemed more motivated by fury. Fury toward the terrorists who had assaulted his beloved commander and left her covered in spaghetti.

"What is the Imperial Court even doing?! A terrorist infiltrated our country! If this isn't a national crisis, then what is?!"

"The Imperial Court has been engaged in meetings from dawn till dusk every day. There's a reason why they haven't acted yet."

"What? What's the reason?"

"There may be a traitor in our midst."

"A traitor…?"

Caostel glared at Vill, puzzled.

"Apparently, someone constructed a Gate of Transference in the soiree venue. You're good with Void Magic, right, Lieutenant Conto? So then you're aware that the ability to teleport hinges upon first setting up two magic gates. In other words, someone got access to the venue before the party and primed a gate there. No outsider could have done that. Incidentally, it seems the second gate was located in a back alley in the capital's skid row area."

"I see. So the Imperial Court is trying to expose the traitor, while at the same time checking to make sure there aren't any more gates."

"Right. That's why they've been having very serious meetings about this."

"Idiots!" Caostel suddenly squawked, like a strangled chicken. "If there's a traitor in our midst, we should root him out and execute him on the spot! Job done!!!"

"Could you calm down a little there?"

"Desperate times call for desperate measures! Now is the time to strike! I'll gather a team and get to work at once! First, we'll go around the entire city and—"

"That would put you in contempt of command, Lieutenant Conto."

He gulped loudly.

"Lady Komari has given her orders. 'Wait until I return.' If you bypass her wishes and act on your own, your head will roll."

"I...I know that. But where *is* the commander? I'm going to see her right now, and I'm gonna get her permission to do something!"

"It seems she's currently monitoring the enemy's movements. From where, I know not. Even I, her closest associate, am not privy to that information."

"I see... Ah, but hold on a minute, Special Lieutenant Villhaze. I'm not about to let that slide. *I'm* her closest associate, not you. Me. Caostel Conto."

"Well, do you know what color underwear Lady Komari wears?"

"??!?!!"

"You don't, do you? So then I'm her closest associate. Anyway, we remain on standby until we receive some kind of word from Lady Komari herself."

"But...will she really come back?"

"What do you mean?"

"The Komari Unit is dangling by a thread. Yohann's been dishonorably discharged, Bellius is currently gravely injured and in a coma. Mellaconcey's taken his paid vacation and gone on an overseas trip. If we lose the commander, too…"

Vill nodded knowingly. Caostel's bluster was all a front. He was genuinely worried.

"It's all right. The Empress herself holds Lady Komari in high esteem. She's as savage as anyone who ever held the Crimson Lord position. She would never, ever abandon her troops."

But in truth, the Seventh Unit *was* on the verge of collapse.

And Komari, currently monitoring the enemy's movements? Please. Our Komari? She really had the bravery for that? Nuh-uh. Vill was simply making stuff up in an attempt to placate the rowdy Seventh Unit soldiers and keep them calm.

Vill left the Crimson Tower, got into a carriage, and headed straight to the Gandesblood residence. She entered the mansion by way of the tradesmen's entrance and ascended the stairs to the second floor as if she had every right to be there. Then she walked down several corridors until she spotted the room she was heading for. Standing in front of the busted door, she called out to the person inside. "Lady Komari?" But there was no answer. Of course.

"Lady Komari, I'm coming in."

Vill entered nonchalantly.

The room was dark. Books were scattered across the floor, their spines splayed open. It appeared Lady Komari still wasn't feeling well enough to pick up after herself.

Taking a deep breath, Vill called her name again.

"Lady Komari, how are you feeling today?"

"…Vill?"

Something stirred over on the bed.

Relieved to have gotten a response at last, Vill started speaking in a low, soothing voice.

"Everyone's worried about you. Why don't you come out of your room, just for a little while?"

"No."

Her response was curt.

"If I go out there, I'm gonna get killed. There's no place in the world for a weak, directionless, cowardly vampire. Being a shut-in is the best thing for me."

"That's not true at all. Lieutenant Conto really wants to see you."

"Who cares! He doesn't know me! He only thinks he does! Hey, everyone, look at the Crimson Lord sitting on the floor covered in spaghetti! I couldn't even look out for Bellius!"

Vill sharply inhaled. So that's what she was upset about?

"Lady Komari…"

"B-besides, if I leave this house, she'll come for me again…"

She. Vill didn't even need to ask. Millicent Bluenight, of Inverse Moon. An old classmate of Lady Komari's, who had bullied her into becoming a shut-in in the first place.

Vill sighed. "All right, then," she finally relented. "We'll just have to wait until you feel better, then."

With a small bow, she left the room.

Lady Komari had been cloistered away for just about a week. Millicent's attack had clearly traumatized her. Or perhaps all the stress had finally gotten to her, and she'd snapped. Either way, this was hardly an ideal situation. She refused to eat the meals Vill prepared, and in her worst moods, she ignored Vill completely.

As the maid rounded a corner, she bumped into Komari's father.

"Ah, Vill. No good, eh?"

"…Unfortunately not, sir."

He frowned with concern.

"I see. Well, there's not much we can do now. No one could have predicted that little madam would show up again to terrorize Komari. Ah, I should never have done what I did."

"…Excuse me?"

"Millicent…she was the vampire girl who bullied Komari three years ago. I was furious. I had her whole family framed for treason and banished from the country. Then she joined a terrorist group to take revenge. Oh dear, what a mess."

"…"

"Well, that aside, please do what you can for Komari. She's weak and fragile, yes, but she's got a good heart. I don't think she'll be able to get by anymore without you around."

"…I understand, sir."

"Good. Well then, I have work to do. Thanks, Vill."

Then, the cause of this entire headache waved jauntily at her and walked off. Vill gazed at his black-cloaked back as he disappeared around the corner. Her fists were clenched by her sides.

It all started from the tiniest of things.

I'd unwittingly done something to antagonize Millicent one day, and after that, it had been too late to set things right.

It wouldn't have been so bad if she'd just given me the silent treatment and had ignored me during team activities and magic practices.

No, Millicent's bullying just kept escalating. Gossiping about me behind my back, cackling shrilly whenever I was in earshot. Breaking my things, before finally escalating into direct physical violence against me.

At first, I tried to laugh it off.

After all, how could the daughter of the esteemed Gandesblood family be a victim of bullying, at school of all places? If either my family or the other aristocrats found out, the Gandesblood name would be dragged through the mud. So I kept it all to myself and refused to ask anyone for help. When Millicent would ignore me, when she would steal my shoes and hide them, when she would scribble horrible things in my textbooks, when she would drop a dirty dishcloth on my lunch, when she would leave dead flowers on my desk...I cried about it all alone. And I never let it show that she was getting to me.

Because bullies are pathetic creatures who can only feel happiness by hurting others.

That's what I'd told myself. To stay strong.

But I soon reached my breaking point.

It had happened that summer, three years ago. Millicent had asked me to meet her in an empty classroom. Stupidly, I went along with her request, and when I arrived, she pounced.

"Hey, will you lend me that pendant of yours?"

I refused, of course.

I always wore my pendant. I'm wearing it now. It's a memento of my mother, who passed away in a fatal accident. A very rare and tragic thing to transpire in this current era of the Dark Core. But pass away she had.

Millicent cackled, amused by my rare show of defiance. She ordered her minions to grab me and pin my arms behind my back. Then she reached toward my neck, grinning as if she'd found a shiny new toy.

That's when I'd snapped.

I felt as though I were a cornered mouse, desperate enough to fight back against a cat. I head-butted the girls who were restraining me with the back of my head to free myself from their grips. Then I ran out, crying. But before I could get far, Millicent cast an incantation (probably a gravity spell), which sent me flying. I hit my face as I landed.

Ha-ha! Look at the crybaby! Need a tissue for that nosebleed?

I shrank as I gazed up at her face, full of malice and hatred.

Let me cut off a finger and I'll let you go. Come on! Just one little pinky!

The pinky finger loophole. It was drastic, sure, but many a bullied child took that route. If you allowed your bully to cut off your finger and keep it, you could walk away free.

But anyway, I don't remember what happened after I'd refused to give her my little finger.

I think she beat me up, without me fighting back. Sometimes I recall differently, however, and envision drawing her blood with a few blows of my own. But at any rate, the next thing I knew, I awoke on my own bed, battered and bruised.

The physical wounds didn't matter so much. They would heal.

The problem was the damage she'd done to my mind.

I was terrified of Millicent, so from that day forth, I'd refused to attend school. The abuse she'd heaped on me had seemed to hit me all at once, as if a dam had broken in my mind. I'd felt paralyzed.

Nothing much happened after that.

I spent the next three years after the incident sequestered in my room.

I stopped going out, stopped seeing people. It was a lonely life, but I spent it reading, and writing my own stories. Stuff like that.

The longer I spent as a shut-in, the deeper the wounds seemed to etch themselves into my psyche.

Daddy and the Empress must have noticed this. And their scheme had worked. It had forced me out of my room and into the Seven Crimson Lords. It granted me normal life again. My new position even enabled me to forget about what had happened…well, more like put a mental block on it. I started regaining my ability to talk to people, as if nothing had ever gone wrong.

But that was all over now.

Because Millicent had come back.

Those cold, dark days of the soul were upon me again.

" … "

Cuddling my dolphin-shaped hug pillow, I trembled as I thought about all the horrible things that would await me in the future. Being a Crimson Lord was something I was starting to get used to, even enjoy a little, but I had to admit it to myself. My true nature was to remain a pathetic recluse for the rest of my days.

So I made up my mind.

I was never going outside again.

Three days had passed.

There was no sign of Millicent. But still I couldn't relax. I felt constantly wired. The slightest creak or slamming door had me twitching with terror.

Vill brought meals to my room three times a day.

Whenever she entered, she would try to talk to me. But the sexual harassment behavior that had always been her specialty had completely ceased. Instead, she acted almost completely normal.

"Lady Komari, I made omelet rice for dinner. Your favorite, isn't it?"

"Lady Komari, it's great weather outside today. Why don't you and I go for a walk together?"

"Lady Komari, I read this great book recently. I'll lend it to you if you'd like."

Just pleasantries like that.

But the "great book" she'd wanted to lend me turned out to be a naughty magazine. I had the feeling she was trying too hard to be normal, and the cracks were starting to show.

Occasionally, I responded to her when I was feeling up to it. But for the most part, I stayed completely silent. Undeterred, Vill kept on trying to get me to talk.

Why was she even bothering with me? Was it sympathy? Pity? Was it because I belonged to a rich family? Were they paying her a lot for this?

That reminds me, she'd mentioned that weird thing once about committing a crime.

"Lady Komari, aren't you planning to write a new novel?"

"..."

"Well...when you do finish a new one, I'd love it if you'd let me read it."

Then with a polite bow, Vill left my room.

Since the door was still broken, I was able to watch her walk away down the hallway.

Just who was she anyway?

Caostel was standing high up on the Artois Plaza Clock Tower's ledge, the tallest landmark in the Imperial Capital, gazing emotionally out at the sky. He was filled with a determination to track down the wench who had attacked Bellius, his brother-in-arms, and had slung spaghetti over the commander, whom he burned with love and respect for.

The situation wasn't showing promise, though.

Two weeks had gone by since the party incident. But there had been no reports of the perpetrator's whereabouts. With no sign of an attack on the horizon, the whole of the Imperial Court seemed to almost relax.

Apparently, the cabinet minister had said: "The enemy hasn't done anything else, so perhaps that's the end of it."

Were the leaders of this country all complete morons?

"Commander..."

Caostel pulled a photograph out from his chest pocket and gazed at it. It showed his beloved commander, dressed in a skimpy bathing suit, blushing. This photograph had really been keeping him going lately.

"Where did you disappear to, Commander?"

His beloved Komari hadn't appeared before the Seventh Unit even once since the attack at the gala. Villhaze had told him that the commander was gathering intelligence on the enemy, but something about that sounded suspicious. That maid was hiding something.

"Commander... Forgive me, Commander..."

Caostel repented.

The terrorist who'd assaulted the party...it had been the fox-faced girl. If Caostel had only been able to apprehend her when she'd appeared in the gardens that night, then none of this would have happened.

In other words, this was all his fault. He would have to take responsibility for this himself. But how?

He made up his mind to locate the commander by himself.

Putting the photo away in his chest pocket, Caostel cast Void Magic, *The Gates of Hell*. Reaching into the portal, he retrieved a small wooden box. From it, he took out a single strand of hair. It was one of the commander's beautiful golden locks, which he'd secretly harvested.

This single strand of hair would allow him to locate the commander. With another Void spell (*The Net of Attraction* this time), he could use magic to locate the vampire who possessed a head of hair that matched this one strand.

However.

Using this incantation would also cause this sacred lock to disappear. In order to locate the commander, he would have to give up his treasure. He'd spent hours, days even, retracing her steps along the hallways, scrambling about on the floor before he'd found that elusive dropped strand.

"Nothing ventured, nothing gained, as they say."

Never mind. There was no other way. And perhaps he could procure himself another piece of hair later on. Caostel gazed down at the Imperial Capital spread out beneath him, trying to reassure himself. Then he began to cast the spell.

Void Magic. *The Net of Attraction*. Instantly, the strand of golden hair evaporated, and an invisible web sprang from Caostel's hand to cover the entirety of the Imperial Capital spread out before him.

He waited for a few moments before tugging his net back in. And what he found was surprising.

His target was located in the Gandesblood mansion.

So she wasn't out tracking the enemy's movements after all! Caostel was triumphant for a few moments. But then why hadn't she appeared before the Seventh Unit? He pondered this for a moment before stopping himself. The commander must have had her reasons. It would be faster simply to ask her himself.

Yes, he planned to head straight to her residence. Usually, it would be the height of bad manners to show up at your commander's abode without being invited first. But these were extenuating circumstances. She would surely forgive him. Oh, but if she invited him up to her bedroom, whatever would he say…? Hee-hee-hee.

Picturing all kinds of delicious scenarios, Caostel sniggered to himself. But just then…

The Correspondence Crystal he always carried began to vibrate with magical power. He answered it, annoyed. All of a sudden, a loud voice rapped in his ear.

"Check it! I found the right potion, it's caused a commotion! Bellius is awake, we're all filled with emotion!"

"What?"

His eyes widened.

So Bellius was well again. That was excellent news. But wasn't this ridiculous rapper supposed to be on an overseas vacation? Wait, did he go on a quest to a faraway land to find medicine?

Well, whatever.

"Mellaconcey, take care of Bellius for me. I'm going to the commander's house."

"Pourquoi, my dude?"

"There's no other way."

"Yo! Intruding on the commander's personal space? It ain't a great idea, and this isn't a race! The terrorist has gone underground, there ain't no sight or sound, so let's all just chill before things go ill."

Caostel ended the transmission abruptly. He had no time for the opinions of others.

Leaping down from the clock tower, he headed to the Gandesblood mansion at top speed.

☆ (Let's go back a bit)

Over lunch, I asked Vill why she kept bothering with me.

The sicko maid shrugged.

"I would have thought it was obvious. It's because I love you more than anyone else in the world, Lady Komari."

It sounded like a lie, but if it was really money or status she was after, then her kind, considerate treatment of me the past few weeks didn't really add up.

Ignoring the curry she'd brought me, I started nibbling on the pear instead, which was for dessert.

"I really don't get it. Are you my long-lost sister or something, Vill?"

"If you want to role-play that, I'm down for it. But we're not long-lost sisters, no."

"Then what is it?"

Vill blushed a little, looking down.

"You know, I've been meaning to tell you this for a long time…"

"…"

"But I was too embarrassed…"

"Okay, you don't have to tell me."

"Hold on! Don't just give up so easily! This is the part where you try to convince me! *Aww, is Vill embarrassed? Tell Aunty Komari everything.* Stick to the script!"

"…"

"Sorry. I forgot, I'm not the comic relief in this story."

Vill sighed deeply then began rummaging around in the pocket of her apron. She pulled out an envelope.

"I wrote down all my feelings in this letter. Please read it when you have a spare moment."

"Yeah, I might. If the mood strikes me."

I rose unsteadily to my feet, still chewing my mouthful of pear as I flopped back into bed. I was feeling a bit lighter today, so I'd decided to talk to her. But now I'd exhausted all of my strength. Spending time around the creepy maid had just made me remember things I'd rather not think about. The Seventh Unit; war; blood.

But Vill didn't leave. Instead, she kept on talking.

"Lady Komari. Lots of people are worried about you."

This again? I rolled my eyes.

"There are a lot of people who are worried about you, and not just because they value your leadership skills and smarts. Please remember that."

She was clearly lying. The Seventh Unit cared about me only because I was a Crimson Lord. Take away all the bluff and bluster, and all you had left was a nondescript, weakling vampire girl. I knew that better than anyone.

"Well, I'll take my leave now. Once you're feeling better, you should return to the Crimson Tower, and..."

Suddenly, she trailed off.

I turned to look over my shoulder, wondering what was up.

That's when I thought my heart was going to leap out of my chest.

"Hello, Terakomari."

"...??!!"

It was Millicent. Standing right behind Vill. Half shrouded in darkness, with a sick grin on her face. She'd thrust a sharp sword into Vill's back.

"Guh...Lady...Komari..."

Her white apron blossomed with red. A jet of blood came shooting out of her mouth, splattering over my uneaten dish of curry. Vill blinked several times, as if in complete disbelief. But a moment later her strength failed her, and she slumped to her knees.

I couldn't even breathe.

My mind was refusing to process reality.

"Oh dear, what's wrong? Cat got your tongue? You could at least say hello after I went to all the trouble to visit. How rude."

"Ah...ah..."

"You were always so squeamish. There's no need to go that pale just because someone got stabbed. Relax, this sword isn't cursed. She'll regenerate in time. Not for a while, though."

"What are you...doing here?"

"What am I doing here?" Millicent cackled. "I told you I'd come back to see you again. You can't have forgotten what I said?"

She started creeping slowly toward me. I was paralyzed by fear.

"Hya-ha-ha! There's no need to look so frightened. I'm not going to kill you in your own bed. If I started slicing you up here, someone would only show up to interrupt us."

Someone? …I almost forgot! This mansion was full of people!

Just as I took in a huge breath to unleash a massive scream, Millicent shot a bolt of magic into my bed, producing up a huge hole. Terrified, I clamped my lips shut.

"If you scream, I'll kill you. If you struggle, I'll kill you. You just sit there like a good girl and listen to what Millicent has to say."

"…"

"That's right. Very good, Terakomari. Okay, shall we get down to it? I didn't come here to assassinate you in your home. I came to set the stage for an even more tragic murder!"

"Set…the…stage?"

"This mansion is full of bothersome flies. So what I need you to do is to get up and come to the location I'm about to name. Can you stand?"

Was she serious? If I went with her, she'd do me in.

As I continued to sit there mutely, she raised an eyebrow and chuckled.

"I see, you're not brave enough to come of your own volition. Well, I predicted this. You always were a complaining, whining crybaby. It beats me how you always used to walk around like you owned the place while being absolute trash at the same time. All right, then, we'll do it this way. Just like how it was three years ago."

Millicent turned and grabbed Vill's arm. Then she dragged her up off the floor as if she were a rag doll.

"I'll take this one with me. If you want her back, come to the abandoned castle at La Nelient when the clock strikes midnight."

"Don't…"

"If you're even one second late, I'll kill Villhaze. Oh, and by the way, make sure you come alone. And if you decide to tell anyone about this…well, you know what will happen, don't you?"

A deep wave of despair crashed over me.

What was I supposed to do about this?

"All right, then, it's settled. Don't disappoint me now, Terakomari."

Then Millicent turned to the windows, which were covered by dark curtains. Casting a magic spell, she shattered the glass with an almighty smash. Sunlight streamed into my bedroom for the first time in days. I was still too terrified to speak. The terrorist hoisted Vill across her shoulder and leaped out of the broken window, disappearing like some sort of bat.

Left propped up in bed, I still couldn't move or speak.

The floor was drenched with blood. Curry was splattered on the walls and the sheets. Millicent had shown up. Vill, murdered. Stabbed. I...

Vill...

I still couldn't believe what had just happened. I didn't want to believe it. But the pain I was feeling was all too real. This was reality. Horrible, horrible reality.

What do I do? What do I do? What do I do? I just sat there, trembling and hugging my knees.

I stayed there in bed for around an hour, cocooned in my blankets.

As I started to calm down, the gravity of the situation began to sink in with horrifying clarity.

Vill had been kidnapped. By a terrorist. There was no guarantee she was even still alive. The perpetrator wasn't motivated by money, so I couldn't use the Gandesblood name as leverage. Millicent had told me to come to the abandoned castle alone. She'd ordered me not to tell anyone else. So there was no one who could resolve this situation besides me.

I was going to have to act alone.

But I was used to acting alone. I was a shut-in who didn't rely on anyone.

Still, what did the sicko maid matter to me?

...

Nothing, right? But then why did I feel so terrible and afraid for her?

Thinking back on my time with her, I felt my chest constrict painfully.

Vill had never once let me down.

She'd stayed up all night hand-digging all those pitfall traps for me so I could defeat Yohann. She'd attacked Millicent at the party to try to save me. She'd risked her life for me. And over the past few weeks, while I'd been cloistered in my room all day and night, she'd brought me three meals a day. The sicko maid had done all of that, for me.

I couldn't turn my back on her now.

I was going to have to save her.

But I was facing the rebel Millicent Bluenight. She was in possession of cursed, Dark Core–canceling weaponry. Could I really go up against such a terrifying foe to rescue the captured maiden like the protagonist of some fairy tale? That was a job for a hero. I should call in the army—entrust this mission to some great commander. Oh wait. Commander…that was *me*.

I laughed bitterly.

A commander on paper alone. How absurd.

I was an idiot. I'd started to get too big for my boots, strutting around in front of the Seventh Unit as a Crimson Lord. Okay, I know I complained nonstop the whole time about how much I hated it and how much I despised working, but…it was actually kind of *fun*, spending my days with Vill and my soldiers. I couldn't deny it to myself anymore. Returning to my shut-in life had made it very clear.

Being alone all the time…it got lonely.

I didn't feel like I was really living.

Staying in my room all day was somehow worse than having to go to war. Worse than spending my days on my toes, wondering if my soldiers were going to turn on me. Worse than snotty classmates bullying me. Because all those things were real.

I really wanted to go outside.

I wanted to take all my trauma from being bullied, ball it up, and throw it in the trash.

But I couldn't. I wasn't strong enough. I wasn't brave enough. My knees still trembled.

If only I really did have combat abilities. I'd run right over there and save Vill in a blaze of glory. But I was a frail, anemic vampire. There was no way I could save her. Yet I couldn't give up on her, either. I was so lost. There didn't seem to be a way forward...

Then my gaze fell on the envelope lying on the table.

It was the letter Vill had left.

She'd mentioned something about putting her true feelings down in that letter.

Carefully avoiding the drips and splashes of blood, I got out of bed and grabbed the envelope. I opened it up to find a completely ordinary-looking letter inside.

Dear Lady Komari,

I hope this letter finds you and your family in good health. Although I see you all every day, so you would think I already knew that. Sorry, just trying to make this seem like a normal letter.

Anyway, let's cut to the chase. You and I first met three years ago, actually. Big surprise, right? You probably don't remember, but I can recall every detail of what happened on that day.

Back then, I was a student at the Imperial Academy, and a poor student at that. I was a true dunce, a dunderhead, a dummy. The strong prey on the weak, so naturally the other students led an intense bullying campaign against me.

The ringleader of their band was Millicent Bluenight.

This vixen had zero empathy, no ability to comprehend the feelings of others. She thought only of herself, and she was the queen bee of the nastiest clique in school. Just thinking about the cruel treatment I received at her hands makes me shiver to this day. No one came to my aid. Everyone was afraid of her, and she ruled the school with an iron fist.

My days felt dark and cold. Then, one rare ray of light shone into my life. That was you, Lady Komari.

I'm guessing you don't remember? One day, while the dreaded Millicent was torturing me, you appeared and reached out a hand to me, a ministering angel come to pull me out of hell. You saved me.

You asked me if I was okay, if I was hurt. You said everything would be okay. You told me not to let them get me down. I've locked all of your sweet words away in my heart to keep forevermore. You were like a true angel to me, one who appeared in the darkest moment of my life. If only there were more people like her, the world would be a better place. That's what I remember thinking.

But then something terrible happened after that. You probably remember this part well enough, so I don't need to go into too much detail, but Millicent's attentions soon switched to you. She despised you for spoiling her fun, so you became her prey from that day forward.

I couldn't do anything about it. I didn't even try to stick up for you when Millicent was tormenting you, as you'd done for me. That is my crime. Cowardice. I wasn't able to repay your kindness. What a terrible person I am. Anyone would agree.

And so, despicable 'fraidy-cat that I am, I hid in the shadows until Millicent disappeared from the country and you became a shut-in. After that, I decided to try to make amends. Why should someone as lovely as you have your life ruined by that bully? The real you, the real Komari, is like a ray of sunshine, a true beacon of goodness. It was all my fault that you became a recluse. Ever since then, I've done everything I can to get stronger. I trained under hellish conditions. But reminding myself it was all for you is what got me through. Yes, there were times when I wanted to give up, to lie down and cry, but remembering your kindness toward me was what always got me back on my feet.

Then, after graduating from the Academy, I managed to get a position as a maid for the Gandesblood family. It was so fortuitous!

Yes, indeed, I had actually been working here at the mansion for a year before we officially "met." I hid myself from you because I didn't want to remind you of the terrible trauma you'd suffered. But I couldn't stop myself from watching you, rooting for you from the shadows. Until...well.

...Everyone has their limits, don't they? When I got word of your appointment to the Seven Crimson Lords, I knew I had to step up and offer myself as your personal maid and steward. Who else could I entrust with that task after all? So let's skip ahead a little. I got them to let me enlist in the Imperial Army (I was given the rank of special lieutenant), and I had myself reintroduced to you as your personal maid. I was worried about how our meeting would go down, but it seemed like you'd forgotten all about me. It was bittersweet, but it made things easier. Well, you know the rest. I apologize for withholding this information from you until now.

This letter has become quite a long one, but there's really not much more I want to tell you. Only that I think you're amazing. You're stronger, nicer, and warmer than anyone I know. You shine like a true diamond. You may have had some troubles and had a period of reclusion, but you can still get back on your feet. Our mental struggles make us better people; they are nothing to be ashamed of. If Millicent comes back again, we can just ignore her together. Or you can ignore her, and I'll handle her by myself. I may have betrayed you once, but I will never repeat the same mistake again. I'm going to do everything I can to help you move forward. But if you say you really don't want to, I won't force you. I'll just stay here by your side.

Ensuring your happiness is my greatest desire, and the only way I can atone for my crimes.

With all my love,
Vill

*   *   *

The paper fluttered to the floor as I finished reading.

Now what?

Tears were beginning to roll down my cheeks.

Millicent had bullied Vill first. Then she'd turned her evil attention toward me. Vill had become my maid to try to make up for that.

Why didn't I remember that? How could I have forgotten something that important?

"Crap..."

You can't just give a person a letter like that and expect them to shrug it off.

Only an insect would be able to read it and not be deeply, intensely moved.

I clenched my fists.

How ironic. We were in the same situation as we were in three years ago. Millicent was tormenting Vill. I was standing here agonizing over whether I should help her. If I did nothing, nothing would happen. But if I saved Vill, Millicent's fury would fall upon me...

Ah, but no.

Things were different now.

This time, I wasn't going to let Millicent have her way with me.

She'd derailed my entire life. I'd spent three years avoiding everyone, shut up in my room. But I wasn't going to let that be my world anymore. I was done.

I wanted to wash away the past completely.

It didn't matter how weak I'd been back then. I was going to save Vill, return to the Seventh Unit, and take up arms again... I mean, I really didn't want to, but I wanted to get my life back. My crazy, madcap life.

I would emerge from my dark room into the sunlight, to smile and laugh and joke with everyone...

"Lady Terakomari. You have a visitor."

I whirled around. A servant was standing in the open doorframe.

Quickly throwing the blankets over the blood on the floor, I tried to act normal.

"A visitor? Who is it?"

The servant frowned, looking uncomfortable.

"He said his name is Caostel Conto. Apparently, he's one of your subordinate officers…"

I quickly changed into my army uniform and headed outside to find the stripped-tree man standing there with a solemn expression. When I asked him what in the heck he wanted, he clutched his cheeks and began to wail.

"Oh, Commander! Finally I get to see you again! Where have you been all this time?!"

I felt a sharp pang of guilt at seeing Caostel so clearly concerned about me. *Great, one more thing to feel bad about.* But it was too late to take it back now. I sucked in a deep breath and looked him square in the eye.

"I'm sorry. I've been…shut in."

"Excuse me?"

Caostel's eyes widened in confusion. I looked at my feet, muttering.

"Feel free to laugh. I was terrified of Millicent. My knees trembled so much, I could barely stand."

"Laugh…?"

"Yeah, it's pretty funny, right? I mean, I—"

"But, Commander, you're outside right now, talking to me. You're not shut in at all."

I blinked.

Caostel wore his usual unsettling grin. But I saw not a trace of disappointment in his eye. That was encouraging.

"Anyway, we can worry about the insignificant details later. First, we need to discuss the current state of affairs."

"Insignificant—?"

But he interrupted me, nostrils flaring in passion.

"Commander! As I'm sure you're aware, that lawless terrorist attacked the Empress's party purely to besmirch your reputation! That is a crime of the highest order. We must set out to track down Inverse Moon so that we can properly exterminate this scoundrel! Unfortunately, however, we've hit a standstill. Without our commander to guide us, the Seventh Unit is like a ship lost at sea."

"More like a ship of fools."

"You are quite correct. We are fools. We weren't able to track down the terrorist in your absence. For that, I apologize deeply. But I must ask you, Commander! Please return to lead us once more!"

I wasn't sure how to respond.

I mean, I didn't even know what to do myself.

"A lowly officer like me has no right to ask where you've been these past two weeks. However, the fact that I've found you now surely means that this is the right time to act! All of us in the Seventh Unit have all been waiting for this moment!"

Caostel suddenly snapped his fingers. With a blast of magical energy, a magic circle suddenly appeared, burned into the grass of the lawn. It was a teleportation gate produced with Void Magic. I recognized the sigils. This kind of portal was a *Summoning Gate*. Caostel was calling someone to this location through magic.

"Commander! I'm so glad to see that you're all right!!!"

I froze. A figure had suddenly materialized over the magic circle... It was Bellius, the canine-headed fellow who'd saved my life back at the party. He was leaning on the shoulder of another man—Mellaconcey— and the two of them began slowly to walk this way.

"Bellius? Are...are you well?"

"I'm fine. A little wound like that won't stop me."

"But you were in a coma for two weeks..."

"A trifling matter. I'm only happy to have been able to shield you, Commander. Ah, but perhaps I was too hasty. After all, a mighty warrior such as you should have been able to well withstand a few blows from that puny terrorist. I apologize for acting so rashly and putting myself out of commission for so long."

"Yo! We're here via portal, this dog dude's immortal! When—"

Suddenly, a fist smashed into Mellaconcey's jaw and sent him flying. It must have hurt Bellius's still-healing hands to have socked the rapper like that, but he merely grunted once before regaining his composure.

"...Anyway, to battle! I, Bellius Hund Cerbero, will follow you to the edge of the world, Commander. Simply lead the way."

"And I, Caostel Conto, am with you, too. Let us bring justice down upon that lawless heathen wench!"

"Check it!"

I felt...deeply moved all of a sudden.

These silly men really did think I was some mighty leader.

"You guys..."

I gazed at them all one by one, hesitating.

"Why do you all...adore me so much?"

I regretted the question instantly. I knew why after all. Because I was such a "strong leader." What other reason could there be? But I kept waiting for my answer. Several seconds passed. I felt like a criminal up on the stand. My subordinates were exchanging *the heck is she even asking us?* looks.

Finally, Caostel spoke.

"Because you're a good person, Commander. You always think about the feelings of the unit. And also because you've got such a cute little bod, despite being so strong, and that contrast is super charming. But mostly the thoughtfulness thing."

Then Bellius gave his piece.

"I am afraid that to speak the frank truth would be improper in front of a lady such as yourself. So I'm going to go with the thoughtfulness aspect as well."

And last it was Mellaconcey's turn.

"Yo, you're the only one who'll rap with me. The others treat me so disrespectfully. So I'll follow you anywhere, Commander. You're the only one who really understands…er."

Ah…

My chest swelled with emotion. Tears were prickling my eyes.

They really were a bunch of dim-witted, criminal-record-having fools, but it was adorable how they were still so willing to follow me. Simply adorable.

I didn't think I'd ever felt this happy before.

"I…I see," I replied, clearing my throat. "In that case, you don't care about my actual strength and whatnot?"

"Strength? Nah, that really doesn't factor into it."

"Huh?"

Caostel clenched his hands together at his breast, continuing.

"Obviously, you're strong. You're a Crimson Lord, aren't you? If you were a weakling, we'd have already mutinied against you, right?"

"…"

"But such concerns are nothing for you to dwell on, Commander! After all, you're the mightiest Crimson Lord in history! Despite that, you have never once acted like a snob; instead, you always put your troops first! That's why everyone is waiting on your word, Commander! Who could fail to love you?"

"…"

Yeah, but this was all predicated on the lie that I was superpowerful.

In that case, I really should just keep on hiding it, shouldn't I? My… true self, that is.

"Y-yeah! You're right! You guys love me because I'm super kind even though I'm also superstrong! Well, I'll just have to show you that your faith has been justified! Let's roll!"

The three of them cheered.

They…really didn't know anything about me.

Yep, they were clueless…but they still believed in me. And they had responded to me as a person…as the leader they knew, not the story they'd been told. I was pretty convinced of that.

So they deserved a payout on that faith they'd put in me.

Okay. I would become their mighty leader. I'd take control of their unit again as the fearsome Crimson Lord, whose name alone could silence even the naughtiest of bratty children. Anything was better than sniveling under the sheets in my darkened bedroom.

Taking a deep breath, I whirled around to face my men, chin raised with pride, one fist clenched against my chest. Just like an commander addressing her troops. Oh wait, that's what I was.

"Thank you! Your words of support have bolstered my spirits. I have decided! We are to track down that lawless terrorist and exact mighty justice upon her!"

"So you know where she is, then?"

"I do." I nodded, before shaking my head immediately. "But you are not to accompany me."

"But, Commander!"

"Commander, why?!"

Their cries of dissent pierced me.

I wish I could have taken them with me, too. Oh, it would be so easy if only I could sic my officers on her. *"Kill the terrorist."* That's all I'd need to say.

But this was my fight.

If I was going to really cast off my shut-in persona and step into the light, then I needed to deal with my trauma myself. I had to do this for me, not because Millicent's threats had forced my hand.

Turning to my officers again, I tried to adopt a confident, arrogant air.

"Sorry, but this is my battle. I need you to return to the Crimson Tower and rally the troops. Explain my mission to them, and then please send me your good vibes and wishes. Knowing I have you all rooting for me will give me all the strength I need to face her..."

Vexations

"Get stronger. More powerful than anyone else."

Her father's lectures had always been straight and to the point.

Millicent Bluenight was certain that these endless lectures had distorted her innocent mind, to the point where they began to seem normal, even reasonable, to her.

Politics ran in the Bluenight blood. Since the Imperial Court was awash with backstabbing and trickery, the Bluenights had only their own strength to rely on. In the Mulnite Empire, might made right, and weak politicians always ended up on the chopping block sooner or later. No wonder Millicent's father was always admonishing her to "get stronger."

He also pulled whatever strings he could to further his daughter's education. The endless extracurricular magic and traditional performing arts classes were fine. They didn't hurt.

No, the thing that really caused Millicent to suffer was the battle training. They'd called it training, but it had been more like systematic abuse. Total hell.

The first time she'd met *him*, Millicent had been eleven years old.

"One day, you'll be the Empress. Do you know what you need in order to ascend the throne?"

Father had called Millicent out to the courtyard to lecture her once again.

"Power, I think?"

"Precisely. Sometimes you really do seem to understand."

Millicent couldn't help breaking into a smile. She did so love those rare occasions when he praised her.

"You need to get stronger. Otherwise, you'll never be the Empress."

"Right."

"But I'm not talking about ordinary levels of might. Those with the capacity to take the throne have *extra*ordinary strength. So, Millicent, you, too, must become…extraordinary."

"What should I do, Father?"

"Your battle master will show you."

That's when Millicent noticed him for the first time.

The strange man standing next to her father.

His presence was so faint and ethereal, she might not have noticed him if her father hadn't pointed him out. He seemed somewhat otherworldly. He had black hair and red eyes. He was dressed in a kimono with long, thick sleeves, one side of which wrapped over the other on his chest and was held together with a thick band of material. Its sleeves flapped in the light breeze. His face was refined, his eyes sharp and shrewd.

"This is Battle Master Amatsu, from The Heavenly Paradise. Starting today, he will be serving as your new combat instructor. Do not displease him."

The man extended a hand, which poked out from underneath his long, flapping sleeve.

"My name is Kakumei Amatsu. Pleased to meet you."

Millicent flinched. Not because she was nervous to be meeting her new teacher, but because this was the first time in her entire life she'd laid eyes on someone not of vampire lineage. And he was the person who would instruct her. Fighting back the feelings of reservation deep within her chest, she reached out and took his hand.

Then the world flipped upside down.

"Gah!"

He suddenly grabbed her arm and twisted it. The pain was unbelievable, and the next thing she knew, her back had slammed against the ground. She realized she was lying in the dirt, gazing up at the sky overhead.

Millicent couldn't process what had just happened. All she could focus on was the pain. She couldn't breathe.

As she blinked, the figure of the man in the robe looming over her suddenly became clear. He had procured a long rod like a laundry pole from somewhere. Spinning it, he brought one end of it down upon Millicent's stomach.

She screamed.

As she rolled around in the dirt, mewling with agony, Master Amatsu looked down at her with distaste.

"Entirely lacking any sense of self-awareness. We'll need to get that fixed right away, or she'll never even have a shot at the Seven Crimson Lords, let alone the Empress's throne, Lord Bluenight. Training her will be an arduous task."

"I'll pay whatever you want. And you have complete freedom to utilize any teaching methods you deem fit."

"Hmm. If you're willing to pay, then I'm willing to put in the time."

Amatsu smirked. Millicent felt a chill pass through her. There was no hint of any humanity in his smile—no kindness, no warmth, no compassion.

And so her training from hell began.

And the evil that would come to be cultivated in Millicent's soul soon began to take root.

Millicent, I believe he said your name was? I am about to teach you to safeguard your mind. In order to be strong, it is most important to cultivate a mindset that cannot be shaken, no matter what.

*   *   *

As soon as she returned from the Academy, her daily lesson in suffering began.

For his weapon, Master Amatsu used what he called a "Meteor Staff," the laundry-pole-type stick he'd used to whack Millicent in the stomach on their first meeting. Millicent was free to use whatever magic or weapons she could find to counter it.

But none of her attacks ever got anywhere near him. Even her Magic Bullet attack, which her magic teachers at school had deemed "most accomplished," could not hit him, no matter how hard she tried. He evaded every shot while barely breaking a sweat, then countered her with a blow that knocked her to the ground.

This went on day after day until nightfall.

If Millicent ever showed any weakness, her father would appear in an instant. *"Get it together!" "You're the heir to the Bluenight name!" "How dare you inconvenience Master Amatsu?!"* Every day was torture, but Millicent couldn't defy her father. All she could do was try to get through it somehow.

The worst of it all was the "Meteor Staff" that Amatsu would use on her.

It looked like an ordinary laundry pole at first glance, but it was clearly cursed with the ability to cancel out the healing properties of the Dark Core. This made the wounds it inflicted exceptionally serious and painful.

Because any injuries it produced refused to heal.

Each day's beatings were overlaid on top of yesterday's cuts and bruises. Terrified of the pain, Millicent took to fleeing instead of fighting, but this only enraged her father, whom she was terrified of as well. So she stopped fleeing and took to desperately swinging at her master, who merely inflicted fresh wounds on her with a cold smile.

Why was this happening to her? One day, at the end of her rope, she asked Master Amatsu this question.

"Your father wants you to have extraordinary strength."

"Extraordinary...?"

"A special ability known as *Core Implosion*. Surely you've heard of it?"

She hadn't. But later on, he explained it to her. Core Implosion was a force that didn't abide by any of the physical laws of this world. With it, you could shatter the very crust of the earth, or even move the stars in the sky.

But using Core Implosion would paradoxically inflict grievous damage upon the wielder; paradoxical, because this went against the Dark Core's regenerative effects. Core Implosion was thus metaphysically unfeasible. If you wanted to wield it, you had to take certain steps to bypass the Dark Core's influence.

"Few are born with the innate power needed to wield this force. But recently, we've discovered that some can achieve it through specialized, rigorous training.

"...Amazing, is it not?" stated Amatsu.

"What kind of training?" asked Millicent.

"Forging a mind that can remain impervious to outside circumstances. For some reason, Core Implosion needs an individual with a special kind of mental state in order to become effective. And the fastest way to strengthen one's mind is to temper the body. Through enduring the endless agony of unhealing wounds, the mind grows strong and hard, like crystal."

Millicent had thought this man was talking nonsense.

But he continued on in complete earnestness.

"I know, I know. You loathe our training sessions with all your heart and soul. But if we can hone and focus those feelings of negativity, we'll be on the path to success. And then your father will be proud of you. So persevere and do your best."

Then he whacked her with the Meteor Staff again.

Not expecting the blow, she received another fresh bruise on her chest.

Listen to me, Millicent. Core Implosion is within our grasp. If we can wield its power at will, then for the first time in history, we'll be able to show people what it means to truly live. *And if you learn how to master it, your father will be proud of you. Doesn't imagining that make you smile? Doesn't it make you feel...alive?*

"Why?! Why can't you use Core Implosion?! Speak!"

Father began berating Millicent as soon as she walked into his study. Afraid, she hung her head in silence.

"It's been a month! A month! You're just not trying hard enough, are you? Amatsu is one of the Five Grand Masters of The Heavenly Paradise! The problem clearly lies with your lack of effort, not his teachings!"

"..."

"And I had a look at your school report card as well. Care to explain? Huh? You've slipped to second in your class! Have you forgotten that you're a member of the noble Bluenight lineage of vampires?!"

Obviously, Millicent's grades had slipped. She had time neither to do homework nor to study, what with training sessions after school every day until nightfall.

"F-Father..."

"Don't talk back to me!" he barked, plopping down heavily in his chair and spinning it around so his back was to her. Then he continued to huff and puff and mutter under his breath. "Gandesblood would laugh himself sick. Damn it all! To have such an embarrassment as an heir! Why, his daughter is far more..."

Gandesblood. A political family that rivaled the Bluenights. Father was always making some snarky comment or other about them.

Millicent stood there frozen in terror.

This time, Father's disgruntled mutterings had been laced with a particularly cruel edge.

Blinking back tears, Millicent fled. She didn't even hear her father call after her.

She had been trying so hard, but to no avail. Why couldn't Father acknowledge her efforts? Was she just not trying hard enough? Maybe she didn't have enough physical injuries yet? Or perhaps her mind was just too weak.

Millicent flew into her room, her body a mess of aches from her many cuts and bruises. Her soul felt like it was bruised, too.

Burrowing beneath the blankets of her bed, she wept. After a few moments, however, she became aware of something slowly approaching the bed.

"Oh, Petro. Are you trying to lick my tears? Thank you."

It was her corgi, Petro, who had been a gift on her tenth birthday. The dog was the only comfort she had in a life that was filled with school, training, beatings, and Father's harsh words.

"I have to keep doing my best, right, Petro? Yeah. It's gonna be okay."

As she stroked his soft back, Millicent found new resolve within herself.

No matter how hard it was, no matter how much it hurt or how badly her soul was wounded, she would endure everything and make her father proud. She would learn to wield the mysterious, elusive power of Core Implosion.

Core Implosion is a marvelous force. But as long as one remains connected to the Dark Core, one cannot evoke it. Do you not see how the Dark Core interferes with the natural order of life and death? Do you not see what a true curse and plague upon society it is?

After that, Millicent redoubled her efforts. All to please Father. She would grow mightier, join the Seven Crimson Lords, then ascend the Empress's throne. She would bring glory to the name of Bluenight.

Recently, she had even learned to anticipate and evade some of the blows from Amatsu. "If you keep going at this rate, you may be able to evoke it after all," he told her. This was high praise indeed. And while the training was as grueling and painful as ever, Millicent felt pleased. She was starting to feel...hopeful.

But her high spirits were soon smashed to pieces.

"You know that girl in the other class? Apparently, her magical ability is exceptional."

Exhausted and sleep-deprived though she was, Millicent couldn't help overhearing gossip in the hallways after class.

"Oh yeah, I know the one. The teacher was going on about her. She can use a kind of ability that ordinary folk can't!"

"You mean advanced-level magic? That *is* impressive."

"No, no, that's not what I meant."

"What, then?"

"It's some kind of rare, crazy power. Cord Explosion? No..."

"Excuse me, do you mind explaining that?"

Millicent couldn't stop herself from going over and confronting her classmate.

That's when she learned that there was a girl in the other class who could use Core Implosion. The very same ability that Millicent had been practically breaking her back in pursuit of...

Suddenly, feelings of hot, burning jealousy and panicked inadequacy overcame her.

She quickly rooted out the girl in question to confront her. She was sitting in a corner of the classroom, her nose in a book. At first glance, she was mousy and nondescript. *This* was the girl who could wield Core Implosion? This...this...*frump*?

"Hey, you. Is it true you can use Core Implosion?"

The girl looked up from her novel. There was fear in her expression.

"That isn't possible, right? 'Cause the only way to do that is awaken it through really harsh training. Right?"

"...It's true. My teacher said so."

The girl's hesitant, trembling voice made Millicent want to scream. She snatched the book from her hands and glowered down at her.

"Show me, then."

"B-but..."

"Go on. Why not? It's not like it can be used up."

Cowed by Millicent's pressuring tone and menacing body language, the smaller girl eventually acquiesced. But still, she seemed hesitant to do it in the classroom.

"If you want to see, we have to go someplace where there aren't any people." The girl's voice was barely a whisper, and Millicent had to strain her ears to make out her words.

They headed behind the school building.

"I really don't want to have to show you this…"

"Just do it."

Reluctantly, the girl reached out her right hand, palm facing upward. Then she said something that Millicent hadn't been expecting.

"Suck."

"What?"

"Suck my blood. My Core Implosion power allows me to see the future of anyone who drinks my blood. It's called *Pandora's Poison*. It will show me what's going to happen for the rest of the day with one hundred percent accuracy."

There wasn't a spell in existence that could tell the future. If what this girl was insisting was true, that meant Core Implosion was truly miraculous.

Millicent was curious…fascinated, in fact. She leaned in and brought her lips to the girl's index finger. Baring her teeth, she bit in, and her mouth filled with the taste of blood.

The change was immediate.

The girl's eyes turned instantly bloodred. Master Amatsu had told her that this was one of the sure signs of evoking Core Implosion.

"I saw it all…"

The girl's expression was…troubled.

"It was…I…"

"What? What did you see? Just spit it out."

"You…you've got a really sad home life, don't you?"

Millicent blinked at her, speechless for a moment.

Then, as the words sank in, she felt anger flare inside her. Somehow, having this mousy girl pity her made her burn with a fury she'd never felt before. Millicent was fine with her life. It wasn't that bad. How dare this little dork look at her with those doleful, empathetic eyes?

She couldn't bear it. She exploded.

Millicent raised her hands and aimed her Magic Bullet straight at the girl's face. At such close range, there was no way the incantation would miss. But somehow the girl managed to evade it. It was as though she'd seen it coming...

"I'm sorry. I'm really sorry. I didn't mean to say that just now. Sorry..."

"Get back here!!!"

The girl set off at a run, fleeing as fast as her legs would carry her.

Millicent shot a dozen Magic Bullets at her, but none hit their mark.

Later, Millicent would lie awake pondering over this moment. She'd blasted the girl's face at point-blank range. What if one of her Magic Bullets had actually struck her? With her power of Core Implosion currently evoked, she had disconnected herself from the Dark Core. Would one of Millicent's attacks have ended her permanently?

What's that? You loathe people with innate abilities? What an amusing thing to say. Yes, yes, focus your abhorrence on this Villhaze girl. But know that your hatred for her will never be sated, even if you manage to kill her. Murdering her won't remove her permanently from this world. Because the Dark Core is always active... Isn't it?

From that day forward, Villhaze became Millicent's archnemesis.

Villhaze was from one of the poorer neighborhoods in the Imperial Capital. Usually, a girl like her wouldn't have been able to enter the same social circle as someone like Millicent. But she'd gotten top marks on the Imperial Academy's entrance exam and had been admitted. Ever since, she'd kept her excellent grades up, and to add insult to injury, it transpired that she was the girl who had recently bumped Millicent off the top spot in the class ranking.

And on top of everything else, she could use Core Implosion.

The thing that Millicent had been training for until she puked up blood…that girl had just been born with it.

She couldn't stand it.

And so she decided to get even with Villhaze.

It was easy enough. The Bluenights were one of the finest families in the Empire.

All Millicent had to do was make one loaded comment in a public setting.

"That Villhaze girl is totally stuck up, if you ask me."

That was all it took to make that little urchin from the poor side of town into the whole school's whipping girl.

There had been a few justice-minded souls who'd tried to sticking up for the weaker girl on principle, but Millicent had soon leaned on her political influences to get them to shut up.

It started with simple shunning. Then came the malicious gossip. Followed by straight-up name-calling. Then on to direct physical violence. The bullying escalated further and further. Millicent knew that if Villhaze activated her Core Implosion skills against her, she'd be able to read Millicent's every move and evade her. To ensure Villhaze didn't somehow slip some of her blood into her food or drink, Millicent surrounded herself with an army of minions at all times.

But the girl didn't even try to fight back. Millicent wasn't surprised. Villhaze had seemed weak and feeble from the start. All she ever did was cry silently in response to Millicent's worst treatment. The tears were more than validation enough for Millicent, though. Somehow they seemed to make up for all the pain she suffered at the hands of Master Amatsu and his brutal Meteor Staff.

Little by little, her soul grew tainted.

*   *   *

Not bad, not bad. I have to admit, you've definitely grown stronger. Your unhealing wounds have steeled your mind and firmed your resolve. You see how the Dark Core is nothing but a hindrance? It stunts and neuters us all, holds us back from what we were truly meant to be…

That year, Millicent had earned the top score on the end-of-semester exam.

On the other hand, Villhaze had plummeted to thirty-first in the rankings. The reason for her sudden downfall was obvious. Millicent's torture campaign had so disturbed her that she hadn't been able to focus on her studies.

Millicent rejoiced. She still couldn't evoke Core Implosion, but she'd clawed her way back to her position as the top student in the Academy. Now Father would have no choice but to reassess his evaluation of her.

"Hya-ha-ha! Guess what, Villhaze, you're ranked thirty-first! How does it feel to be a loser?"

Kick. Punch. Stamp.

Villhaze didn't even try to move out of the way when she saw Millicent striding down the hallway toward her. How was it fair that a feeble weakling like this could evoke Core Implosion? It only added fuel to the fire of Millicent's fury.

"Get up. You're supposed to be superstrong, right? You can use Core Implosion, right? Surely you ought to be able to kill us all dead right here. Why don't you try it, huh? Loser!"

But Villhaze said nothing in return. She merely lay on the ground as they kicked her and stamped on her. If the healing and regenerative powers of the Dark Core that acted on everyone hadn't been around, even this shrinking mouse would have been forced to try to evade the blows. Millicent scowled, reeling from the familiar pain that Master's cursed staff had inflicted all across her body, her unhealing wounds.

"Hey, Millicent. I think we should just leave her. She's obviously lost her mind."

"Yeah, it's no fun if they don't cry out or try to fight back."

Her minions were beginning to lose interest. True, the girl was hardly much sport for them. Millicent racked her brain for a few moments. Then she had an idea.

"Let's just kill her, then."

Her minions raised their eyebrows, entertained by the prospect. That's when Villhaze visibly paled for the first time.

Thanks to the power of the Dark Core, killing a person wasn't really considered worthy of a murder charge, since they would just regenerate anyway. But to deliberately exploit that loophole just for the pleasure of hurting another person...that was monstrous. Anyone with basic common decency would agree.

Now that she had her minions on board once more, Millicent raised her right hand.

It was elementary light magic, a Magic Bullet. One direct blow to an opponent's forehead would be enough to strike them down.

"D-don't!"

Villhaze's expression clouded over with fear.

Yes. That's the face I wanted to see. How dare she possess what I've been so desperately seeking, all without putting in a shred of effort? How dare she overtake me in the student ranking when she's nothing but a grubby commoner from the slums? She deserves to die. Die. Die. Just lie down and die, why don't you...

Millicent's mouth stretched into a demonic grin.

The seeds of evil that had grown within her soul had begun to blossom.

But just then...

"Stop it!"

Someone grabbed her other arm.

Millicent turned, blinking, feeling as though she were staring directly at a beam of light.

But it wasn't that. It was a girl. A very pretty girl with blond hair and red eyes.

Despite the bravery of her actions, she was visibly trembling. And yet her gaze was still filled with determination.

Terakomari Gandesblood.

Millicent's true archnemesis. The girl who would turn her life completely on its head and send her cascading down the path of true darkness.

Hmm. Yes, indeed, you do have talent. I shall tell your father that you are almost ready...almost ready to finally invoke Core Implosion.

Millicent was furious that someone had interrupted her bullying, her sole source of joy. But the moment she'd realized that this intruding girl had been a vampire of her own social standing, not to mention the daughter of an aristocratic family that had long been enemies of the Bluenights, she'd backed down immediately.

Actually, that had been the best course of action. Besides, Millicent's spirits were still pretty high. She hadn't managed to kill Villhaze, which was a bummer, but she'd finally been able to get a reaction out of her. That girl had looked like she was about to pee her pants! What was more, once Millicent went home, she would be able to tell Father all about how she was once more top of her class. He would be so pleased. So she decided to leave dealing with Terakomari for another day. Reflecting on the day's events, she walked home with an uncharacteristic spring in her step. However...

"Top of the class? That should go without saying!"

When Millicent excitedly shared her news with her father, his reaction was less than stellar. In fact, he shouted at her, spittle flying out of his mouth.

"Never mind that childish nonsense! What about Core Implosion? Can you use it yet?!"

Millicent choked back tears.

"Master Amatsu says I'm nearly ready. I should be able to use it soon."

"Enough lies!" This time his saliva landed on her face. "Master Amatsu is deeply aggrieved by your complete lack of effort! If you had a shred of talent, you would already be able to evoke Core Implosion by now! He's asked for more money to go on training you!"

This news struck Millicent like a blow to the head.

Had Master Amatsu really said that?

"Why are you so stupid and useless?! A daughter of the esteemed Bluenight lineage ought to be able to activate Core Implosion at least once or twice! This is yet another thing Gandesblood will be able to hold over my head and mock me for!"

"Gandesblood...?"

"Right. Armand was bragging about his daughter yet again today. His second eldest daughter. Apparently, she has 'special abilities.' Your complete opposite, hmm? Compared to Gandesblood's girl, you're a total failure!"

An outsider listening in might have started to feel an ironic sense of pity for Lord Bluenight upon hearing this jealous, insecure rant.

But that thought still hadn't occurred to Millicent. Instead, she'd blamed herself. She was awash with misery. She turned her back on her father and ran away blindly down the hallway, ignoring the eyes of onlookers.

Why did nothing ever work out for her? Why wouldn't Father ever praise her? Why didn't she have any talent?

But there was no one to answer her cries. It felt like the entire world was conspiring against her.

That was when Millicent began to see things from a different angle.

No. This wasn't her fault at all.

It was all because of *her*. That little witch, Terakomari.

Why hadn't she realized this before? All of this pain was on Terakomari. Because her father was constantly comparing the two of them.

It was her fault.

If Terakomari wasn't around, things would be different...

Eager to hide away, Millicent hurried up to the door of her room, muttering curses. But when she got there, she found something black and lumpy lying before her door.

"Petro?"

She recognized the corgi immediately. He was the one member of her family who understood her. He'd probably come to soothe her, knowing that his mistress was in pain. Feeling a huge sense of relief, Millicent hurried over to him.

"…Petro?"

But he didn't turn around.

Petro was sprawled on the floor, unmoving. A wave of dread assaulted Millicent. She could feel her heart rate increasing as she scooped him up in her arms. He was so cold. He wasn't moving. There were no signs of life.

"Huh…?"

"It looks like that dog is dead."

She felt a presence looming over her from behind. She whirled to find the man in the long robe. Where had he come from? He was glaring down at Millicent with his usually frigid gaze as she clutched her dead family member in her arms.

"It must have been sick. That's a real shame."

"It doesn't make any sense! He was fine this morning!"

"The Dark Core's influence doesn't extend to pets. It's not like this is a rare occurrence."

Despair overwhelmed Millicent. It had been too sudden. She hadn't even gotten to say good-bye. Tears rolled down her cheeks. But Amatsu still had more to say.

"A friend of mine has the ability to reverse time. Core Implosion, of course, you understand. But unfortunately, I can't ask him to come all the way here just for a dead dog. So there's no reviving your little friend. A shame. But you know, if *you* had a special ability of your own, you might have been able to save Petro. But you don't, do you? Like I said…a shame."

"But…but…"

"It's absurd, isn't it? The Dark Core. If it can't even save the person you really love. Well, a dog in this case. And yet it safeguards the worst of humanity, when really their lives deserve to be flushed down the drain. Do you really think this is the way things ought to be?"

Amatsu's lecture was too complicated for Millicent to comprehend. She was still too stunned from the loss of Petro to think straight.

It was all over for her. She had lost her only friend. There was no one to praise her. No one to offer her kindness. All that was left was her empty existence…her miserable life of beatings and cruel words. There was no point living that way…

But just as Millicent was about to lose all hope…

She felt a warm hand come down on the top of her head.

Shocked, she looked up, and her jaw fell to find the coldhearted Amatsu looking down at her with a warm smile.

"Do not waste tears. The pursuit of strength is all that matters. People grow weak when they forget that."

His gentle tone struck a chord in Millicent's heart.

"Don't you despise this world for making you suffer so? Don't you want to get revenge? Don't you want to kill them all? Ah, except for me, of course. If you could only harness that hatred, nurture it within your soul, then I know that you could become mighty beyond all measure. I'll help you to achieve that. I'm the only one who's on your side now, you know."

Millicent gazed up at Amatsu, her jaw hanging open.

He had never spoken to her this kindly before. It was as though she had been dying of thirst this time entire, and now he'd offered her a cup of clean, cool water. Like he was her savior.

"What…what should I do?"

"Do as you wish. We have free will after all, do we not? Love those who are dear to you. Kill those you find disagreeable. Whom do you most want to exterminate, Millicent?"

She knew the answer right away.

The cause of all her suffering.

Terakomari Gandesblood.

"Then kill them, no matter what it takes. I'll give you all the power you need to pull it off."

As she gazed into his solemn eyes, Millicent could hear her heart throbbing in her ears.

In the end, Millicent had been easily swayed to darkness.

I'll be honest here. You have no talent. Core Implosion won't come to you. But you're not a hopeless case. You have other talents, many of them. So don't feel too disheartened. But Core Implosion...it isn't going to happen for you.

Amatsu arranged a funeral for her corgi. After chanting over the body in a strange language, he nodded to the attending priest. "May Petro rest in everlasting peace."

After that, Millicent went through a sort of spiritual transformation.

Her father's teachings had been correct. This was a dog-eat-dog world. She needed to be strong if she wanted to survive. If she wanted to learn how to kill.

Master Amatsu was as strict as ever. Every day brought fresh bruises. The pain was never-ending. But unlike before, Millicent's mind had opened to the teaching. She focused everything on her goal of getting stronger. She dedicated herself to the training.

But there was no peace for her sickened soul.

Villhaze.

Terakomari Gandesblood.

The mere fact that these two existed, with their inborn talents, affronted Millicent to her core.

And she especially loathed Terakomari.

Her social standing was equal to Millicent's. But she had that gorgeous face. And she was kind and brave, the sort of girl who would step in when she saw someone else being bullied. On top of that, she apparently had some special ability. Maybe even Core Implosion. There was so much to envy about Terakomari. She didn't even know how good she had it. If there was any vampire in the land that Millicent secretly, desperately longed to be, it was her.

And the worst thing of all was that by simply existing, Terakomari caused Millicent's father to be disappointed with her. To scream at and rebuke her endlessly.

Terakomari needed to die.

No matter what it took, Millicent was going to murder her.

Henceforth, she resolved to do whatever Amatsu told her.

There was no need to hold back. Master Amatsu had given her permission.

Terakomari was an insult. An affront. She didn't deserve to exist.

So Millicent launched an intense bullying campaign against her, just as she'd done against Villhaze. She got all her minions on board. Even though Terakomari was an aristocrat's daughter, she didn't have as large a social circle as Millicent had, so it was relatively easy.

"Ha-ha-ha! Look! Look! If you don't like it, why don't you evoke Core Implosion or something and stop us, hmm?"

Millicent had lured Terakomari behind the school building, where she launched her attack.

If Terakomari used Core Implosion, well, that was no big deal. Millicent would just use one of her minions as a human shield. In fact, she's incorporated that into her plan to find out what kind of special ability Terakomari possessed before she killed her.

But Terakomari didn't even try to defend herself.

She refused to do anything with her power.

But while Villhaze had crumbled, Terakomari refused to break. Even if they punched and kicked her, that fire in her eyes never seemed in danger of dampening. She was like a shining beacon of pure light. One that made Millicent's darkness seem even more absolute in contrast. It infuriated her. Utterly infuriated her.

But what truly made Millicent lose it was what Terakomari had muttered during one of her beatings.

"I feel sorry for you."

Millicent could hardly believe her ears. Was this girl insane? Why would she say something like that to her?

But Terakomari kept on talking as she lay prone on the ground at Millicent's feet.

"Is there something that's bothering you, Millicent?"

She wanted to scream at Terakomari to shut up. *"You're the cause of all this, you stupid wench! Because of you, my life is a living hell! You don't know anything about other people's pain! So don't you dare look at me with pity in your eyes! I'm strong. Stronger than you'll ever be!!!"*

But even as she screamed at her, Millicent was filled with a sense of wonder.

To say that even in the face of all this physical violence...the girl had a kinder spirit than Millicent could have imagined.

She would need to break that spirit.

Desperate to find a weak point she could use against Terakomari, Millicent dug into her background. She needed something that couldn't fail to be effective.

"Hey, nice pendant. Give it to me."

Millicent had hit the bull's-eye. Finally, Terakomari trembled. In fact, she seemed so desperate, so panicked, that Millicent had gotten a rush off her reaction. She remembered cackling harder than she ever had before, looming over the girl. That...that was the last thing she remembered.

The memory of what had transpired after that had never returned to her.

She woke up on an infirmary bed.

But in this world, infirmaries were more like temporary storage facilities for people who were awaiting regeneration. In other words...

Millicent had died. But she had no idea why, or what could have possibly happened. She'd only been toying with Terakomari. How could she have died from that?

After lying there in shock for a while, one of the Imperial officials showed up to talk to her.

"Millicent Bluenight. You are hereby banished from the Empire for the crimes of mass murder and treason."

Millicent was paralyzed with disbelief. She couldn't even begin to process this.

The official went on. He informed her that on the day she'd tried to steal Terakomari Gandesblood's pendant, there had been a huge massacre at the Imperial Academy. A hundred people had been wiped out. At first, Millicent assumed she'd been one of the victims, but apparently that hadn't been the case; in fact, the newspapers were all reporting that the perpetrator of the massacre had been none other than Millicent Bluenight herself.

"What's the meaning of this?!"

"Ask yourself that question. You are no longer a vampire of the Mulnite Empire. So now you have two choices. Incarceration in the dungeons for the rest of your life. Or leaving the country immediately. What's it to be?"

Millicent simply blinked.

Now there was only one thing she knew.

Fear. The metallic tang of it in her mouth, the sensation of a fist closing around her heart.

Bloodred eyes. Blood drops spurting. A little finger, stained bright red. The moment she had touched Terakomari's pendant, something monumental had occurred.

That's when Millicent knew the truth.

Terakomari had killed her.

"That can't be…!"

At the very last moment, she'd played her ace in the hole.

Millicent couldn't process it. She'd been so sure that she'd be able to counter any attack Terakomari came up with, even if it did involve Core Implosion. After all, she'd been training day in and day out until she vomited up blood. She was the strongest student at the Academy, wasn't she? How could stunted little Terakomari have done this to her?

And yet…she had.

She'd TKO'd Millicent Bluenight with a single counterattack.

"Oh…ohhh…"

As anguish overtook Millicent, her tears began to flow.

How could it have ended like this?!

Was this the difference between hard training and inborn talent, after all?

But Millicent didn't have much time for crying. Before she knew it, she was being escorted to the border.

She was still half in disbelief.

However, after endless digging, she'd uncovered the real truth.

This had all been a plot against her.

Terakomari herself had slaughtered all those people. But her father had been desperate to shield his little princess from the public's reaction. So he'd resorted to playing a dirty hand. He'd managed to frame Millicent for the crime to get his daughter off scot-free. At the same time, he'd also destroyed the house of Bluenight, his greatest political rival.

It was a ridiculous story, a tale no one should have believed.

But Terakomari's father, Armand Gandesblood, was a crooked politician, who would stop at nothing to further his own political ambitions. That was what Millicent's father had always impressed upon her during his many rants. To make matters worse, Armand had apparently been one of the current Empress's favorite little pet students when the two were at the Academy together.

With the Empress backing up his claims, Armand could have sold the public any story he felt like.

At any rate, this was how Millicent had come to be banished from her homeland.

Her father and Amatsu, too… She had lost track of the both of them.

After her exile, Millicent sobbed all the time. She wept even harder than she had when Petro died. She wandered the towns of the unfamiliar outside world, living like a vagrant. At night, she curled up into a ball and sobbed. And with every tear she shed, her hatred grew more and more oppressive.

Hatred for her own weakness.

Hatred for this cruel, unfeeling world.

Hatred for Terakomari, who had killed Millicent with such incredible ease.

Yes…*Terakomari*.

She had spurred Millicent's downfall.

Millicent couldn't bear to have been defeated without even getting the chance to strike. She would have to murder Terakomari to set things right. This time around, she would crush that runt and her stupid Core Implosion power. Yes. Millicent would destroy her. And it was right when she'd made up her mind that a devil had come to pay her a visit.

"Millicent. You don't seem to be faring too badly out here alone after all."

Black hair. Red eyes. Flapping robes. A quick, swift way of moving, as fast as the wind. Millicent would never have forgotten him.

It was her old battle master, Amatsu.

He flashed a demonic grin at her.

"Well, I certainly never expected things to end up like this. But our reunion has to be fate. So, Millicent…would you like to come with me? I'd like to officially invite you to join Inverse Moon. I can guarantee you'd be most welcome."

From that day forward, Millicent had kept fighting. Her father's words—"Get stronger"—were always in the back of her mind. But this time, she wasn't trying to grow more powerful for the sake of the

Bluenight reputation. No, she was getting stronger for herself. So that she could assassinate Terakomari and feel reborn for the first time. To that end, she immersed herself in Inverse Moon activities along with her mentor, Amats.

She'd never worked harder at anything in her life.

And then, one day three years later, she'd stumbled upon her rival's name in the newspaper.

NEWEST CRIMSON LORD SPEAKS: "I'LL TURN THE ENTIRE WORLD INTO OMELET RICE"

At first, she was certain it had been some kind of joke.

But at the same time, she was greatly disturbed.

Her hands shook as she clutched the article. Memories she'd been blocking out came flooding back. And the old rage boiled up inside her once again. Millicent's days as a terrorist had been grueling and blood-soaked (even though she'd chosen that life, sometimes she wondered what she'd gotten herself into). But while she'd been suffering, Terakomari had been strutting around as a commander in the army, a Crimson Lord no less. Millicent was so incensed and offended, she could barely breathe.

So she returned to her homeland for the first time in three years to gather information on Terakomari. She even headed to the Imperial Palace itself, just to see with her own two eyes how her rival was getting on.

She'd found the girl laughing.

As though she was having the time of her life.

Not only did she have all the power, but now she had personal fulfillment, too?

Millicent almost lost her mind with rage.

She bit her own lip so hard that blood dribbled forth.

She was going to kill her.

Millicent was going to KILL KILL KILL KILL KILL KILL KILL KILL KILL KILL KILL KILL KILL KILL KILL KILL KILL KILL KILL KILL KILL KILL KILL KILL KILL…

She was going to freaking KILL HER!

But before she did that, Millicent was going to break Terakomari mentally and emotionally. She was going to make her wish she'd never been born. Punish her for strutting about, showing off like she was some great commander. And she would off Villhaze, too, just to wrap up all the loose ends and settle all her old school scores.

And when all that was done, Millicent would start over. She would go straight and live a decent life.

She swore it.

Vexati

The Vexations
of a Shut-In
Vampire Princess

Yohann Helders was trembling with fear.

For the past two weeks, he'd been staying in the abandoned castle in La Nelient. Now he'd discovered the body of a maid he recognized, nailed to a cross in the chapel located in the heart of the castle.

Blood oozed steadily from where the nails pierced her palms.

Although Yohann couldn't make any sense of the scene, a deep sense of foreboding was unfurling slowly within his chest.

"Hey…what the heck is that all about?"

He turned to Millicent, who was standing beside him. She'd gotten him to follow her here, promising him that she had something "amusing" to show him. But Yohann had no idea what was so amusing about this.

"Can't you tell? That's Villhaze—Gandesblood's maid."

"I know that. She's a sicko, always trailing around after Terakomari. What I want to know is, what is she doing *here*?"

"She's my hostage, duh."

Grinning, Millicent slowly advanced on the maid. She was unconscious, and her head was slumped forward. Millicent reached up and stroked her chin gently.

"I've got the maid, so Terakomari is sure to follow. She's a weakling, yes, but she's nothing if not compassionate. She'll never turn her back on her little companion."

Yohann wasn't on board with this. For one thing, he wasn't sure Terakomari would be brave enough to risk her life for anyone, even if it was a friend of hers. Second, Millicent Blueknight was seriously starting to creep him out.

Their conversation back in the bar had gone like this:

"If we can slaughter Terakomari during the Empress's party, where all the high-society fat cats are gathered, then we'll be able to publicly shame her. No, even better than that. We'll be able to expose the true 'might' of the pathetic, so-called Crimson Lord to every vampire in the country so they can see her for the con artist she really is!"

"Then I'll sneak in and assassinate her," offered Yohann.

"No. That would make you guilty of treason. I'll be the one to actually slay her. I just need you to get me access to the gala."

Yohann had been loath to miss the chance to get into the action, but he hadn't wanted to be guilty of treason, either, so he'd agreed to Millicent's plan. He'd used his army background as leverage to sneak into the venue, where he'd set up a magic gate for Millicent to use later.

But in the end, she hadn't been able to take out her target. All they'd managed to do was ruin the Empress's party. And Terakomari's approval rating remained high even after the ruckus had died down.

After that, Yohann had started to cool off a bit and think more clearly.

When he considered it logically, there were few benefits to be had from teaming up with terrorists. If he wanted to exact revenge, he could get it for himself. If he was going to kill Terakomari, he wanted to do it with his own hands. He had no need for trickery. After all, he was the famed perpetrator of that prison massacre, wasn't he?

Unfortunately, Yohann was already in way over his head.

He couldn't go back to the Seventh Unit, not after all that. And the big brains at the Imperial Palace had figured out that Yohann had been the one who'd constructed the magic gate by examining the magical residue that had been left on the scene.

There was no place in the Mulnite Empire for him anymore.

And so he was stuck with this psychopath, Millicent Bluenight.

"Listen. If I can manage to kill Terakomari, then…"

But Yohann suddenly trailed off. The sight before him left him speechless.

Millicent had just shoved a cursed blade into the maid's shoulder.

It was a sharp, shiny, silver knife, imbued with the power to neutralize the Dark Core's regenerative influence.

The maid's face contorted in agony as crimson blood spurted from the hole. Seeing this, Yohann panicked and dashed forward.

"What are you doing?!" he screamed, grabbing Millicent by the shoulder. "You're going to kill her for real!"

"Kill her for real? You have no idea what you're talking about, do you?"

Yohann froze, a deep feeling of dread seizing him.

Her voice was so cold and inhuman, it made him think of snow blizzards in the bleak midwinter.

"I'm bored. I wanna amuse myself until Terakomari comes. You got a problem with that?"

"B-but there's no need to use a cursed knife, is there? The wound won't heal if you do that…"

"…Weren't you the one who was talking about wanting to get revenge on Terakomari? Doesn't that involve murdering her?"

"Yeah, but it's not like *really* killing someone."

"I'll terminate *you* if you don't stop annoying me."

Yohann felt like a scared rabbit, hypnotized by the eyes of a venomous snake.

She slowly turned to fix her cold-blooded murderer's gaze on him.

"It looks like you're not prepared to be an Inverse Moon coconspirator. But let me ask you this: What's the point of butchering someone if they won't stay dead? Go on. Tell me."

"It…it can be useful for wars and stuff."

"Uh-huh. You know, I thought you were like me, but I was wrong."

Millicent grinned faintly before plucking the dagger out of the maid's shoulder and switching it to her left hand. Yohann watched her, sweat sliding down his forehead. Not being a true killer himself, Yohann could never have predicted what would happen next. Without a second's hesitation, Millicent buried the knife up to its handle in his chest.

The neighborhood of La Nelient was a slum comprising most of the Imperial Capital's poorest district. Usually, I wouldn't have dreamed of setting foot in a place like that, but today I was fired up and feeling brave enough to face it.

The air was stagnant, and the town was gray and gloomy.

I kept my eyes averted from the ramshackle houses lining the roads, but fortunately, no one tried to speak to me.

Perhaps my Mulnite Imperial Army uniform intimidated them. And it wasn't the regular uniform, either. It was custom-made, with the full moon crest that identified me as a high-ranking commander.

I made my way through town, heart pounding. Finally, my objective came into view up ahead: the abandoned old castle.

According to the official records, it had once been a vacation home for some rich guy. But he'd disappeared without a trace one day, so now its sole inhabitants were tramps and wild animals.

Taking a deep breath, I passed through the gates.

I was on my way to confront Millicent directly. Though I was obviously prepared, I still found myself trembling with fear. I wanted to turn and run home with my tail between my legs.

But as much as I wanted to, I couldn't do that. I promised myself that I would try to make a clean break with my past.

I took another deep breath and stepped through a large hole in the castle wall to gain access to the building. It was dark and dreary inside, like a graveyard. Maneuvering my way through the rubble and pieces of broken furniture, I continued onward until I came across a strange door. At one point it must have been quite elegant, what with its ornate carving, but now it was a mess of rust and mold.

I paused in front of the door. Somehow I knew.

This was the place. Beyond this door, Vill and Millicent awaited me.

Swallowing hard, I placed my shaking hand on the entrance and pushed against it.

The portal creaked slowly open to reveal what looked like an old church. So the guy who'd owned this castle had been a religious type. That was interesting. As I took a step inside…

"So you've come, Terakomari."

The sound of my name in the gloom made my heart leap almost out of my chest.

When my vision came into focus, I saw Millicent, standing by the altar. She was holding a silver knife in her right hand, while the other was thrust into her pocket. Her reptilian eyes glittered as they gazed straight into me.

I was so terrified, I was certain my knees were about to buckle.

But when my gaze shifted to who was behind Millicent, I forgot my fear completely. Shock and concern replaced all my other emotions.

My maid was nailed to a cross.

"Vill!"

"Whoa, whoa, no need to panic. She's not dead yet. She will be soon enough, though.

"…Hya-ha-ha!" Millicent's shrill laughter pierced the air.

I clenched my trembling hands into tight fists, glaring right at her.

"…Return Vill to me."

"Now, now, no need to be so hasty. Not when you and I finally have the opportunity for a nice private chat. You must have a thing or two you want to say to me?"

"Not really."

"Well, I do."

She jumped down from the altar and started heading toward me with heavy footsteps.

"Listen, Terakomari. Do you have any idea how much I've suffered since that day?"

"What day? What are you…?"

"It happened exactly three years ago. The day I tried to take your pendant."

"…"

I remembered. The event that had caused me to become a shut-in.

After that day, Millicent had stopped attending the Academy…

"My life's been upside down since that day. Your jerk father framed me and my entire family for treason and had us cast out of the country."

"What?"

"I was chased out of the Academy, chased out of the country, I lost contact with my family, became homeless…and then finally I joined the terrorist group…Inverse Moon. While you were enjoying a cushy shut-in life in your mansion, I was crawling about in the gutter!"

Millicent continued to rant, fidgeting agitatedly with the knife.

"You're the cause of everything that went wrong for me, Terakomari. Yes, I found my brethren in Inverse Moon after I got banished from the country. But that was just a happy coincidence. Although I do agree with their ideologies. The power of Core Implosion, and our slogan: *Life in the Shadow of Death Is Mankind's Long-Cherished Desire*. But the true passion burning within me has nothing to do with terrorist ideology. No, it's my desire for vengeance that has sustained me these three long years. My lust to permanently kill you. That is all I really care about."

"Wh-what? But you started picking on me to begin with!"

"And I'll finish it. My soul is burned black with hatred for you. If I continue to do nothing, I know it will incinerate completely and crumble to ash. So that's why I picked this auspicious date to lure you to me for the final showdown. Now we can settle the old score, once and for all. Yes, this is my ritual rebirth ceremony, where I will wipe you off the face of the earth and begin my new life, my soul washed clean."

"…"

Finally, it all made sense to me.

Millicent wasn't so different from me after all. She hadn't been able to process the trauma of what had happened three years ago; she'd struggled through life with so much unresolved. In that case, there was no chance we'd come to a peaceful resolution. The thick wad of bank notes I'd brought on the off chance I could pay her to leave me alone would be of no use.

"I get how you feel. I understand how you must want to kill me for real."

"Don't try to empathize with me. You can cry and beg and use your little tactics all you want, but you'll never get away. I'm going to murder you slowly, with my bare hands. Yeah. I'm going to scramble you up like an omelet. One that oozes bright red, ketchup-like blood. Your favorite dish, isn't it? Omelets over rice?"

"What? No, I actually much prefer Salisbury steaks, and—"

"Then I'll grind you up like hamburger meat!!!"

"Wait, I don't follow…"

"Silence, Terakomari! Don't antagonize her any further!"

I heard a desperate squawk from a corner of the chapel and turned to see the blond youth…Yohann Helders. He was staggering in the shadows, bleeding from the midsection. He was the last person I would have expected to see here. But Yohann continued to gaze at me with earnest, panicked eyes.

"She's nothing but an insane murderer! A runt of a vampire girl like you has no hope against her! If you value your life, you'll run!"

"What are you doing here?"

"Never mind that! Just flee! She's insane, and she's got cursed weapons! Look! See this chest wound? It hurts! It won't heal!"

"I see…"

I clenched my fists.

"I'm sorry I was too late. I'll come and help you shortly. Just hold on."

Yohann's jaw dropped.

Then it closed again. "You're a fool!" he yelled, bursting into tears. "You're the biggest idiot alive! I teamed up with this psychopath to assassinate you, did you know that? There's nothing you can do anymore! She's completely cold-blooded! Millicent is on a whole different level compared to those army brawlers. Just forget about the maid and run awa-GLUH!"

Yohann's body flew into the air.

Millicent's Magic Bullet hit him in the legs and knocked them out from underneath him, leaving him crawling on the ground, squealing.

I gasped.

Millicent was truly evil. She saw people as nothing more than cockroaches.

"Shut up, worm. Terakomari and I are about to duel to the death. Her death."

Millicent threatened Yohann with her silver knife, a cursed weapon that would block the regenerative powers of the Dark Core. If she cut his carotid artery with that, he would permanently expire.

There was no way I could let that happen.

Seeing one of my soldiers being threatened this way, I felt an indignant fire begin to burn inside my belly.

It was…rage. Rage like I'd never experienced before in my life.

I dug into my uniform pocket and withdrew a vibrant stone, which I immediately threw.

"What?! A Magic Stone?!"

Millicent's eyes widened.

The Magic Stone flew before landing at Yohann's feet and exploding.

"Yaaaaargh!!!"

Yohann screamed as the blast knocked him flat. But now he was safe from Millicent's assault. I'd managed to take him out with the Magic Stone before she'd had an opportunity to use one of her cursed weapons on him. He would be all right now—safe, at least, until he regenerated.

"Gack, gahhh! …Ha-ha-ha! Very nice, Terakomari! So you did come here prepared to throw down!"

As the smoke cleared, a skinny silhouette came into view.

Sweating, I thrust my hand back into my pocket again. I hadn't been able to bring that many Magic Stones with me, so I wanted to neutralize Millicent quickly before I ran out of options.

As my field of vision cleared, she and I locked eyes. She was grinning like a shark.

And then, before I even knew what was happening, a rain of Magic Bullets came flying at my face.

Around this time, Komari's father, Armand Gandesblood, came sprinting into the Imperial Palace.

Komari had disappeared from the house all of a sudden. And what's more, he'd discovered a large amount of blood in her room. Obviously, something terrible had happened.

"Empress! It's Komari! She's missing!"

Armand burst into the audience chamber and began yelling without any preamble. But the Empress's reaction made him skid to a halt, and soon he was scowling at how casually she was draped across her throne, with her long blond hair and big boobs and utter disregard for the usual process of aging. "Gone, you say?" she inquired.

"Yes. She just disappeared! I don't even know how long she's been missing!"

"And you're only realizing this now?"

"What?" Armand was confused.

The Empress heaved a huge sigh.

"You always were a shockingly dim-witted man-thing, weren't you? Komari left the Gandesblood mansion an hour ago. Millicent captured Villhaze to use as bait. Your daughter has gone to save her by heading into the belly of the beast all by herself. My informants reported everything directly to me."

"Th-then why...?"

"Why am I still sitting here, you mean? Well, let me ask you this... what good will it do her to have me intervene?"

"But if you don't, she'll get killed! You're just going to turn your back on her?!"

"I'm not going to turn my back on her. Komari is my child. Mine and Yulinne's."

"Don't distort facts. Komari is my daughter."

"Never mind the reproductive semantics. You've been far too over-protective of that girl. None of this would have happened if you hadn't gone nuclear on the Bluenight family. Letting Komari handle this herself is the best thing for her. She needs to make a clean break with the past, and she needs to do it by herself. This is a fine opportunity if you ask me."

"That's...that's too harsh!"

"Now, now, don't misunderstand me. I'm a vampire, not a demon. I'll step in if things start looking grim; you can count on that. But I don't think it will be necessary."

"I don't get it."

"But you should know this better than anyone. That girl isn't normal. In fact, when it comes to weirdness, she tops even me."

"..."

There was a short, loaded silence. Then...

"Excuse me! Empress! Urgent news!"

A female servant came crashing into the audience chamber in total dismay. Her cheeks were bright red, and she was panting hard. The Empress twitched a brow in response.

"What's wrong? Why are you so red and sweaty? Would you like to hop in the bath with me, hmm? Or I could lick it off for you..."

The servant ignored this blatant sexual harassment in favor of delivering her message.

"The Seventh Unit! They've gone wild! Rogue! They've invaded the lower-class district of the capital!"

"La Nelient, eh? Slumming it, are we, Commander?"

Dusk had fallen, and a mob was advancing through the capital and picking up speed.

The group consisted of all five hundred vampires from the Seventh Unit. The Komari Unit.

They were an unruly bunch who lacked the discipline to keep in formation, all running and jostling together with their bloodlust shooting sky-high. Little did they notice the alarmed townspeople who rushed to lock their doors as they passed. They were too focused on their mission.

"Hmm. We'll pay for this later, mark my words," Bellius muttered darkly to himself. Yet he, too, was jogging along with the mob while ignoring the lingering pain in his belly. He wanted to fight alongside the commander just as much as the rest of his crew. Caostel grinned beside him.

"Who cares what they do to us? The commander has been seized with the urge to slaughter! We can't just sit back at HQ twiddling our thumbs while she embarks on a monumental duel all alone!"

Bellius was the only one who'd given any real thought to what might come after this insurgency. The others, however, had been overtaken by battle fever and their desire to reach the side of their beloved commander. The Seventh Unit was a band of scofflaws so nefarious that parents would threaten naughty children with a visit from them. They thought nothing of turning their backs on authority and pursuing their own goals.

Right now, they were advancing on the lower-class district of the Imperial Capital, known as La Nelient.

Yes, they knew exactly where their beloved commander was.

When she'd run off earlier, she'd neglected to inform her officers where she was going. But Caostel had remembered his *Web of Attraction* spell. All he'd needed to power it was a piece of Komari. Sadly, however, he'd lost his much-beloved strand of hair in the process. As he was wailing loudly about this, Mellaconcey suddenly interrupted him by pushing a golden lock into his hand.

"I gotcha, bro!"

"Huh?"

"Check it! The commander's bedroom is what I infiltrated! What I found was a pillow hair, nothing X-rated! So I pocketed the hair, no one even saw me there, and now we can get our commander relocated!"

Mellaconcey, of course, met a swift pummeling from the other troops, who were completely fed up with his rapping schtick by now.

At any rate, the commander's position had been easy to deduce after that. She'd warned them not to follow her, but there was no way they were going to obey that order. After all, Squad Komari was a band of outlaws. They were always ready to break the rules and cause chaos. They lived for anarchy. The commander could lecture them, stamp on them, or wring their necks if she liked. None of that could put them off once the battle-lust swept them up.

"Hold on, Commander! We are coming to assist!"

""""RAAAAAGH!!!""""

The crowd of vampires, the Komari Unit, raised their voices as one in a booming battle cry as they continued their rampage through the streets.

I slid under a bench, narrowly avoiding Millicent's magical strike. As I cowered, a rain of Magic Bullets ate holes in the walls, pews, and door of the chapel.

"Come now, Terakomari! Don't just cower under the benches like a little church mouse! I'm going to kill your darling maid, you know!"

"Curses…!"

Waiting for a bullet to zip past my nose, I gathered my courage and scurried out from under the bench. At this, Millicent grinned widely. As she readied another Magic Bullet, I whipped out another Magic Stone, this one a *Barrier Wall*, and threw it on the ground.

A magical wall sprang up between us out of nowhere, which Millicent's Magic Bullets instantly studded.

She blasted bullet after bullet at the wall, but the *Barrier Wall* held firm.

Good. I produced another Magic Stone. Next up, something with some oomph. Maybe even the strongest one I had, to stop Millicent in her tracks…

"Guh!"

A dull pain flared in my shoulder.

She got me. Somehow. A hole must have opened in the *Barrier Wall*. Then Millicent deftly shot a bullet right through the hole and struck me in the shoulder. My Magic Stones fell from my pocket and scattered across the floor. As I scrambled to pick them up, the *Barrier Wall* shattered to pieces, accompanied by an immense crash.

Crap, I thought, but it was too late.

I heard another *bang*, signaling a fresh attack.

A Magic Bullet tore into the flesh of my other shoulder. The force of the impact sent me flying backward, and I rolled across the ground before smashing into the wall and slamming my head on the stone.

Mewling, I tried to rise to my feet, but I couldn't manage it.

The pain hit me a few seconds later.

It was like being on fire. Blood was pumping from my shoulder, almost in rhythm with my heartbeat. Tears began to flow. Even though I clutched the wound, the pain just wouldn't cease. For the first time ever, I felt the encroaching shadow of death, and all the fear that came with it.

"What are you even doing? Relax. I'm not going to wipe you out this soon. Where would be the fun in that?"

Twirling her silver knife, Millicent cackled.

Of course. It had only been a Magic Bullet, not one of her cursed weapons. The power of the Dark Core would heal my injuries in time.

It still hurt, though. Like, a lot! And it wouldn't stop gushing. Why was I having to go through so much pain? Why did I…?

Just then my gaze went to Vill, hanging on the cross.

She was a pitiable sight.

Her body was covered in various wounds, a small river of blood puddling beneath her. Her hands and feet were nailed to the boards, and the weight of her body looked to be opening those cuts even more as time passed.

Compared to what Vill was going through, crying over a little shoulder pain like this seemed silly.

Let Millicent kill me in a place like this? No way.

"Ah-ha! You can still stand? Very good, Terakomari!"

Clutching the wall, I managed to drag myself to my feet. My entire body ached, and my legs were trembling. I felt numb with fear. But I refused to let this foul terrorist get away with what she'd done.

"You'll never beat me!"

Millicent practically hopped with glee.

"Oh, how fascinating! You've got more moxie than I credited you for! Now, where do you want the next hit? In the chest? The belly? Or should I mess up that lovely face of yours? You're an absolute knock-out beauty, right? Well, how about if I absolutely knock you out, you scrawny wench?"

"...Don't forget the part about me having a rare scholarly intellect as well."

"Are you...are you completely insane?!"

"Are YOU?! You psycho terrorist!"

Flinging a Magic Stone with all my might, I set off at a run. I was aiming to get as close to her as possible, where my stones would be most effective, and she wouldn't have the space to unleash her Magic Bullets.

"Hya-ha-ha! A kamikaze attack? You really have lost your marbles, Terakomari!"

She fired another bullet at me, which grazed my ear. I couldn't even feel it. I didn't have time. I ducked as another came right at me.

"Explode, Magic Stone!"

I squeezed my eyes shut as the Magic Stone I'd just hurled suddenly exploded.

Then came a blinding flash of light.

This stone was called *White Flash*, a special type of light magic meant for temporarily blinding your opponent.

"You...you impudent little witch!" Millicent hissed, one arm covering her eyes. With her free hand, she blasted Magic Bullets wildly all over the room. The benches, stained glass, and holy statues were immediately peppered with holes. *Stay firm, Komari! You've almost got her!*

Dodging and weaving between the rounds, I finally reached Millicent.

She opened her eyes and stared at me.

But I'd already shoved a Magic Stone up against her stomach.

"What are you...?"

"Magic Stone! *Shock Wave!*"

A blast went off, and the force of the shock wave blew her backward. I remained on the move, chasing after her even as she flew. When she landed on the floor with a heavy *thud*, I activated another Magic Stone, *Falling Rocks*. As it activated, a heap of rubble began to form, hovering precariously high up above, right on top of her.

"Eat it, Millicent!!!"

"What the—"

But it was too late. The heap of rubble came slamming down on Millicent like a ton of bricks. Her scream was awful. The sound of her bones breaking was impossibly loud, like dry sticks crackling on a fire. But I wasn't done yet. Just for good measure, I conjured up another heap of *Falling Rocks*. The pile of rubble fell like meteors, crushing Millicent into the stone floor.

The entire chapel shook from the force of the impact.

This time, Millicent didn't scream. There was a brief clattering, as if she was still stirring under the rubble heap, but then it ceased. She moved no more.

But I still couldn't relax. I was already readying another Magic Stone. She was clearly dead.

But I was still terrified, and I couldn't be sure I'd won.

Terrible, tenacious Millicent, going down that easily? No way. *Surely low-level Magic Stone incantations couldn't have taken her out...was* what I kept telling myself. Mostly, I didn't want to believe that I'd actually just killed someone.

But Millicent remained silent. And very still.

I let out a huge gasp of air and crouched down on the floor.

I did it. I did it! Finally I could be reborn and leave my shut-in past behind.

But no…it was too early for celebrations. I leaped to my feet and ran over to Vill, strung up above the altar like a martyr.

"Vill! Are you all right?!"

She gave no response, merely hanging there as blood oozed from her many wounds.

I could pull her down and carry her home on my back. Just as I was about to climb up on the altar, it happened.

Something hit me in the back of my legs.

"Huh?"

I looked down, blinking.

Sticking out from the back of my calf was a silver dagger.

A blood-drenched hand gripped its hilt. I traced the arm to see Millicent's demonic face, her eyes burning into mine.

"Hya-ha-ha!!! Nice moves, Terakomari!"

I couldn't even croak in response. My throat had locked up.

She plucked the blade from my leg with a sickening sound. Unable to stand a second longer, I plunged to the ground. And there I lay, too shocked to move. She had stabbed me. With that silver knife. The cursed weapon, the one that canceled out the Dark Core's influence…

The pain was searing. And it was traveling up my spine.

I could hear myself screaming.

Tears spouted from my eyes. Drool hung out of my mouth. The sensation was unbearable. It felt like my flesh was on fire. And this wound would never heal. This pain would never end. As that realization struck me, fear overtook me, and I almost passed out. But my reflexes were still firing, so I found myself rolling across the floor, trying to get away from Millicent.

"Huh? Terakomari? Where do you think you're going?"

"Gluck!"

Millicent's boot landed hard on my stomach, knocking the wind out of me. I looked up. She was standing over me, grinning down.

"Why…?"

"Why am I still alive? Hya-ha-ha! Are you an idiot?! You think low-level Magic Stones could ever kill me?"

Then she reached down and grabbed me by the neck.

I flinched, averting my gaze. I couldn't bear to look at her demonic visage up close. There was a pile of rubble across the room. Millicent must have cast a protective incantation at the last moment. But that didn't matter now.

"Does it hurt? It does, doesn't it? It must. Look how much you're bleeding!"

"S-stop it…"

"Make me!!!"

Fireworks were going off behind my eyes. She must have punched me. I found myself rolling across the floor again. Though I tried to scramble to my feet, the pain in my leg was too much. Stumbling over, I crashed down on the stone floor once more.

Millicent's guffawing was almost obscene.

"Ah, you're really trying your hardest, aren't you, Terakomari? I didn't even credit you with getting this far."

Her boots clacked over the stone floor as she approached me. I couldn't stop shivering.

The silver dagger flashed.

"You're the same sniveling worm who tried to kill me three years ago. You always were a stuck-up crybaby brat. You haven't changed a bit. Oh, you tried to change, that's obvious, but your efforts were futile. You should just let yourself get exterminated like a bug. That way, not a trace of your miserable existence will be left behind."

I was sobbing now. Snot streamed down my face, but I didn't care about dignity or shame anymore.

My whole body throbbed. The shot to my shoulder, the stab wound on my leg, my cheek where she'd punched me. And the mental wounds. They all hurt so much.

"You're just going to lie there weeping? You think that's going to get you anywhere? The world's not that kind! You don't know anything about the world, but after I was banished from the country, I learned fast! I learned that no one's coming to help you if you cry. The only thing you can ever rely on is your own strength!"

"Sh-shut up...I'm...not crying. I'm not..."

"Quit trying to look brave!!!"

Millicent shot another Magic Bullet into my side. I must have been suffering from nerve damage because I felt no pain there. But then she advanced on me again, her face twisted. She raised her boot and slammed it against my stomach.

"Guhhh!"

I wasn't able to dodge it. All I could do was clutch my stomach and roll around in agony.

"Hya-ha-ha! You're pathetic!"

Grabbing a handful of my hair and pulling me up by it, Millicent continued to cackle.

"Ha-ha! Shall I turn you into an omelet now? Hmm?"

"Seems like you...like omelets...more than I do..."

"So what if I do?!"

She smashed my face into the floor.

My vision went white for a few moments, and I completely lost all my bearings.

"How about you get on with it and whip out your Core Implosion already? That'll hurry things along. I've been preparing for three years, so even if you do use it, it won't inconvenience me that much, I reckon."

I had no idea what she was talking about.

When I didn't respond, Millicent screamed at me again.

"What? You need some special trigger to evoke it? Or you just don't feel like using it? You lost your will to fight, is that it?"

"…"

"Say something!"

She screamed in my ear so loudly that it felt like my head would split open.

Then she spat with fury and disgust.

"You really seem totally unaware of everything. You came here to confront me because you were planning to rely on Core Implosion, right?"

"I don't…know what that is."

"So why did you come here, then? Surely you didn't think you could overcome me using your basic, low-level magic skills, hmm? I mean, you can't seriously be that stupid, can you?"

I could, actually.

Anyway, it wasn't a question of winning or losing.

It was about living or dying…

"I came here for…Vill."

The words came out in a sob. Bloody spittle flew from my lips.

But I kept speaking.

"I came here to rescue Vill. I know I'm short, and I'm clumsy, and I can't use magic, and I'm a stupid, useless waste of a vampire… I was so afraid to come here that my legs were quivering the whole way. I tried to turn back so many times…but I don't want to run away anymore!"

It hurt to breathe.

But still, I kept going.

"I can't waste any more of my life shut up in my room! That's why I showed up! I know I'm frail, I know it! But I had to try! I had to do my best for my friends, who have always cared for me!"

"…"

Was it my imagination, or did Millicent just take a step back?

It probably was my imagination.

Because she immediately erupted into fury and started screaming at me again.

"Do your best? Cut the bullshit! If we could all just get what we wanted by doing our best, then no one would ever have to suffer!"

She kicked me in the stomach again. I wanted to say something else, but I couldn't form the words.

Millicent sighed, gazing down at me with disgust.

"Pathetic. You're truly pathetic. How can you face me, knowing you're that weak? I don't get it. But whatever. I'll put you out of your misery soon enough. After that…yeah, I'm going to crush the Mulnite Empire. This country is full of nothing but weakling losers like you. I'll kill every last one of them."

"…"

She was a demon. She had no soul.

Millicent had said something about me and her not being so different, but she was so wrong about that. She hadn't changed at all from three years ago. She hadn't even tried.

She was nothing but a murderer whose moral compass had warped beyond all repair. She found joy in nothing but inflicting pain on others.

My body hurt so badly, I couldn't seem to move.

But just as I was about to give up for real…

"All right, I think I'll kill the maid first. Watch closely, Terakomari. Your beloved maid friend is about to turn into a cold slab of vampire meat."

What?

Kill…Vill?

"Ah, it looks like she's still asleep. I'd prefer to execute her while she's awake. Then I can savor the look of agony and terror on her face. Hmm. Maybe she'll wake up if I cut her a little?"

Millicent took a step forward.

Turning the silver knife over and over in her right hand, her face a mask of demonic intent…

Wait.

I can't let you do this.

I can't give up. Not now.

"…Stop."

Millicent paused.

Slowly I staggered to my feet. Gathering the last dregs of my courage and anger, I raised my head and stared right into her devilish eyes.

"I won't let you hurt Vill. I'm…going to take you down."

She smacked her lips.

"Look, could you just get on with it if you're going to attack me? You don't have to announce everything first. Get it together; unless you want to go down like a worm."

"I'm not going to…die. I'm not gonna let a scumbag like you take me out."

No, there was no way I could give up.

Because Vill had always been there for me after all.

I couldn't just abandon her.

Besides, I was an commander. A Crimson Lord! What commander could stand down while one of her officers was being executed?

So I had no other choice. I was going to have to kill Millicent Bluenight.

"Raaaagh!!!"

My battle cry was pretty impressive, but I only had enough strength to limp weakly toward her.

I didn't have a specific plan in mind. I was just running on impulse. If only I could get off one good shot to the kisser… I just had to gather all the strength I had left and…

"You piss me off!!!"

Her roundhouse kick struck me right in the face. Since I hadn't been able to brace myself against it, I tumbled backward. Still, I refused to give up. Slipping a little in the puddle of blood beneath me, I staggered to my feet once more.

"I'm not done yet. I can still fight."

"Shut UP! You piss me off so bad!!!"

A barrage of Magic Bullets came flying my way. One hit my cheek. One pierced my shoulder. One grazed me in the side. Blood was spurting from my many wounds. But I still wouldn't give in. The injuries would heal soon enough. She could break my arm, she could cause me to bleed internally…I didn't care. I would just keep going.

"I won't let you do this! I'm taking Vill, and we're going home!"

"Oh, shut up, Miss High-and-Mighty! You shut-in LOSER!"

"I'm not a recluse anymore! I'm going to defeat you, then walk an entirely new path in life!"

"Walk a new path? I'll break your legs like little sticks! See how far you can walk then!!!"

"I won't let you beat me! You're a nasty person who delights in tormenting others!!! I'm not letting a scumbag like you get the best of me! I'm going to see you get what you deserve!"

"Hah! Come on and try it, you little…!!!"

Millicent raised both hands. I could sense magical power charging up inside her. Yikes. This wasn't looking good…but it was too late. A Magic Circle had formed itself in front of her. Then, with an ear-piercing sound, a laser shot up from the Magic Circle.

This was advanced-level magic…the *Heretic Ray.*

I couldn't run from it. Not only was I not fast enough, I also couldn't bear to turn my back on Vill and leave her there.

"…!!!"

The next thing I knew, the blast hit me full-on.

Everything went white. I almost lost consciousness completely, but I managed to just about hold on. Fresh wounds opened. My blood vessels popped. This time, I was definitely a goner. I was sure of it. My body rocketed through the air.

The next thing I knew, I was lying on the stone floor, gazing up at the ceiling.

I couldn't move. At all. Couldn't even twitch my fingers.

She must have completely destroyed my pain receptors because I couldn't feel a thing, even though my body was in complete tatters.

I was…going to succumb.

I couldn't bear it. It was so unfair. I couldn't defeat Millicent. I couldn't save Vill. I was going to die a weakling, a shut-in loser vampire. And there was nothing I could do about it.

I hated that it was going to end like this.

After I'd been so strong and shown such un-Komaristic bravery, too...

What kind of an ending was this?

"Lady Komari..."

But as I wept to myself in total despair, I heard a voice.

At first, I thought it was a hallucination. But it wasn't. Apparently, I'd rolled right under the altar. When I looked up, I realized I was looking right up Vill's skirt.

She was wearing...black panties.

Wait, why was I looking at this?! I'm not a pervert! I just...lost my mind from being near death. Yeah.

"Lady Komari."

I shook my head. This was no time to be worrying about panties!

My maid had regained consciousness.

"Vill...I'm sorry... I couldn't...save you."

Blood dribbled from my lips. After that, my words completely stopped. I tried, but all that came out was a wet, wheezing sound.

She smiled at me, bloody tears dripping down her cheeks.

"Thank you. You came to my rescue once again."

No. You've got it wrong, Vill.

I hadn't been able to do anything. I'd just recklessly sprinted out of my bedroom right into my own death trap. What a rare scholarly intellect I had. Not.

"Don't look so sad. You did great. And you're not a shut-in vampire anymore. You can hold your head up and live with pride now."

No, I couldn't. I really was a useless, frail, shut-in vampire. But Vill seemed to read my mind just then. Her smile widened.

Then I blinked in shock.

With immense strength, Vill just tore her right hand free from the nail that had bound it to the cross. The nail popped off, and a fresh river of blood began to flow from her tattered hand. It looked super painful. She grimaced for a moment, but then her usual calm expression returned.

"You're the strongest, kindest person in the world. But you don't have any self-confidence. That's why you always look so worried."

She slowly raised her reddened right hand.

Her white fingers trembled in the air above me, so pale, like the belly of a dead fish.

Then a droplet of blood trickled down to the tip of her finger…

"Still alive, are we, Terakomareee?!!!"

A sudden, deranged shout shook the room.

Obviously, it had come from Millicent. I couldn't see her, but I could hear her murderous footsteps treading closer and closer.

"Stop right there, Terakomareee!!! I'm going to slice you up with my *Silver Blade of Doom!*"

Oh gosh, she really was going to butcher me. But I couldn't get my body into gear. It had given up.

Suddenly, everything went sharply into focus.

I saw Vill's trembling finger. The deep red droplet of blood. The source of all magical power. A vampire's finest source of nourishment. My most hated food.

"Please forgive me, Lady Komari. You can punish me as hard as you like later."

The apology was merely a formality.

A scarlet droplet of blood fell from Vill's fingertip.

It fell straight down with incredible speed, landing and splashing on my lips.

High above the ruined castle, the skies turned bloodred.

The entirety of a person's future, condensed to a tiny grain of light, embedded into her brain.

What a thrilling sight it was. She had never before seen a future so grand and vast. Of all the futures she'd viewed since she'd obtained her power of *Pandora's Poison*, never before had she encountered an individual with such potential. Terakomari Gandesblood could go anywhere. Do anything. It was all right there.

Ah, yes. She saw everything.

No matter what happened, Lady Komari would never be broken.

She smiled. It was a grin of deep relief. To know that the woman she adored so much had such a beautiful, glittering future ahead of her.

"Komari. You're going to win. I swear it."

As those words left her lips, Villhaze shut her bloodstained eyelids and went limp.

"So as I was saying, Empress, we need to mobilize the army to the downtown area at once!"

"It is mobilized. Well, the Seventh Unit is."

"That's not the army! That's a band of savage vigilantes!"

"How dare you speak badly of the Empire's loyal soldiers? Ah, hold on a second."

The Empress raised a finger, silencing Armand as she lazed on the throne. Frowning, she looked upward. Armand blinked at her. This was an emergency. What was she doing? He waited in exasperation for her to resume speaking.

The busty blond Empress grinned.

"It seems the die is already cast."

"What? Empress, I don't understand."

"Try using your brain. I just sensed a huge magical surge, coming from the outskirts of the city. In other words...Komari has ingested...*blood*."

"What?!"

Cold sweat slid down his cheeks. In that case, there would be no going back.

But the Empress was still smiling triumphantly.

"The issue is settled, then, isn't it?"

"...Are you insane? Do you have any idea how hard I've worked to keep that girl away from drinking blood all these years?"

"Calm yourself. An incident like the one that happened three years ago won't occur this time. Probably."

"But..."

"Don't you have any faith in your own daughter? Since becoming a Crimson Lord, she's met so many people and has cast off the shackles of her loser persona. The girl she is now...that girl has heart. She won't lose herself just from ingesting a little blood. Although her physical form might be affected a bit..."

"..."

Armand gnashed his teeth.

Komari hated blood...because he'd hypnotized her into believing she did.

She didn't know this herself, of course, but the girl possessed a fearsome and terrific power.

Core Implosion. An extremely rare ability. It allowed one to deliberately cancel out the Dark Core's influence and tap into their latent, natural power. A highly unorthodox and shadowy skill.

In Komari's case, she could only invoke her abilities by partaking in the blood of someone else's veins.

Until this point, Komari had evoked Core Implosion only three times.

The first time had been when she was three years old, when she tasted blood for the first time at the dinner table. Not a single vampire present in the Gandesblood residence at the time survived that incident.

The second time had been when she was ten years old. A newly hired maid served Komari a dish with blood in it, and the girl slaughtered her before she even had time to blink.

The third time had been when she was twelve. During a skirmish with a bully at school, blood had gotten into Komari's mouth somehow or another. The bully died before she even knew what had happened. To make matters worse, Komari went on to indiscriminately slaughter the staff, the pupils, the members of the Third Unit who'd been sent in to help, as well as the Crimson Lords.

In other words, blood turned Komari into a ruthless, indiscriminate murderer. But now this woman, this half-mad Empress who'd manipulated things *on purpose* to spark another such incident, was lounging on a chair and smiling blithely at Armand.

"The Seven Crimson Lords specialize in the art of murder. The existence of any weaklings in the group brings down the reputation of the Empire. But I appointed Komari as a Crimson Lord not just to bolster her confidence, but also because she really is an *excellent* candidate for the job."

"You're insane."

"Ah, yes, I can't wait to see it! Show me, Terakomari! The sublime Core Implosion technique, unprecedented in the entirety of the Empire's thousand-year history, *Blood Curse*!!!"

She gazed upward with a rapturous expression on her face.

High above the palace skylight shone a gorgeous crimson full moon.

The vampires of the Komari Unit, having breached the walls of the abandoned castle, arrived at the chapel to be greeted with a stunning sight.

A *bizarre* sight.

The floors were awash with the blood of a person or persons unknown. A blue-haired girl was standing in the middle of the chapel holding a silver knife. She was unmistakably the terrorist who had attacked the Empress's party.

Usually, the soldiers wouldn't hesitate to attack her on sight. But right now they were stunned and silent. All were gazing at the girl strung up at the back of the church, above the altar.

It was the maid, nailed to a cross.

And below her, their beloved leader, Commander Terakomari Gandesblood, lay slumped.

Could the commander really have fallen to the terrorist girl?

As the troops stood there shifting uneasily, fear and doubt beginning to gnaw at their minds, they noticed a sudden movement.

The commander was stirring, slowly rising to a sitting position like a corpse rising from the grave. Her clothes were tattered and torn, she was smeared liberally with blood, and her expression was as frigid as ice…

Her tiny rosebud lips moved.

"I'm gonna kill you."

Then, a gust of scarlet-colored magical energy swept through the church with a roar. And not just through the church. Through the entire castle, through the entire slum district, through the Imperial Capital, and then throughout the entire Empire, staining the skies above a deep crimson.

The Seventh Unit froze.

Confusion, anxiety. Obviously, they were experiencing those emotions. But above all else, what made the vampires tremble was an overwhelming sense of awe and delight.

The commander had turned the skies red.

The true power of Terakomari Gandesblood…unveiled to them all at last.

"Commander…"

One of the soldiers in the mob gasped her name, and a wave of voices quickly followed.

"Commander!" "Commander Komari!" "Finally, the commander has unleashed her full power!" "Please, exterminate the terrorist, Commander!" "Ko-ma-rin! Ko-ma-rin! Ko-ma-rin!"

The vampires were getting more and more fired up, and their individual yells soon turned into a united chant as the people called for their leader. In the midst of all the fervor that was currently shaking the walls of the church, Commander Komari herself simply stood silently, her cold gaze fixed on her bitter enemy.

©riichu

★

Millicent was frowning.

How could Terakomari be standing after the colossal beating she'd just given her? And how had she attained the awe-inspiring, plainly overwhelmingly destructive magical power that was currently emanating from her like an aura?

Behind her, the cheers grew louder.

The chapel had suddenly filled up with vampires clad in army uniforms. Where they came from, Millicent had no idea. She must have called in her troops… Millicent turned back to face Komari, grinding her teeth together.

"Terakomari, remember when I told you I'd kill you if you blabbed about our secret meeting? That cross up there is rigged up with bombs. All I have to do is shoot one tiny magic beam at them and then—"

Millicent stopped talking and gasped.

She was gone.

Terakomari had vanished.

Millicent looked around in confusion and dismay. This couldn't be. Where had the girl escaped to? She'd been standing right there a second ago! Millicent felt a cold bead of sweat slide down her back as…

…She recoiled from a powerful blow to the stomach.

"Guh! Gah!!!"

Millicent let out an anguished scream but somehow managed to stay on her feet.

Eyes widening, she looked down at her stomach. A gaping wound had formed there, from which blood had already started to gush. It felt as though her guts had been ripped from her body. Was that what Komari had been trying to do?! When the realization dawned on her, she pulled back her lips in a roar.

"The heck do you think you're doiiinggg??!?!?!!"

The soldiers whooped and hollered in approval. Millicent turned back around to find Terakomari now standing about ten feet away.

Her red eyes were sparkling. And they looked even redder than before…a deep, crimson hue. Her right hand was raised, dripping with Millicent's blood. She looked like some sort of monster. There was nothing left of her that resembled the weak little bullied girl she'd once been.

Komari didn't speak. She simply stared at Millicent.

"What the heck? Is this…is this Core Implosion…?"

"…"

"Say something! Look, you've ripped out a chunk of my stomach! How are you planning to make up for that, huh?!"

"…You."

"What? Can't hear you!"

"…Gonna *kill* you."

Terakomari stamped, sending a shock wave of crimson-colored magical energy shooting toward Millicent at breakneck speed. Stiffening with terror, Millicent immediately started firing off Magic Bullets. Jets of light emerged from her outstretched fingertips, lighting up the dim church. But they didn't reach Terakomari. Twisting and turning with unnatural, otherworldly movements, she evaded each one. *Damn it all.* She was too fast.

"Ack!"

A fist flew toward her face.

Though it was only the fist of a little girl, small and knobby, Millicent somehow knew that it had the power to knock her dead. She flung herself to the side, and the mitt ended up smashing into the stone wall behind her.

Then it exploded with an immense blast of magical energy.

The blast tossed Millicent into the air like a rag doll. She flew across the room and landed flat on her butt.

Looking up, she saw a gaping hole where the wall used to be.

Her jaw dropped. This couldn't be happening. There had to be some mistake.

She'd plotted for three years in the hopes of witnessing Terakomari's

Core Implosion powers; dreaming that defeating a more powerful Terakomari would prove that Millicent herself had grown stronger since their last battle.

But she'd never expected this.

Millicent had never dreamed that Terakomari's Core Implosion would be this terrible, this almighty.

Clutching her stomach, Millicent staggered to her feet. Her enemy was rubbing her fist and cricking her neck this way and that. Behind her, the vampire goons were still chanting *"Ko-ma-rin! Ko-ma-rin! Ko-ma-rin!"* like a bunch of idiots.

This was insane.

"This is insane! Insane, insane, insane!!!"

She was going to kill Millicent? It was Terakomari who deserved to die! Die like vermin crushed into the dirt after what Terakomari had done to her. Yes, Millicent was going to tear her full of holes, rip out her guts, and crush her brains!

Staggering backward, she drew together all of her magical power and tapped into the deep reserves lying dormant within her. She could feel her veins bulging with the effort, but she paid that no heed. All she cared about was murdering Terakomari. She had to kill Terakomari. Terakomari needed to die.

"Milliceeent…"

Terakomari slowly turned to face her.

Her face was a grinning mask.

"You…pitiable soul."

That's when Millicent really snapped.

She started screaming like a banshee.

"You snotty little brat, I'll kill youuu!!!"

Millicent's magical energy burst forth in a blaze of light.

It was a high-level light spell called *Wicked Flare of Annihilationism*.

A thick laser beam sliced a channel through the floor. This would finish her. The corners of Millicent's mouth rose in a triumphant grin.

But then something surprising happened.

Just as the laser beam was about to make contact with Terakomari, it suddenly veered sharply off course.

"What the…"

Some kind of interfering force seemed to have knocked it off its trajectory. A thunderous roar filled the church. The laser beam shot straight up, eating into the ceiling. But it didn't stop there. It blazed its way through the upper floors as well, coming out of the roof and disappearing among the clouds.

It had left a huge hole in the castle roof.

Through the opening, the light of the full moon filled the church with its bloodred light.

Millicent gazed at Terakomari, quivering with fear.

A Magic Circle had opened in front of her. That was the advanced-level magic spell *Crystal Deflector*. Any attack that touched the Magic Circle would bounce away from its intended trajectory. It was an extremely rare defensive skill.

"How? How can you wield such magic all of a sudd—guh!"

Suddenly, Millicent's left arm received a colossal blow.

What followed was unimaginable pain.

Screaming, Millicent tried to look down at her limb to assess the damage. But she couldn't. Because her left arm wasn't there. It had been blown clean off. It was now lying in the corner of the church like a limp, white worm.

She'd been struck with low-level magic…just a simple Magic Bullet. That wench had used Millicent's signature attack against her.

Millicent was incandescent with rage. Terakomari would pay. Millicent was going to beat her to death. With her one remaining limb.

"?!"

But something suddenly struck Millicent as strange.

Her legs refused to move. It was as though someone was holding on to them…

"Yeek!!!"

Millicent let out a horrified shriek. A crimson-red hand had risen from a puddle of blood near her foot and had latched on to her ankles with an iron grip.

"What the heck is that?!"

The thing's hold on Millicent grew stronger.

But it wasn't merely gripping her. It was crushing her, as though trying to snap the bones in her ankles. Millicent fired Magic Bullets down at it in desperation, but it seemed to be composed of blood, so no matter how many holes in the thing she opened, it grew no weaker. Soon Millicent ran out of strength and could no longer conjure any more bullets.

"Get off! Get off!" she shrieked, but it was to no avail.

Her ankle bones snapped and crunched.

Millicent crumpled to the ground, wailing in pain. Her snapped bones were sticking out of her skin at crazy angles. She almost fainted.

What the hell was going on?

She'd never heard of magic like this before.

"This is insane! It's insane, it's just insane!!!"

Muttering and rambling to herself, Millicent looked up at Terakomari. A cold glint shined in her enemy's eye as she slowly approached.

A blood-drenched girl, illuminated by the light of a crimson moon.

Millicent twitched in terror.

Then she was hit with the strangest sensation of déjà vu.

But it wasn't from mental memory. It was from *muscle memory.*

This feeling…it was the same that she'd had three years before, when she'd touched Terakomari's pendant with her fingertips.

Millicent had dedicated the past three years to paying Terakomari back for that moment.

But she had no idea…

…My efforts…were all for naught?

…I was never going to be able to defeat someone with might like hers…?

"Wow, Commander!" "You really gave it to her!" "Terrorists are the scum of the world!" "Commander, you're so cool!" "Marry me, Commander!" "Komarin! Komarin! Komarin!"

Behind her, the vampire goons were shouting their heads off.

Then Terakomari loomed over her.

"It's over."

Terakomari reached her hand out slowly.

Millicent felt like she was about to split in two from fear.

…Fear? Me, cowering before…Terakomari?! Give me a break! That… THAT is insane!!!

That's when Millicent realized something.

It wasn't over yet. She still had a chance.

She still had her cursed knife, her *Silver Blade of Doom*, clutched in her right hand.

She didn't hesitate.

"DIE, TERAKOMAREEE!!!"

She swung the knife upward, but it didn't reach her foe's neck as planned.

A disembodied right arm flopped uselessly to the floor with a flumping sound. Millicent's right limb.

Somehow it had been neatly amputated at the shoulder.

"Ah…"

Despair washed over her in a huge, dark wave.

She had no further tricks up her sleeve.

As she accepted her defeat for the first time, an immense fear of demise engulfed her. She was trembling all over, oozing cold sweat as she flopped onto her back and glared at Terakomari with hatred and resentment.

"You…how…?"

She wasn't certain herself what she was asking.

In the face of Terakomari's immense power, all her efforts had come to nothing. Millicent wanted to scream and wail from how unfair it all was. She despised Terakomari for being so blessed—the fates clearly loved her, since they'd granted her such incredible abilities. Millicent was so jealous, she couldn't stand it.

She gazed at her old enemy, her mouth agape, her eyes filled with disbelief.

Such incredible power. Such an indomitable will…

But she'd realized something.

Terakomari was falling apart.

Her clothes were torn. Her face was smeared with blood and tracked with tears. Her stomach and shoulder were still oozing blood. And the wound the *Silver Blade of Doom* had inflicted was clearly still causing her considerable pain.

She looked a real mess.

Millicent had caused all that.

If Terakomari had been aware of her Core Implosion abilities and had been able to use them freely from the start, then she would never have endured Millicent's tormenting to this extent.

Right. Terakomari hadn't been born perfect after all.

In essence, what Terakomari had said about herself was true. Fundamentally, she was a boring, plain weakling of a vampire. With no particular talents or skills, an embarrassment to her race.

But that runt of a vampire had made it all the way here without using any special skills.

Core Implosion was intrinsically linked to one's mental fortitude.

Hadn't Master Amatsu told her something like that?

I had to do my best for my friends, who have always cared for me!

She recalled Terakomari's words from earlier in their fight.

So…that was probably a big part of it, Millicent thought.

If only I had been able to strengthen my mind like her. I wonder if things would have been different…

Why had she bullied Terakomari? Because she'd been having a hard time at home? That had been stupid.

In her lust for power, she'd even joined a terrorist organization.

The cause of all of her misfortunes…had been her own weakness of spirit. If only she'd chosen a different path, her future might have played out differently. It could have turned out much better than this.

No.

What good was it to consider the past now?

Millicent realized that she was crying.

Not because she was frustrated in defeat. Not because she was afraid to die.

But because Terakomari had become so powerful. She was shining like a bright light.

I wanted to be like that one day...

"Prepare yourself."

Slim fingers closed around Millicent's neck.

The crimson-colored vampire leaned in, speaking in a dispassionate voice.

"I'm going to put you out of your misery."

"Wait...GURK!"

Millicent had no further time for repenting.

A wave of absolute despair washed over her as Terakomari ripped her head from her shoulders and completed Millicent's annihilation.

※

Six Nations News, May 21st, Morning Edition

GIRL DETAINED! MULNITE EMPIRE TERRORIST GROUP "INVERSE MOON" MEMBER APPREHENDED

BY MELKA TIANO

The Mulnite Imperial Government, which has been dealing with serious terrorist attacks in recent years, announced on the 20th that they have apprehended a young woman believed to be a member of the anti–Dark Core terrorist group, Inverse Moon. The offender, who is believed to be a vampire from the Mulnite Empire, was killed and captured by Crimson Lord Commander Terakomari Gandesblood while hiding out in a ruined castle in the La Nelient slum quarter. This is the first time a member of Inverse Moon has ever been apprehended; the Mulnite Empire has claimed a victory for all of the Six Nations, while striking fear into the hearts of terrorists the world over. (…Continued from front page) Crimson Lord Commander Gandesblood, who apprehended the perpetrator, is to be honored in a special ceremony. Gandesblood, who many say is the most powerful Crimson Lord in history, as well as the youngest, is expected to continue her duties as a commander. The recent "Komarin Boom" is also expected to continue as her approval ratings have never been higher. We here at Six Nations News are excited to see what Commander Komari does next…

Vexations

I awoke to find myself lying in bed.

My head felt fuzzy, and my body ached all over.

The ceiling above looked unfamiliar. What was I doing sleeping in a strange place? Had I been kidnapped? It was possible. My family was rich and had vast political influence. And I was a total knockout beauty…

"Lady Komari. You're awake!"

Confused, I looked over.

The creepy maid was sitting in a chair by my bedside. I stared at her. She wasn't wearing her maid uniform right now. Instead, she was in hospital pajamas, and both of her arms were bandaged. She didn't look like the sicko maid anymore. Just a regular sicko. Wait, wait, never mind that right now.

"Vill?! Are you all right?!"

As I rushed to sit up, pain shot through the lower half of my body, and I fell back against the pillows. Ouch. That hurt so bad. It felt like someone had stabbed me in the calf with a pair of scissors.

"Please, lie still. Your wounds still haven't healed."

"It hurts! What is this?! Why does it hurt so bad?! It feels like my leg is on fire!"

"You were stabbed with a cursed weapon. Don't you remember?"

Come to think of it, I did.

Yes. I went to the abandoned castle all by myself and fought with Millicent. Got pretty banged up, too. I was about to give up…realizing I couldn't manage to save Vill…when…wait. If I could feel pain, that had to mean…I survived?

"Vill? Are we in heaven?"

"No, not yet. You won, Lady Komari."

"What?"

"You beat Millicent Bluenight. You infiltrated the castle, took down the terrorist, and saved the captive…me."

"Wait, what? What are you talking about?"

I obviously lost…right?

Millicent had shot me full of Magic Bullet holes, stabbed my leg with her silver knife, and then finally sliced me up with a laser. There was no way I could have come back from that. Only great mages in fantasy novels can turn that kind of situation around.

Vill was gazing into my eyes.

"Do you know about Core Implosion?"

"Implosion? Wait, that's what you were telling me about in the bath that one time?"

"Yes. Core Implosion is a very special, very powerful force that is entirely distinct from magic. People with Core Implosion abilities can cut off the Dark Core's influence to tap into demonic forces ordinary people can't even comprehend."

"Huh. No, I've never heard about it before. But what of it?"

"You used it."

"Huh? Say what?"

According to Vill, this was what happened.

I'd been born with a special type of Core Implosion power, known as *Blood Curse*. Whenever a drop of blood passes my lips, I explode with dark magical energy and powerful abilities. Just when Millicent had been about to execute me, Vill had fed me a drop of her blood, thus awakening my Core Implosion. Then I suddenly became all-powerful and used my skill to pummel Millicent into hamburger meat.

I see, I see... Wait, what the—?!

"I don't remember any of that!"

"Well, you seemed to go a bit over the top. After you twisted Millicent's head off, you fainted. The Seventh Unit thugs carried you on their shoulders back home, and for a while there, we all thought you were going to croak!"

"Hold on, there's so many things I wanna ask, but I can't think straight!"

"I'll explain everything at leisure later. All you need to know right now is that you're kind of a demigod, Lady Komari. You have the power to crush any foe in existence. Millicent was nothing compared to you."

"That's unbelievable, though! I'd find it easier to believe if you told me she'd tripped on a flagstone and had died from hitting her own head on the altar!"

Vill chuckled.

"Yes, it is quite hard to wrap your head around. But you're under no pressure to believe it if you don't want to. I'm just so happy that you're here, and you're safe..."

"..."

Why was she acting like everything was all fine and dandy?

And this was much too embarrassing. I wasn't used to her being so...open about her emotions with me. I much preferred her evil machinations on my body. Ah, wait, no I didn't.

I turned away from her, trying to think of how to change the subject.

"You look really well, Vill...even though you were on the brink of death..."

"I'm a soldier, too. I can handle a few war wounds."

"I see..."

I didn't know what else to say after that. My head still felt fuzzy.

I knew this wasn't heaven, but everything seemed kind of hazy and floaty.

"Lady Komari…" Vill hesitated. "Lady Komari, you won. The terrorist was arrested. Right now, she's chained up in the underground jail. She won't bother you anymore."

"R-right…"

"So there's no need for you to keep holding on to the past."

"…"

It was as though a cool breeze were blowing away the cobwebs of my past.

I didn't have to worry about all that anymore. It was such a relief…

The past three years the shadow of Millicent had loomed over my life.

I didn't want to go outside. I didn't want to spend time with people. I had so many painful memories…so I withdrew myself. And the feelings just got worse and worse. Shut up in my dark bedroom, wallowing in my misery, enabling my own prolonged victimhood.

But those days were over now.

I had managed to take the first step along an entirely new path.

"But just because I defeated her, it doesn't mean my mental wounds will automatically heal…"

"You may be right. However…"

"I want to talk to Millicent. At some point."

Vill blinked at me, shocked. I was surprised by my own feelings, to tell the truth. But somehow I just got the feeling it was something I needed to do.

"She hates me. I think she always will. But I want to change. I don't want to be afraid of her anymore. I think I need to try to get some sort of closure. Otherwise, I won't be able to make a clean break with the past."

"That's very admirable. But it also sounds like you're just saying what you think you ought to say."

"Maybe I am."

I smiled wryly. Until recently, I would never have sought out a conversation with anyone, let alone someone I knew harbored bad feelings toward me.

That had to mean I'd made huge progress already, right?

"But I think it would be good for me to get out and about."

"I understand. Then I shall schedule three battles every two days."

"Why do you always have to take things to the extreme?!"

I huffed angrily in bed.

This sicko was as ignorant of my feelings as ever! Hmm, but even if she was able to comprehend them, I had the feeling she'd still ignore them. What a jerk she was. But at the same time, I had to concede that in her own creepy way, she had always tried to care for me. I couldn't get too mad at her.

"Lady Komari?"

"What?"

"Thank you for coming to save me."

I looked around at her, surprised.

She was wearing her usual cool expression, but her cheeks were uncharacteristically pink. I think she'd been waiting for the right chance to say that to me.

"You're welcome."

I gazed up at the ceiling as I spoke. The words sounded clumsy on my lips.

"...It feels like everything got settled before I even knew what was really going on. Is it settled for real, though? I'm not dreaming, am I?"

"No. You're awake."

"Hmm, it doesn't feel like a dream, now I think about it. It's just hard to comprehend. How did the army manage to arrest Millicent?"

"You unleashed Core Implosion and saved my life, Lady Komari."

"Yeah, but I mean... Oh, never mind. I guess what's important is that we're both alive and well."

I could think about the details later.

I turned my focus back to Vill.

"What about you? What are you going to do now?"

"…Eh?"

"The score from three years ago has been settled. You don't need to act as my maid anymore."

If what she wrote in the letter was true, Vill had come to be my maid as a form of repentance. (Not that I needed her to repent or anything in the first place…)

But now that the past was finally over and done with, there was no need for her to attend to me anymore.

I peeked at her, wondering what her reaction would be.

The sicko maid was gazing at me, mouth agape, looking like the world was about to end.

"But… You can't mean… You don't need me anymore?!"

"Er, I didn't mean it like that…"

"That is *so* mean, Lady Komari! How could you take my duties away from me?! If you do that, I'll have nothing left! I'll be forced to break into your bedchamber and pilfer your panties to satisfy myself!"

"Can't you just steal money like normal people?! I'm really gonna dismiss you from your post if I find you pawing through my underwear drawer!!!"

"Ack…dismissal…I'd rather die… I've devoted my life to you, Lady Komari, but now…"

"All right, all right! You can stay with me! Okay? I need you as my maid, Vill."

"Are…are you proposing…?"

"In your dreams, sicko!!!"

I yelped, kicking my legs. Ouch. That was a bad idea.

She really was a complete nightmare of a maid.

But still…part of me really enjoyed our banter.

Arguing back and forth with her like this…it always seemed to lighten my mood. It always made my problems seem to get smaller somehow.

With Vill by my side, I really felt like I could be reborn and start over as a whole new person.

Yeah, I really thought I could.

I wanted to withdraw. Be a shut-in.

I really, honestly, and truly felt that.

"Urgent news! Captain Mellaconcey has captured the enemy commander! I repeat! Captain Mellaconcey has captured the enemy commander! We win!!!"

The messenger's voice rang out, and all the vampires who were surrounding me began to yell and cheer. Engulfed by the noise, I allowed myself a tiny little sigh of relief.

"That was a close one. I can't believe they all charged in a single formation."

"Seriously. I thought we were all gonna die..."

I relaxed, sinking deep into my throne.

Yes, I was back on the battlefield.

We, the Mulnite Imperial Army's Seventh Unit, had just finished our third engagement against the Lapelico Kingdom's Chimpanzee Corps. They were the ones who'd declared war on us, of course. Commander Hades Molekikki was desperate for a grudge match against me, and I hadn't been able to come up with a suitable excuse to get out of it.

We'd trained well and had hatched a battle plan beforehand, of course, but we probably shouldn't have bothered. They launched an all-out kamikaze assault on us. The moment the battle began, Molekikki gave the order for an all-out, united charge. Full of bloodlust, the beast-folk came at us without a second's hesitation, with their commander front and center. That had made it easy for Mellaconcey to launch an impromptu bombing raid with explosive magic to take out the Chimpanzee himself and smoothly bring the bout to a close.

If the Chimpanzee had reached us, I probably would have been killed. Vill had told me something crazy about my having Core Implosion power, but I still didn't really believe her. I mean, me? All-powerful? Please. But my soldiers had apparently witnessed me "making mincemeat of Millicent." Maybe it had been a group hallucination? They always seemed like they were out of their minds on some dodgy substance or other. Magic mushrooms from the forest...?

So, then, how had I managed to prevail over Millicent? It had probably been a delayed effect from one of the Magic Stones I'd hit her with. Had to be.

Or at least, that was what I told myself. I really needed to stop dwelling on it so m—

"Gah! I didn't even get a chance to fight!"

The blond-haired youth by my side, Yohann Helders, clucked his tongue angrily. He was as hotheaded and rash as ever. Shaking his fist at the blue sky, he continued to grumble.

"Curses! My first real battle in ages! What am I supposed to do with the battle fever that even now threatens to engulf my soul?! Shall I burn down all these fields?!"

"Hey, brat. How did you worm your way back into this unit anyhow?"

Bellius folded his arms across his chest and glared at Yohann. The dog-headed man was back in top form, and during yesterday's training he'd been swinging his ax around merrily and decapitating his opponents with ease.

Yohann snorted confidently.

"If you've got a problem with it, Bellius, take it to the commander. She's the one who personally reinstated me into the Seventh Unit."

""What?""

Bellius froze. Caostel, who had been listening to the conversation, also froze, and the two of them stared at me in shock. Ah. Well. I mean, I'd deliberated over it for quite a while... Everyone makes mistakes, right? And hadn't Yohann repented? I figured there was no harm in pardoning him. Besides, he came to me and personally apologized.

"I'm terribly sorry, Commander. I'll never plot to kill you again. I mean, uh...I'll protect you instead. You may be weak and useless, but you've got grit. I'll help you become a great warrior, a truly mighty Crimson Lord. Ah, but don't get me wrong! I'm not doing it 'cause I like you or anything! It's purely transactional! Let me back into the Seventh Unit, and I'll be forever loyal to you! I'll protect you with my life! All I ask is...that you let me be near you!"

I mean, how could I have turned him down?

Even though he knew my true nature, he'd still agreed to follow me. And he'd even sworn to protect me with his life. Who could abandon such a good, loyal soldier as that?

"Commander! How could you pardon Yohann?!"

"He teamed up with a terrorist against us all! He's dangerous!"

A crowd was gathering, and its members had begun to mutter their discontent. The thrill of victory hadn't managed to distract them for long. "Pah!" I spat, throwing my head back and putting on an air of confidence and bravado, with just a hint of superiority.

"Are you really all so quick to condemn a man who made a simple mistake?"

"...But Commander. Yohann's crime is terribly grave..."

"Is it? He only colluded with a known terrorist a little bit. You guys are all way too quick to blame people!"

"...?!"

The vampires all gawped at me in shock.

"She's so...magnanimous!" "So openhearted!" "Commander Tera-komari is truly the best of us all!" "Her outlook on life is so sagacious!" "When the commander speaks, I can almost hear a thousand of our enemies shriek in fear!"

Can you, now?

...Ugh, please. Stop looking at me with those adoring eyes, all of you!

"I see. So the commander's generous nature has saved Yohann's skin."

"Precisely. But relax. If he does any more terrorism in the future, I'll come down on him like a ton of bricks! Even a saint's patience sometimes runs out, they say! And my patience has its limits, too! So don't worry! I'll take personal responsibility for Yohann and off him myself if the need arises!"

"HAAAIIILLL!!!"

The vampires screamed in approval, which caused me to jump. I wasn't expecting them to cheer just then.

But anyway, I was relieved they seemed willing to accept my decision regarding Yohann. Plus, I'd managed to secure myself a loyal bodyguard.

But that aside...

"All right! We won the battle, so we now return to Mulnite in triumph! Let us report our victory to the Empress! And then let's kick back and chill!"

I wanted to go home as soon as possible and crawl into bed.

However...

"No, Commander! We have to start training for the next battle straightaway!"

"...Huh?"

"Caostel is right. We must make haste and prepare!"

"Yeah!" "We need to head home and start prepping for the next fight!" "Arrrgh! I can hear the bootfalls of our enemies approaching!" "The bloodlust is upon me!" "Let's dooo it!" "Let's gooo!" "Hunnnnng!" "Nyunnng!" "Hyaaaah!" Graaagh!" "Rawwwr!"

....

......

...Was this a zoo?

"Lady Komari, you should probably forget about resting for a while. It's fight time now."

" ..."

I watched my soldiers roar and bellow and stamp their boots in a fit of combat frenzy. Then I despaired.

I really, really couldn't understand how their minds worked. An indoorsy girl like myself really wasn't a good match for this group of brawlers. Taken individually, they weren't so bad, but put them together, and they were darn near uncontrollable. If I did anything to rain on their parade, I was certain they'd turn on me and rip me limb from limb.

And so even though I hated doing it with every fiber of my being, with every cell of my body...I raised my voice and made another patented Komarin speech.

"Very well! Your passion has inspired me! We return to Mulnite to immediately begin planning our next engagement! As promised, I will keep you all sated with the blood of your enemies! I am your commander, Terakomari Gandesblood, who shall paint the skies above all Six Nations crimson with blood! Follow me, for all else is ashes!"

The roar this time was so loud, it almost knocked my head off.

Then they all started up their "Komarin" number again.

Surrounded by my adoring soldiers, I gazed up at the sky, resigned to my fate. It was a beautiful deep blue. Turn this pretty sky bloodred? Yuck.

Sigh.

Maybe I really should have stayed a shut-in after all...

But my fate was already sealed... I was destined for further trials as Commander Komari, the Shut-In Vampire Princess...

Afterword

Hello, I'm Kotei Kobayashi.

My editor told me I could take up as many pages as I liked for the Afterword, but I actually don't have that much to write. Still, I'd like to take this opportunity to talk about myself a little bit.

One of my greatest inspirations for starting to write novels was the *Shiji*, or *Records of the Grand Historian*, by Sima Qian.

Now, I'm not claiming that I read all of it, everything from "Annals of the Five Emperors" all the way to the "Autobiographical Afterword of the Grand Historian," or anything so dramatic as that! But I did eagerly devour the sections we covered in my high school classics classes on Xiang Yu.

The first time I read it, I just thought, *So he got dismembered in the end...ew.* But through reading and rereading it in preparation for the end-of-term test, I suddenly realized what a crazy and dramatic tale it was. It was so...irrational. I started to get this weird feeling of dread, like my sixth sense was tingling or something.

Everyone knows the famous Xiang Yu section of *Records of the Grand Historian*, of course, and it's widely recognized as being an example of great Classical Chinese literature. But for it to strike a chord with a high school kid like me who knew nothing of Classical Chinese literature, good or bad, well, that's a very powerful thing. It got me thinking that, one day, I'd like to write a similar novel/composition.

But I think that sort of East Asian tragic fantasy tale could spring only from the pens of those who had actually lived in those times.

After I entered university, the first real novella I wrote was a historical Chinese romance, a retelling of what happened when Zhang Lian of the Han Dynasty went to assassinate Qin Shi Huang, founder of the Qin Dynasty. Personally, I thought I did a pretty good job of capturing that Ancient Chinese atmosphere and the conflict between characters, but all I heard was *"These characters are so cute!"* and *"The main character is REALLY cute!"* No one seemed to notice the other stuff at all.

So I figured I'd better play to my strengths and write a more Western-style novel, something with a bit more oomph. For this book, *Vexations of the Shut-In Vampire Princess*, I decided I'd be satisfied as long as the main character turned out cute. So I set out to write a comical fantasy with a heroine whom people would love. I really hope that readers enjoy the humorous mismatch of layabout Komari and the extreme situation she's placed in. And if you find yourself thinking, *"Man, Komari is so cute!"*— well, that would make me very happy, too.

I would also like to take this opportunity to thank a few people:

The illustrator, riichu, whose wonderful artwork brought this story to life so vividly.

Everyone at the GA Bunko Editorial Department, who chose this work for the Eleventh GA Bunko Prize (Merit Award).

Yoten Sugiura, my supervising editor, who taught me so many things while I was still a clueless newbie.

Everyone else involved in the publication of this work.

And finally, all the readers who picked up a copy of this book.

I extend my most heartfelt thanks to all of you.

Thank you so much!!!

Until next time! (If there is a next time, of course!)

Kotei Kobayashi